Penguin Books
The Talking Trees
and Other Stories

Sean O'Faolain was born in 1900 and educated at the National University of Ireland. For a year he was a commercial traveller for books but gave it up to fight on the side of De Valera in 1921. He was a member of the Irish Republican Army for six years, taught for a further year and then studied for three years at Harvard University. For four years he taught at Strawberry Hill Training College for Teachers, after which he turned to writing and went back to his native Ireland, where he now lives in Dublin. He has written some twenty books, including *The Irish* (a Pelican book) and travel and literary criticism, novels, biographies, and several books of short stories. He has also contributed to all the well-known periodicals in Great Britain and the United States. His latest publications are an autobiography, *Vive Moi!* and a book of stories, *The Heat of the Sun*. Sean O'Faolain is a D.Litt. of Trinity College, Dublin. He is married, with two children. His wife has written several books of Irish folk-tales and his daughter published her first book of stories in 1968.

Sean O'Faolain

The Talking Trees

and Other Stories

Penguin Books

Penguin Books Ltd, Harmondsworth,
Middlesex, England
Penguin Books Australia Ltd, Ringwood,
Victoria, Australia

This collection first published in Great Britain by Jonathan Cape 1971
Published in Penguin Books 1973

The author wishes to thank the following for permission to reprint stories which first appeared in their pages: Ladies' Home Journal, Playboy, The Atlantic, Saturday Evening Post (*who published 'A Dead Cert' under the title 'What a Stunning Night!' and 'Feed My Lambs' under the title 'A Fool of a Man'*), The Sign (*who published 'Our Fearful Innocence' under the title 'This Shallow Bay'*) *and* The Critic (*who published 'Hymeneal' under the title 'I'll Write Wan Terrible Book'*).

Made and printed in Great Britain by
Richard Clay (The Chaucer Press), Ltd, Bungay, Suffolk
Set in Linotype Pilgrim

Contents

The Planets of the Years

I confess that I did not enjoy that winter of 1967 in Cambridge, Mass. My husband had too much to do and I had nothing to do: a common complaint, I have since gathered, with visiting professors' wives. Every morning while I faced an empty day he could go off happily to Widener Library researching for his biography of Henri Estienne, a character about whom I knew nothing except that he was a sixteenth-century French wit whose most famous *mot* is 'If youth but knew, if age but could'. I never got to like H.E., as we called him. His *mot* is out of date anyway, and his equally famous observation, that God tempers the wind to the shorn lamb, is complete baloney. I far prefer the man or woman (*Anon.*) who said that God never opens one door but he shuts another. And I like the other sad one, too, that says we are all as God made us, and some of us even worse.

When my happy man left me in the morning I rarely saw him again until dinner time, and after dinner he so often buried himself in the study with H.E. that before the winter was out I took to calling him The Man Who Lives Upstairs. To be fair, he did, early on, introduce me to Boston, especially to its museums, and to two or three other disoccupied foreign wives. (American wives are never disoccupied.) But after that, apart from airily recommending me every morning to the delights of Boston, the only thing he did for me was to take me on Saturday nights to the Symphony, occasionally to a play, and, to my surprise – Are all newlywed wives constantly making these surprising discoveries about their husbands? – I found that not even H.E. could keep him away from a Western in Harvard Square or a Humphrey Bogart revival in Brattle Street. The only other way I could seduce him from H.E. was to make love with him – I will *not* tolerate the phrase make love 'to', it is a ridiculous preposition – and as we were only four months married we made love a lot. It is my happiest memory of Cambridge, Mass. Still, no matter how much in love you are you cannot fill a whole winter's day that way. Certainly not in Widener Library. I was often lonely and mostly idle.

And then there was the house. It belonged to a friend of my husband, a professor in M.I.T., who in his turn was spending a sabbatical in Europe with, I am sure, his not at all disoccupied wife. I ought to have loved it, and in many ways I did. It was well furnished, well heated, well lit, contained lots of books, and it was delightfully roomy, far too big, really, for two people – it ought to have been full of noisy children. It was almost too quiet, tucked away on a side street flanked by a large if rather dank garden which I chiefly remember for the way its tall elms used to float up like seaweed every evening at twilight during those exquisite moments when the lights of the city are slowly turning the sky into a sullen, iridescent pink. I loved the house for its agreeably old-fashioned air of having been lived in for generations. I even liked the dust, the discarded matches, the lost coins, the bits of Christmas or Thanksgiving tinsel shining at the bottom of the hot-air registers in the floor. In fact, I liked everything about it except its situation – a long way up Massachusetts Avenue, bordering, across the railroad track, on the garish, noisy shopping centre of Porter Square, and the crumby neighbourhood behind it that looked anything but salubrious by day and, so my Cambridge friends warned me, was not particularly safe at night. Not being an American I suppose I dare mention the word Negroes. I do not mind mentioning Greeks, Italians and Syrians too. Like everybody in the world, I am nothing if not a racist – in so far as I accept every race but prefer my own. And I do not always trust the Irish either.

Now, I am not a nervous woman, but whenever The Man Who Lived Upstairs left Cambridge for a night to give a lecture elsewhere, and I lay in bed, reading myself to sleep, longing to have him by my side, hearing nothing but an occasional late car whistling along Mass Avenue, or the snow plopping softly from the roof, I could not help remembering that even back home in crimeless Ireland my parents' home had already been broken into three times in the previous three years. I could not also help thinking that the front door was partly glazed and that the downstairs windows were protected only by the weakest of hasps. Anyone who wanted to could, as the police say, have 'effected an entrance' without difficulty, and, the house being so tucked away, he could have done it unheard and unseen. Was that shuffling noise really the snow? On dusky afternoons I sometimes found myself rather shamefacedly putting the chain on the door.

Late one such snowy afternoon in November, I was alone in the house, writing home to my sister in Ireland. 'How I wish,' I had just written, 'we were together now, Nancy, gossiping over a drink or a pot of tea . . .' On the impulse, I had just risen to comfort myself with a solitary tea tray when, as I passed through the lighted hall towards the kitchen, I was startled to see two dark figures outside the glass door, outlined against the far street lights. I stood still and watched them. For quite a while they did not stir. Then the doorbell rang tentatively. I went forward, and saw through the muslin curtains what looked like two women. One was very small, the other was rather tall. I removed the chain and opened the door.

The small woman was ancient. Whenever I think back to her now I always see an old peasant woman wearing a black coif, bordered inside with a white goffered frill that enclosed a strong, apple-ruddy face netted by the finest wrinkles. I know this is quite irrational. She cannot have been dressed that way at all. I am probably remembering not her but my old grandmother Anna Long from the town of Rathkeale who came to live in our house in Limerick city when I was a child, and who was the first person I ever heard talking in Irish. The tall woman was middle-aged, and dressed conventionally. It was she who spoke first.

'I am sure,' she said diffidently, in unmistakable Boston-American, 'you will think this a very strange request that I am going to make to you. This is my aunt. She lives with me in Watertown. I brought her in to lunch in Cambridge for her eightieth birthday, and I promised her as a special treat that I would show her this house. You see, she got her first job here when she came over from Ireland sixty-three years ago . . .'

Here the old woman interrupted her niece. She spoke with a surprisingly rotund voice as if she were an oracle intoning from within the recesses of a cavern; but an oracle with an Irish brogue as thick as treacle and as rich as rum.

'We meant, ma'am,' she rumbled, 'only for to look at the outside of the house. But when I saw the lighted hall I made my niece ring the doorbell. For thirty-five years this was my door. It was a door-knocker we had. I'd love, ma'am, for to have wan tiny little peep into the inside of the house.'

I at once took her hand and drew her into the hall. At that moment nobody could have been more welcome.

'I was just putting down the kettle,' I said to them both. 'We'll have a nice cup of tea and be talking about home.'

When they had banged the snow from their boots I led them into the front drawing room. Tea, however, the old woman would not take, perhaps out of pure politeness, or from the delicate fear that I was only trying to compound her intrusion. She would not even sit on the chair I offered her. (I thought afterwards that in all her years as a servant she had never sat down in that house except in her kitchen or her bedroom.) Peering around her like a cat in a strange room, she started to talk about herself – again out of politeness? to cover her peering? – interrupting her flow only to say, every so often, like the warning croak of a bird, how much it had all changed:

''Tis changed entirely! We never had rugs on the floor like that. Carpets we always had, all over the house. Of course, when I landed in Boston it was the year nineteen-oh-four, and that is sixty-three years ago, and sure the whole world is changed since then! I was just turned seventeen. It was the month of January and I will never forget to my dying day the snow falling and falling. I never seen the like of it in all my life. From behind Slieve Callan I came, in the County Clare, and many's the time I seen Callan white with snow. Ye have the electric. Gas we had. But that Boston snow beat all I ever saw. It was like snow that started falling a long time ago and didn't know how to stop. Oh, dear! The blinds are changed too! It was my uncle Paudh met me off the boat, God rest his soul, and glad I was to get shut of it until I saw where he took me. To his home in South Boston. And a black, dark place

South Boston was in them days. I was frightened out of my wits at all the rattle of the horsecars, and the trams, and the railway roaring like thunder and lightning all night long. I didn't sleep one wink with the fright and the strangeness of it all. Ma'am! Could I have a little peep at the back drawing room, if you please?'

We moved into it.

'Oh, vo!' she said disapprovingly, peering down over the hummocked snow, indifferent to the beautiful sunset in the rusty sky, 'Look at the garden! Flowers we had, all the year round. We had a glasshouse. I can see no glasshouse! Have ye no glasshouse? The way I got the job was through my uncle Paudh's son, Patsy Coogan, my own first cousin. He was a coachman that time to a man named Newsom, a Quaker man, had a big country house out in Arlington. He had the job all lined up for me in this house with the three Misses Cushing. Are you sure there is no glasshouse? He came for me with the carriage the very next morning, and if I was frightened before, I was five and forty times more frightened the way we drove, and we drove and we drove. I that never saw any but the wan street of Miltownmalbay until I took the train straight down to the Queenstown docks ten days before. I was lost! There was no end to the streets. I was sure Patsy was lost too and was only taking me around in circles. I kept saying to him, "And where are we now, Patsy?" And Patsy kept saying, "In Boston! Where else?" I never in my life felt so cold as I did in that old horse carriage. It is very warm in here, God bless it! And no fires! It is the way ye have the central heating. The three Misses Cushing always insisted on a roaring log fire in every room. I was so cold I began to cry with the cold until Patsy said, "What the divil ails you and you going off to live in the finest house in Cambridge, Mass?" I said, "And where on earth is Cambridge Mass?" He got right cross with me. "Where is it?" he roars at me, "but in Boston! Where else?" Ma'am,' she pleaded, 'the one place I really wanted to see is my old kitchen.'

I led them into the kitchen.

'Oh, glory! Mind you, ma'am, I'm not faulting it. It is very nice. But somehow it is gone very small on me. God bless us, all the changes and innovations! I wouldn't know it at all, at all!

Tiles on the floor we had. And where is my kitchen trough gone to? An electric stove! But where is my old kitchen range? Oh, the grand meals I cooked on that old range! For all the dinner parties! Yards long it was. And as bright as a battleship. Where can it be gone to? Am I in the right house at all?'

I showed her where I could only presume it must once have been, behind a walled-up part of the kitchen lined now with shelving.

'It was at that black divil of a range I learned how to cook. Oh, you have no idea of the kindness of the three Misses Cushing teaching me how to cook. The goodness of them! The patience of them! Though, mind you, many's the rap of the rolling pin I got on the knuckles from Miss Caroline when she'd be bad with the megrim. The best of good food they had! Would you believe it, this was the first house where I ever ate fresh meat. And is it how ye have the table and chairs for to eat in the kitchen?'

'Like we have ourselves,' the niece said crossly. 'At home in Watertown.'

'Three breakfast trays I took up every morning, winter and summer, to the three Misses Cushing. At half past six I would rise, and it was dark and cold them winter mornings, to light the range, and the divil of hell it was to light sometimes, and clear out the three fireplaces, and set and light the big log fires, and make the three breakfasts and, while the kettle was boiling, to steal up like a mouse so as not to waken my ladies, and put a match to the three fires in their bedrooms that I set the night before, and come down then and carry up the three trays at the tick of eight o'clock. Oh, the three loveliest, kindest ladies you ever met! Saints they were! I never in my life met such goodness. They thought nothing was too good for me. When I think of the darling little bedroom they gave me up under the roof, it was like a babby house, only for being like an icebox in the wintry nights.'

'You must have been very happy here,' I said comfortably, and realized at once that I had made a mistake by the way her head jerked like a bird cocking an ear to a worm underground. I had used a word she would never use. I was being sentimental about an experience that had been outside, and apart and beyond all sentiment. 'I mean,' I said hastily, 'you were contented here.'

'Ho!' she smiled. 'I was contented all day and every day as I never was before or since. I found my first and only home in this blessed house.'

'You have a nice home now,' her niece said. But once more the old lady paid no heed to her.

'Ma'am! There is one last thing I'd love to see. The stone trough in the basement.' (She pronounced it *throw*, as if she was still living in the wilds of County Clare, or in Anglo-Saxon Wessex.) 'Oho, then, the baskets and baskets of washing I did in that old black trough! And no hot water either only for what I'd drag down the stairs from the kitchen range.'

Was there a stone trough in the basement? I could not remember. Or had there ever been? But this time the younger woman rebelled, looked at her watch and looked out at a neighbouring house pouring two beams of light between the black trunks of the elms.

'It is too late, Auntie. The dark is falling. And there will be more snow. Don't encourage her,' she whispered to me. 'She could never make her way down those stairs.'

'Maybe I could help her?' I whispered.

The old lady was not listening. She had gone to the window, her mouth breathing moist patches on the cold pane.

'Marmee, her name was,' she whispered.

'Who?' I asked.

'The cat they gave me.'

It was only when she turned and began to sway, and we both ran to support her to a chair, that I realized the tiring day they must both have had.

'I won't let you go without the cup of tea!' I ordered, and put on the kettle, spread out the supermarket oilcloth, the rented china, the American biscuits and the Danish spoons, while her niece knelt beside her and looked worriedly at her pallid face and rubbed her knobbly hands. 'I only wish,' I laughed, 'that I had a nice hot slice of soda bread for you, cooked in the bastable, and tea smelling of the turfsmoke.'

They looked at me uncomprehendingly. Had they never seen

a bastable pot or smelled turfsmoke? The old woman's eyes and mind had begun to stray from me on the long journey homeward.

'Did you never go back to Ireland?' I asked. 'Didn't you ever go home?'

'Home?' she asked, and dropped her voice a pensive octave. 'Home?'

'I took her home,' the niece said curtly, 'in 1957. When my husband was killed working in the subway. It was my first visit to Ireland. And,' she said bitterly, 'my last.'

'Didn't you enjoy it?' I asked the old woman, and wet the tea, and sat beside her while she sipped it. I so wanted her to talk to me about Ireland!

'Slieve Callan,' she murmured, and I saw its whiteness rising like music under the low clouds moving imperceptibly from twenty miles away across the wrinkled Shannon. 'Letterkelly,' she whispered, and I saw a dozen roofs huddled under the white mountain. 'Miltownmalbay,' she said, and that would be her nearest market town, with every slate in its one street rattling under the wind across Spanish Point, where, I had so often been told, three ships of the Armada went down under tons of sea. 'County Clare,' she sighed, and I saw its grey lava, its tiny lochs and its cowering white cottages with their pigs' eyes of windows glinting in the sun.

'No, girl,' she said, 'I did not enjoy it. It was not the way I remembered it to be. Whenever you go back to any place,' she said, and I marvelled at the phrase, 'across the planets of the years, nothing is the way it was when you were young. Never go back, girl! I thought when I was going back that, maybe, I might stay there and end my days there. But it was not me they wanted. I took home all my savings. One thousand dollars I had. The savings of fifty years. They were dragging it out of me and dragging it out of me until it was all but gone. Ayeh! God help us! They were poor and they couldn't help it. When it was all gone I said to my niece here, "Now, we must go home." '

I looked at her niece, she looked sullenly at me, we both looked at the old woman.

'You are Irish,' the niece said after a while.

'Yes,' I said. 'I am Irish.'

She nodded, and the three of us looked out at the falling night and we understood everything.

We rose. The niece carefully muffled the old woman against the cold. As we went to the door they thanked me again and again for showing them the house. The farewells ended when I said, 'Good-bye, now, and come again any time ye like,' and closed the door, and replaced the chain.

I watched them through the muslin curtains cautiously descending the wooden steps to the brick pavement. They moved away carefully and slowly, arm in arm, towards the bright headlamps flying along Mass Avenue, and the bright windows of Sears, Roebuck across it, and the friendly telephone kiosk that I liked so much because it remained bright all through the night. At the end of the street they halted, turned for a moment and looked back. I saw with their eyes this lighted door behind which I stood unseen. The whole house behind me would be dark against the city's glow. I knew better than to fancy that the old woman would be rejoicing in her last backward look. She would be uttering her vatic croak, 'All changed!' Or the exhausted niece might even be saying crossly, 'Are you sure it was the right house at all? It didn't look so very grand to me!'

As they moved out of sight large flakes were sinking silently through the penumbra of a street lamp. I saw a black mountain mourning under a white veil. Somewhere there had been a lost childhood. Somewhere, at some time, in some house, there had been a vision of home. I returned to the letter I had been writing in the drawing room.

'How I wish we were together now, Nancy, gossiping over a drink or a pot of tea ...' I wrote on quickly. 'I could be telling you my great news. I have suspected it for weeks but I only heard today from the doctor that it is true. Oh, Nancy, the spring will be here soon, and after that the months won't be long passing until it comes, and then the four of us will all be together, in Ireland ...'

How gently the lighted snow kept touching that window-pane, melting and vanishing, and, like love, endlessly returning across the planets of the years.

A Dead Cert

Whenever Jenny Rosse came up to Dublin, for a shopping spree, or a couple of days with the War Union Hunt, or to go to the Opera, or to visit some of her widespread brood of relations in or around the city, or to do anything at all just to break the monotony of what she would then mockingly call 'my life in the provinces', the one person she never failed to ring was Oweny Flynn; and no matter how busy Oweny was in the courts or in his law chambers he would drop everything to have a lunch or a dinner with her. They had been close friends ever since he and Billy Rosse – both of them then at the King's Inns – had met her together twelve or thirteen years ago after a yacht race at the Royal Saint George. Indeed, they used to be such a close trio that, before she finally married Billy and buried herself in Cork, their friends were always laying bets on which of the two she would choose, and the most popular version of what happened in the end was that she let them draw cards for her. 'The first man,' she had cried gaily, 'to draw the ace of hearts!' According to this account the last card in the pack was Billy's, and before he turned it she fainted. As she was far from being a fainter, this caused a great deal of wicked speculation about which man she had always realized she wanted. On the other hand, one of her rivals said that she had faked the whole thing to get him.

This Saturday afternoon in October she and Oweny had finished a long, gossipy lunch at the Shelbourne, where she always stayed whenever she came up to Dublin. ('I hate to be tied to my blooming relatives!') They were sipping their coffee and brandy in two deep saddleback armchairs, the old flowery chintzy kind that the Shelbourne always provides. The lounge was empty and, as always after wine, Oweny had begun to flirt mildly with her, going back over the old days, telling her, to her evident satisfaction, how lonely it is to be a bachelor of thirty-seven ('My life trickling away into the shadows of memory!'), and what a fool he had been to let such a marvellous lump of a girl slip through his fingers, when, all of a sudden, she leaned forward and tapped the back of his hand like a dog pawing for still more attention.

'Oweny!' she said. 'I sometimes wish my husband would die for a week.'

For a second he stared at her in astonishment. Then, in a brotherly kind of voice, he said, 'Jenny! I hope there's nothing wrong between you and Billy?'

She tossed her red head at the very idea.

'I'm as much in love with Billy as ever I was! Billy is the perfect husband. I wouldn't change him for worlds.'

'So I should have hoped,' Oweny said, dutifully, if a bit stuffily. 'I mean, of all the women in the world you must be one of the luckiest and happiest that ever lived. Married to a successful barrister. Two splendid children. How old is Peter now? Eight? And Anna must be ten. There's one girl who is going to be a breaker of men's hearts and an engine of delight. Like,' he added, remembering his role, 'her beautiful mother. And you have that lovely house at Silversprings. With that marvellous view down the Lee...'

'You can't live on scenery!' she interposed tartly. 'And there's a wind on that river that'd cool a tomcat!'

'A car of your own. A nanny for the kids. Holidays abroad every year. No troubles or trials that I ever heard of. And,' again remembering his duty, 'if I may say so, every time we meet, you look younger, and,' he plunged daringly, 'more desirable than ever. So, for God's sake, Jenny Rosse, what the hell on earth are you talking about?'

She turned her head to look out pensively at the yellowing sun glittering above the last, trembling, fretted leaves of the trees in the Green, while he gravely watched her, admiring the way its light brought out the copper-gold of her hair, licked the flat tip of her cocked nose and shone on her freckled redhead's cheek that had always reminded him of peaches and cream, and 'No,' he thought, 'not a pretty woman, not pretty-pretty, anyway I never did care for that kind of prettiness, she is too strong for that, too much vigour, I'm sure she has poor old Billy bossed out of his life!' And he remembered how she used to sail her water-wag closer to the wind than any fellow in the yacht club, and how she used to curse like a trooper if she slammed one into the net, always hating to lose a game, especially to any man, until it might have been only last night that he had felt that aching hole in his belly when he knew that he had lost her for ever. She turned her head to him and smiled wickedly.

'Yes,' she half agreed. 'Everything you say is true but...'

'But what?' he asked curiously, and sank back into the trough of his armchair to receive her reply.

Her smile vanished.

'Oweny! You know exactly how old I am. I had my thirty-fourth birthday party last week. By the way, I was very cross with you that you didn't come down for it. It was a marvellous party. All Cork was at it. I felt like the Queen of Sheba. It went on until about three in the morning. I enjoyed every single minute of it. But the next day, I got the shock of my life! I was sitting at my dressing table brushing my hair.' She stopped dramatically, and pointed her finger tragically at him as if his face were her mirror. 'When I looked out the window at a big red grain boat steaming slowly down the river, out to sea, I stopped brushing, I looked at myself, and there and then I said, "Jenny Rosse! You are in your thirty-fifth year. And you've never had a lover!" And I realized that I never could have a lover, not without hurting Billy, unless he obliged me by dying for a week.'

For fully five seconds Oweny laughed and laughed.

'Wait,' he choked, 'until the lads at the Club hear this one!'

The next second he was sitting straight up in his armchair.

'Jenny,' he said stiffly, 'would you mind telling me why exactly you chose to tell this to *me*?'

'Aren't you interested?' she asked innocently.

'Isn't it just a tiny little bit unfair?'

'But Billy would never know he'd been dead for a week. At most he'd just think he'd lost his memory or something. Don't you suppose that's what Lazarus thought? Oh! I see what you mean. Well, I suppose yes, I'd have betrayed Billy. That's true enough, isn't it?'

'I am not thinking of your good husband. I am thinking of the other unfortunate fellow when his week would be out!'

'What other fellow? Are you trying to suggest that I've been up to something underhand?'

'I mean,' he pressed on, quite angry now, 'that I refuse to believe that you are mentally incapable of realizing that if you ever did let any other man fall in love with you for even five minutes, not to speak of a whole week, you would be sentencing him to utter misery for the rest of his life.'

'Oh, come off it!' she huffed. 'You always did take things in high C. Why are you so bloody romantic? It was just an idea. I expect lots of women have it, only they don't admit it. One little, measly wild oat? It's probably something I should have done before I got married, but,' she grinned happily, 'I was too busy then having a good time. "In the morning sow thy seed and in the evening withhold not thine hand." Ecclesiastes. I learned that at Alexandra College. Shows you how innocent I was – I never knew what it really meant until I got married. Of course, you men are different. You think of nothing else.'

He winced.

'If you mean me,' he said sourly, 'you know damned well that I never wanted any woman but you.'

When she laid her hand on his he understood why she had said that about Billy dying for a week. But when he snatched his hand away and she gathered up her gloves with all the airs of a woman at the end of her patience with a muff, got up and strode ahead of him to the levelling sun outside the hotel, he began to wonder if he really had understood. He even began to wonder if it was merely that he had upset her with all that silly talk about old times. A side-glance caught a look in her eyes that was much more mocking than hurt and at once his anger returned. She had been doing much more than flirting. She had been provoking him. Or had she just wanted to challenge him? Whatever she was doing she had manoeuvred him into a ridiculous position. Then he thought, 'She will drive to Cork tonight and I will never be certain what she really meant.' While he boggled she started talking brightly about her holiday plans for the winter. A cover-up? She said she was going to Gstaad for the skiing next month with a couple of Cork friends.

'Billy doesn't ski, so he won't come. We need another man. Would you like to join us? They are nice people. Jim Chandler and his wife. About our age. You'd enjoy them.'

He said huffily that he was too damned busy. And she might not know it but some people in the world have to earn their living. Anyway, he was saving up for two weeks' sailing in the North Sea in June. At which he saw that he had now genuinely hurt her. ('Dammit, if we really were lovers this would be our first quarrel!') He forced a smile.

'Is this good-bye, Jenny? You did say at lunch that you were going to drive home this evening? Shan't I see you again?'

She looked calculatingly at the sun winking coldly behind the far leaves.

'I hate going home – I mean so soon. And I hate driving alone in the dark. I think I'll just go to bed after dinner and get up bright and early on Sunday morning before the traffic. I'll be back at Silversprings in time for lunch.'

'If you are doing nothing tonight why don't you let me take you to dinner at the Yacht Club?'

She hesitated. Cogitating the long road home? Or what?

'Jenny! They'd all love to see you. It will be like old times. You remember the Saturday night crowds?'

She spoke without enthusiasm.

'So be it. Let's do that.'

She presented her freckled cheek for his parting kiss. In frank admiration he watched her buttocks swaying provocatively around the corner of Kildare Street.

Several times during the afternoon, back in his office, he found himself straying from his work to her equivocal words. Could there, after all, be something wrong between herself and Billy? Could she be growing tired of him? It could happen, and easily. A decent chap, fair enough company, silent, a bit slow, not brilliant even at his own job, successful only because of his father's name and connections, never any good at all at sport – he could easily see her flying down the run from the Egli at half a mile a minute, the snow leaping from her skis whenever she did a quick turn. But not Billy. He would be down in the valley paddling around like a duck among the beginners behind the railway – and he remembered what a hopeless sheep he had always been with the girls, who nevertheless seemed to flock around him all the time, perhaps (it was the only explanation he ever found for it) because he was the fumbling sort of fellow that awakens the maternal instinct in girls. At which he saw her not as a girl in white shorts dashing to and fro on the tennis courts, but as the mature woman who had turned his face into her mirror by crying at him along her pointed finger, 'You are in your thirty-fifth year!' How agile, he wondered, would she now be on the courts or the ski runs? He rose and stood for a long time by his window, glaring down at the Saturday evening blackness of Nassau Street, and heard the shouting from the playing fields of Trinity College, and watched the small lights of the buses moving through the bluing dusk, until he shivered at the cold creeping through the pane. He felt the tilt of time and the falling years, and in excitement understood her sudden lust.

As always on Saturday nights, once the autumn comes and the sailing is finished and every boat on the hard for another winter, the lounge and the bar of the Club were a cascade of noise. If he had been alone he would have at once added his bubble of chatter to it. Instead he was content to stand beside the finest woman in the crowd, watching her smiling proudly around her, awaiting attention from her rout (what was that great line? *Diana's foresters, gentlemen of the shade, minions of the moon?*) until, suddenly, alerted and disturbed, he found her eyes turning from the inattentive mob to look out broodily through the tall windows. The lighthouse on the pier's end was writing slow circles on the dusty water of the harbour. He said, 'Jenny, you are not listening to me!' She whispered crossly, 'But I don't know a single one of these bloody people!' He pointed out the commodore. Surely she remembered Tom O'Leary? She peered and said, 'Not *that* old man?' He said, 'How could you have forgotten?'

Tom had not forgotten her, as he found when he went to the bar to refresh their drinks.

'Isn't that Jenny Rose you have there?' he asked Oweny. 'She's putting on weight, bedad! Ah, she did well for herself.'

'How do you mean?' Oweny asked, a bit shortly.

'Come off it. Didn't she marry one of the finest practices in Cork! Handsome is as handsome does, my boy! She backed a dead cert.'

Jealous old bastard! As he handed her the glass he glanced covertly at her beam. Getting a bit broad, all right. She asked idly, 'Who is that slim girl in blue, she is as brown as if she has been sailing all summer?' He looked and shrugged.

'One of the younger set? I think she's George Whitaker's daughter.'

'That nice-looking chap in the black tie looks lost. Just the way Billy used always to look. Who is he?'

'Saturday nights!' he said impatiently. 'You know the way they bring the whole family. It gives the wives a rest from the cooking.'

It was a relief to lead her into the dining room and find her mood change like the wind to complete gaiety.

'So this,' she laughed, 'is where it all began. And look! The same old paintings. They haven't changed a thing.'

The wine helped, and they were safely islanded in their corner, even with the families baying cheerfully at one another from table to table, even though she got on his nerves by dawdling so long over the coffee that the maids had cleared every table but theirs. Then she revealed another change of mood.

'Oweny! Please let's go somewhere else for our nightcap.'

'But where?' he said irritably. 'Not in some scruffy pub?'

'Your flat?' she suggested, and desire spread in him like a water lily. It shrivelled when she stepped out ahead of him into the cold night air, looked up at the three-quarter moon, then at the Town Hall clock.

'What a stunning night! Oweny, I've changed my mind! Just give me a good strong coffee and I'll drive home right away.'

'So!' he said miserably. 'We squabbled at lunch. And our dinner was a flop.'

She protested that it had been a marvellous dinner; and wasn't it grand the way nothing had been changed?

'They even still have that old picture of the Duke of Windsor when he was a boy in the navy.'

He gave up. He had lost the set. All the way into town they spoke only once.

'We had good times,' she said. 'I could do it all over again.'

'And change nothing?' he growled.

Her answer was pleasing, but inconclusive – 'Who knows?'

If only he could have her in the witness box, under oath, for fifteen minutes!

In his kitchenette, helping him to make the coffee, she changed gear again, so full of good spirits (because, he understood sourly, she was about to take off for home) that he thrust an arm about her waist, assaulted her cheek with a kiss as loud as a champagne cork, and said fervently (he had nothing to lose now), 'And I thinking how marvellous it would be if we could be in bed together all night!' She laughed mockingly, handed him the coffee pot – a woman long accustomed to the grappling hook – and led the way with the cups back into his living room. They sat on the small sofa before his coffee table.

'And I'll tell you another thing, Jenny!' he said. 'If I had this flat twelve years ago it might very easily have happened that you would have become my one true love! You would have changed my whole life!'

She let her head roll back on the carved moulding of the sofa, looking past him at the moon. Quickly he kissed her mouth. Unstirring she looked back into his eyes, whispered, 'I should not have let you do that,' returned her eyes to the moon, and whispered, 'Or should I?'

'Jenny!' he ordered. 'Close your eyes. Pretend you really are back twelve years ago.'

Her eyelids sank. He kissed her again, softly, wetly, felt her hand creep to his shoulder and impress his kiss, felt her lips open. Her hand fell weakly away. Desire climbed into his throat. And then he heard her moan the disenchanting name. He drew back, rose and looked furiously down at her. She opened her eyes, staring uncomprehendingly around her and looked up at him in startled recognition.

'So,' he said bitterly, 'he did not die even for one minute?'

She laughed wryly, lightly, stoically, a woman who would

never take anything in a high key, except a five-barred gate or a double-ditch.

'I'm sorry, Oweny. It's always the same. Whenever I dream of having a lover I find myself at the last moment in my husband's arms.'

She jumped up, snatched her coat and turned on him.

'Why the hell, Oweny, for God's sake, don't you go away and get married?'

'To have me dreaming about you, is that what you want?'

'I want to put us both out of pain!'

They glared hatefully at one another.

'Please drive me to the Shelbourne. If I don't get on the road right away, I'll go right out of the top of my head!'

They drove to the Green, she got out, slammed the car door behind her and without a word raced into the hotel. He whirled, drove hell for leather back to the Club, killed the end of the night with the last few gossipers, drank far too much and lay awake for hours staring sideways from his pillow over the grey, frosting roofs and countless yellow chimney pots of Dublin.

Past twelve. In her yellow sports Triumph she would tear across the Curragh at seventy-five and along the two straight stretches before and after Monasterevan. By now she has long since passed through Port Laoise and Abbeyleix where only a few lighted upper-storey windows still resist night and sleep. From that on, for hour after hour, south and south, every village street and small town she passes will be fast asleep, every roadside cottage, every hedge, field and tree, and the whole widespread, moonblanched country pouring past her headlights until she herself gradually becomes hedge, tree, field and fleeting moon. Arched branches underlit, broken demesne walls, a closed garage, hedges flying, a grey church, a lifeless gate-lodge, until the black rock and ruin of Cashel comes slowly wheeling about the moon. A streetlamp falling on a blank window makes it still more blank. Cars parked beside a kerb huddle from the cold. In Cahir the boarded windows of the old granaries are blind with age. The dull square is empty. Her wheeling lights catch the vacant eyes of the hotel, leap the useless bridge, fleck the side of the Norman castle. She is doing eighty on the level uplands under the Galtee mountains, heedless of the sleep-wrapt plain falling for miles and miles away to her left.

Why is she stopping? To rest, to look, to light a cigarette, to listen? He can see nothing for her to see but a scatter of farmhouses on the plain; nothing to hear but one sleepless dog as far away as the moon it bays. He lights his bedside lamp. Turned half past two. He puts out his light and there are her kangaroo lights, leaping, climbing, dropping, winding, slowing now because of the twisting strain on her arms. She does not see the sleeping streets of Fermoy; only the white signpost marking the remaining miles to Cork. Her red tail-lights disappear and reappear before him every time she winds and unwinds down to the sleeping estuary of the Lee, even at low tide not so much a river as a lough – grey, turbulent and empty. He tears after her as she rolls smoothly westward beside its shining slobland. Before them the bruised clouds hang low over the city silently awaiting the morning.

She brakes to turn in between her white gates, her wheels spit back the gravel, she zooms upward to her house and halts under its staring windows. She switches off the engine, struggles out, stretches her arms high above her head with a long, shivering, happy, outpouring groan and then, breathing back a long breath, she holds her breasts up to her windows. There is not a sound but the metal of her engine creaking as it cools, and the small wind whispering up from the river. She laughs to see their cat flow like black water around the corner of the house. She leans into the car, blows three long, triumphant horn blasts and before two windows can light up over her head she has disappeared indoors as smoothly as her cat. And that, at last, it is the end of sleep, where, behind windows gone dark again, she spreads herself under her one true lover.

Neither of them hear the morning seagulls over the Liffey or the Lee. He wakes unrefreshed to the sounds of late church bells. She half opens her eyes to the flickering light of the river on her ceiling, rolls over on her belly and stretching out her legs behind her like a satisfied cat, she dozes off again. He stares for a long time at his ceiling, hardly hearing the noise of the buses going by.

It is cold. His mind is clear and cold. I know now what she

wants. But does she? Let her lie. She called me a romantic and she has her own fantasy. She has what she wanted, wants what she cannot have, is not satisfied with what she has got. I have known her for over twelve years and never known her at all. The most adorable woman I ever met. And a common slut! If she had married me I suppose she would be dreaming now of him? Who was it said faithful women are always regretting their own fidelity, never their husbands? Die for a week? He chuckled at her joke. Joke? Or gamble? Or a dead cert? If I could make him die for a week it would be a hell of a long week for her. Will I write to her? I could telephone.

Hello, Jenny! It's me. I just wanted to be sure you got back safely the other night. Why wouldn't I worry? About anyone as dear and precious as you? Those frosty roads. Of course it was, darling, a lovely meeting. And we must do it again. No, nothing changes! That's a dead cert. Oh, and Jenny! I nearly forgot. About that skiing bit next month in Gstaad. Can I change my mind? I'd love to join you. May I? Splendid! Oh, no! Not for that long. Say . . . just for a week?

He could see her hanging up the receiver very slowly.

Hymeneal

I

Away back in 1929, a few months before they got married, Phil and Abby Doyle had bought a red-and-yellow brick house, semi-detached, with a small garden in front and a useful strip for vegetables at the rear, on the North Circular Road. It stood about halfway between the Dublin Cattle Market and the entrance to the Phoenix Park – to be precise a bare 1300 feet, or 80 perches, from the Park Gate, as Phil had once carefully established in his schoolmasterish way by means of a pedometer attached to his left leg. All in all it was a pleasant quarter, so convenient to the city that Abby could be down in O'Connell Street by tram within ten minutes, and yet sufficiently remote for almost unbroken quietness. On still summer nights she could sometimes hear the morose growling of lions from the Zoological Gardens, the crazed laughter of monkeys. Early in the morning, if the wind was from the east, she might hear the mooing of cattle and the baaing of sheep from the Market. Otherwise the only obtrusive noise was when an occasional freight train from Kingsbridge came trundling along the loop north of the city down to the quays and the cargo steamers for England. But the greatest attraction of the North Circular for Abby was that when her sister Molly married Failey Quigley in the following year, they had bought an identical house next door. Abby, it soon transpired, was to have no children, so that when Molly's family got too long-tailed for their little terrace house, and Failey became a Member of the Dail, and ultimately a Cabinet Minister, she was all the more relieved that they moved only five minutes away, to a larger house, at the corner of Infirmary Road.

There they all remained, then, close together for more than thirty-five years, as much familiars of the North Circular as its postmen, busdrivers, doctors, shopkeepers, milkmen, dustmen, priests, beggarwomen, policemen and park-keepers; co-citizens of Oxmanstown, veterans of the Arran Quay Ward, seasoned Dubliners. Abby could have walked blindfold between Doyle's Corner and the Park Gate. She knew every dog with its nose out through the bars of its garden gate, every crack in every pavement, every step up or down, as well as she knew every vagary of her house – the secondhand Frigidaire that grunted up to her so comfortingly during the night, her one-bar electric stove that warmed her toes in the morning (if she remembered to stick the scrubbing brush under its loose wall-plug), the four permanently stuffed jets of her gas stove, the electric bulb in the middle of the kitchen ceiling that she knew how to light and put out with a tap of her broom handle, or the plants in her tiny glasshouse outside the kitchen window, all stolen from the People's Gardens or the Botanics and dropped into the pouch of her umbrella with the quick sideways look of a born babysnatcher, every one of them to be palm-touched afterwards with maternal love in their tiny indoor garden. Outside and inside number 26 Saint Rita's Villas, she had put down her roots for life in the North Circular.

Unfortunately, when his retirement was about a year away, Phil had been forced to make some unsettling observations. Of these the most inexorable was that Abby was getting a bit beyond housekeeping; and on his modest pension he could never afford a full-time servant. On the other hand, as the cost of living went up and the value of his pension went down, the house had quintupled in value. Now, if ever, was the time to sell it and move out of Dublin to some place cheaper.

After much searching he found exactly what he wanted west of the Shannon in County Clare, about a mile from the tiny village of Corofin, some thirty-five miles from Limerick, and less than twenty from the Atlantic coast. It was a small old whitewashed cottage, standing on a quarter-acre of reedy ground, with a stout slate roof (only a few of its slates were missing), two and a half rooms, cement floors and an open turf-shed leaning against the gable under a rusty corrugated iron roof. Without saying a word to Abby he bought it. He had the holes in the floor filled in, the broken glass in the windows restored, the walls whitewashed, the woodwork painted blue, a dry closet built at the end of a path to the rear and a cold bath installed in the half-room. The fine new zinc cistern that he raised outside, level with the roof, would supply plenty of soft rainwater. For drinking water there was a well about a hundred yards away. For heat they had two fireplaces. In the nearby bogs turf abounded. For light they would use petrol lamps. Absolute perfection!

When it was all done he took some coloured photographs of it and for months he kept them in his wallet to peep at as secretively and happily as a youth might peep at a picture of his first girl. Then, at last, one night, like a conjurer, he whisked them out of the air and fanned them out on Abby's lap.

'Our new home!' he cried triumphantly, standing over her – six feet two and thin as a rake handle – 'Isn't it the perfect answer? Isn't it lovely? You will garden. I will fish, and shoot, and take long walks. Every night we will sit on each side of a blazing turf fire, you with a cat, me with a dog, as cosy as two kittens in a basket. You will be sewing or knitting. I will be writing my Autobiography. And when the night ends we'll fall asleep lulled by the lovely pattering of the rain on the tin roof of the turf-shed. Perfect peace. Philosophic calm. Fresh air. Lovely country. Content and serenity without end.'

Abby slowly put on her specs and looked carefully at the pictures, one after the other. Then she went through them again. When she had looked at them several times she held them between her palms without raising her head or saying a word. She was forcing herself to remember that whenever Phil got some lunatic idea into his head there had always been only one thing to do – let him alone and he might, he just might begin gradually to forget it. Cross him and it was stuck in his head forever.

'Well?' he cried at last. 'Isn't it wonderful? Isn't it what the doctor ordered?'

She slowly lifted her head and looked at him with eyes as moist and humble as a dog so old that even its whiskers have gone white.

'It looks very nice, Phil. Very nice. For the summer. But the rain, Phil? The rain battering on the tin shed?'

In a fury he snatched up the pictures.

'Chalk and cheese!' he roared, meaning that that was what they always were.

He roved up and down the room like a caged cheetah. He kicked the chair. He kicked the table. He took up a cushion from the sofa and hurled it to the end of the room. Then he stood in front of her with his ten fingers splayed flat against her.

'Say no more!' he said. 'I understand! You have made yourself perfectly clear! Don't say one other single word! But for God almighty's sake will you tell me what it is that you don't like about our cottage?'

'You haven't even told me, Phil,' she whispered meekly, 'where it is.'

' 'Tis in West Clare! And please don't try to tell me that you, who were once a National School teacher, don't know where West Clare is.'

Abby had been reared in Dublin. Anywhere beyond the Liffey, or west of the Phoenix Park or south of Bray was, to her, a wasteland.

'Oh, of course, Phil,' she wailed humbly, 'I often *heard* of West Clare! I even heard a song about it. *Are ye right there, Michael, are ye right? D'ye think that we'll get there before the night?* All about some queer railway they have that has to balance itself on one track like an acrobat. Phil! Will we have to travel to West Clare on that awful railway?'

He sank into his armchair and bowed his head in his hands. Bloodshot he looked up at her. He spoke to her gently.

'Abby! The railway that you are trying to describe was called the Artique railway. It was an engineering experiment made by a Frenchman in 1889 away down in the County Kerry. It was abolished twenty-five years ago.'

'But, Phil, in the song they have the railway in West Clare. I'm almost certain of that, Phil! I can sing it for you.'

Which, pipingly and inaccurately, she began to do while he contemplated her, undecided whether to admire the power of female stupidity or the profundity of female deceit. At the end her voice broke and she was singing croakingly through a veil of tears.

'And as the train draws near Kilrush / The passengers get out and push . . . Are ye right there, Michael, are ye right / D'ye think we'll get there before the night? / Oh, it all depends on whether / The ould engine holds together . . . / But we might, then, Michael . . . So we . . .'

He went and sat beside her and touched her wrinkled paw, remembering how sweetly she used to sing for him long ago.

'Abby,' he whispered, 'that old railway was broken up, donkeys' years ago, too. Listen to me, Abby! Let me tell you, calmly, simply and quietly, about West Clare. County Clare is one of the loveliest counties . . .'

She dried her eyes with one hand while he held the other and talked and talked about County Clare – to her as he thought, to himself as he was despairingly to discover, both that night and on every other night that he tried to interest her in Clare's fauna and flora, its archaeology, its geology, its ecology, its methods of husbandry, and all the wild sports of the West. Her trouble, he realized in the end, gazing at her opaque eyes, was not that she could not take in what he was telling her. It was simply that she thought that the less she knew about Clare the farther she kept it away from her. He might, he saw, as well be trying to sell her an unfurnished shack in the Great Mohave Desert.

2

For some twenty-five years before Phil had been due to retire from his post as Inspector of Schools he had planned his pensioned years around The Book as exultantly as an executioner sharpening his axe to wrap it around the neck of his favourite enemy.

'On the night,' he would say to Abby, 'of the day that I hand in my gun, to whatever half-witted idiot will at that time be Minister for Education, I am going to sit down on that chair, by that window, at that table, and I'm going to start writing The Book.'

Unmuzzled at long last, he was going to expose, in his Autobiography, all the miseries and humiliations, botcheries and bunglings, all the chicaneries, evasions and general lunacies that he had had to suffer in silence at the orders of one fool of a Minster after another through forty years of serfdom.

'Mind *you*!' he would roar at her. 'This book isn't going to be just any old book. There never was, there never will be a book like my Book. It's not going to be a Book at all! It's going to be a landmine. It's going to be an atom bomb. The day my Book comes out you will hear an explosion like the Trumpet of Judgement reverberating from one end of Ireland to the other, and the next thing you will see,' spreading his arms like wings and letting his voice fall to the gentlest whisper, 'will be the entire Department of so-called bloody Education floating over Dublin like black snow.'

It was all ready. It was all waiting, locked in his bookcase. Two hundred and fifty blank pages of it, bound in black cloth, with the words *Chapter One* written on the top of page one, and the title neatly typed and pasted across the black cover: *I Was Speechless for Forty Years*. On nights when he felt particularly hard pressed by some harder-to-bear-than-usual ministerial folly he would run his fingers lovingly down the spine of it, sigh expectantly and feel calm again.

Not that Abby ever heard him utter all these wild words of his in one breath. Normally Phil was a staid, disciplined and good-humoured man, who had made countless friends all over Ireland and enjoyed countless happy days with them. All the same, over the years, and over and over again, Abby had heard every one of those separate words, always in total and tactful silence; having learned by experience that if she uttered as much as one word in reply, even if she did no more than sigh a gentle 'Oh, Moses!' – her one and only expletive – he would at once start reciting what she called the Pome. And the Pome was even harder to bear than his wildest guff about the Book.

This poem was a set of satirical verses entitled *The Patriot* which she privately called 'That accursed ould rawmeysh of a thing by Frank O'Connor that started it all off.' These malevolent verses Phil – if crossed, or imagining he was crossed –

would recite at her in a voice like a tuba at full blast, slowly goose-stepping up and down the worn carpet of their little sitting room in the North Circular.

> BEJASUS! (forte) Before ye inter me (maestoso)
> I'll show ye all up! (fortissimo)
> I've everything stored in me memory, (con brio)
> Facts, figures enough (veloce)
> Since I first swore an oath of allegiance (spiritoso)
> As a patriot boy (diminuendo)
> To avenge me maternal grandfather (sforzando)
> They hanged at Fermoy . . . (vibrato)

On down to the last sibilant bellow of,

> Ye think ye'll escape me? (capriccioso)
> Ha! 'Tis true that me sight's a bit shook, (scherzo)
> I was never no hand with a pen, (allegro)
> But I'll write One Terrible Book (pianissimo)
> Before, with gun-carriage and pipers – (affettuoso)
> Ye dastardly crew! – (parlante)
> Ye bring to his grave in Glasnevin (legato)
> The ONE man that was true! (tremolo)

The only time Abby had ever spoken out about the Pome was one night after she had complained to her sister Molly that he must have recited that accursed pome to her at least once a month for the last twelve years, which made some one hundred and forty-four times in all – enough, Molly commented, to make even a gravedigger get a bit fed up with *An Elegy Written in a Country Churchyard*.

'But it's your own fault!' Molly had flashed at her out of her black gipsy's eyes. 'You're too soft with him! I tell you, if my Failey did that to me I'd soon put a stop to his gallop. Why don't you just tell him to put a sock in it? The man must be mad. But, sure, those fellows in the Department of Education are all mad. 'Tis well known! 'Tis given up to them! Every one of them is half-crazy from having to deal with priests and bishops from morning to night. You can't tell me anything about those fellows. If I didn't put my foot down on Failey at least once a month he'd be making speeches at me every night of the week – speeches that he'd never dare to give out in public but that I have to listen to just to let him blow off steam. The next time Phil Doyle recites that old stuff to you just tell him to put it where the woman told the monkey to put the nuts.'

Three nights later, like the fool she was, Abby took Molly's advice. When Phil had completed the Pome she gazed up at him pensively, allowed him his marital due of one minute's silence and then gave a babyish little titter.

'Phil! Do you know what I think whenever I hear that pome? I think that it's a very nice pome. But somehow it always reminds me of that other lovely pome, "*The curfew tolls the knell of parting day, the lowing herd . . .*" '

'That thing,' he roared at her, 'has no guts in it!'

'Maybe,' she persisted tremblingly. 'But 'tis apt, Phil! 'Tis very apt. I mean if you ever do get around to that book of yours, and I'm sure, Phil, it will be a very nice little book too, it will be our parting day with a lot of friends. That is if, God help me, I ever live to see it.'

'See it?' He charged at her with his finger pointing at her like a bayonet. 'You wait! And you know, too, who's going to get the worst lash of my whip in it – your lovely brother-in-law. Our longest reigning so-called Minister for Education. Ireland's beardless Palmerston! The original inventor of Total Inaction and Absolute Non-intervention in Anything Whatsoever! The blind boshtoon! The total botch! The braying polthacawn! Oho! If I was never to write another word but that fellow's obituary I'll show him up for the eedjut he is, was and always will be. He's going to be the linch-pin of my Book. The core, and kernel, fulcrum and omphalos of it! You just wait and see!'

Shaking like a poplar leaf, she still dared to persist.

'Oh, Moses! Is it poor Failey? Who was always and always so fond of the pair of us!'

'Fond?' At that Phil laughed in three descending, mocking brays, like the devil in *Faust*. 'Ho, ho, ho! That's a new one. Fond? I don't want fondness! I want action. But will I get it from Failey? Any more than I ever got one spark of it from any single one of his rubber-stamp predecessors? Let me give you one simple example. Look at this frightful case that cropped up only last week in Mullaghabawn East over a teacher named Hooligan! A fellow that, as every living soul in Mullaghabawn East, and West, well knows, hasn't been sober since he switched from his mother's paps to his father's poteen. And his wife as bad as him. Fighting in the schoolroom, the pair of them. Before the children's eyes. Throwing mollyers of stones at one another in the schoolyard. Calling one another bitch and bastard at the tops of their voices! But do you think your fond, and fair and lovely Failey will take any action about that? And why not, pray? Answer me! Why not?'

Wishing to the Lord God she had never opened her mouth about either the Pome or the Book, or that she had Molly there to talk up to him, she moaned:

'Phil! What do I know about any Hooligan or Booligan? You're the one who knows everything about these things.'

'You know damn well why Failey won't take action.'

'I don't, Phil. I'm sure it's some awful reason. I suppose 'tis because her mother is his aunt, or his cousin is his nephew, or his sister is the Reverend Mother of Mullinavat, or her uncle is a titular bishop in Africa, or . . .'

'Failey will take no action because he hasn't the GUTS, that's why, and he never had, nor never will have, and that's why!'

At which point in their sad comedy – where any normally intelligent member of the audience would have begun to roll up his programme and fish for his coat, and the doorkeepers would be signalling out to the cloakroom girls – what must Abby do but produce her last little weapon, pull the trigger and let her feeble fan of protest puff out of it:

'Failey,' she whispered, 'is *kind*! It's through his kindness,' she began to weep, 'that you weren't retired like everybody else at sixty. And that leaves the pair of us with our one last year of peace and comfort here in Dublin. *And leaves the world to darkness and to me.*'

Curtain! With Phil falling back into his armchair behind his shivering newspaper; gassed, silenced, chokingly whimpering to himself at the insoluble mystery of why in God's name he had ever married a woman who knew nothing whatesoever about Education; and, if *she* was like that, in spite of listening to him day in and day out, how could he ever hope to liberate anybody or anything at all in Ireland? It was not, however, the end of their row. It never was. That always came as a final apotheosis, showing Phil deep in hell, growling through Greek fire and blue smoke – that is to say, locked upstairs in the bathroom, obscening at her as he never in his life obscened at anybody in public, strangling her with his two fists, shoving her head down into the W.C. and pulling the chain on her for good and all. That done, he straightens his four-inch stiff collar, tidies his thin dust of hair and emerges on the landing to call amiably down the stairs, 'Abby! What about a nice little cup of tea and a few of those old arrowroot biscuits of yours?'

'Well,' Molly duly asked her, 'did you shut him up about the Pome?'

'I did,' Abby lied. 'I said the reason Failey kept him on, and every lunatic like him in the Department, was out of sheer kindness and nothing else.'

'And what did his Royal Irish Lordship say to that?'

'He said, "He kept me on because he knows I'm the best Inspector of Schools in Ireland." '

The two of them smiled wisely at one another. They knew that Failey had kept Phil on only because he adored him. The best storyteller, the funniest yarner, the only decent bit of company in the whole Department, the one man who knew the country inside out and from edge to edge, ever parish priest in it, every jarvey, every tinker, every taxi driver, every bush in every bog, every sparrow on every telegraph wire, a man always ready with a comical tale about every one of them, a man to be welcomed with open arms whenever he came into the office in Marlborough Street, shaken heartily by both hands, ordered to 'sit down there, my old pal from far-off days and tell us the latest lunacy from the hinterland,' and straightway given a generous jar from the bottle of Irish that Failey kept in his bottom drawer for the few, the very few visitors that he could more or less completely trust. The sisters knew furthermore, having told him of it themselves, that Failey knew about the Book and that he did not like the smell of it at all.

'Not,' he once privately confided to Abby, 'that I care a damn what he puts into it. Give and take, I'm used to hard knocks. But Phil isn't. And he'll get plenty of them if he ever writes that book!'

To the end Abby built high hopes on those words. Maybe, she innocently hoped, Failey might extend Phil's retiring age to seventy, and by then all this lunacy about leaving Dublin would have 'frizzled out'. She spent her last few months pleading with him not to take her away. He spent them reassuring her that it was best to go. Then, his time up, he led her westward across the Shannon.

3

It took them a whole day to get from Dublin to the cottage. They went by taxi, by train to Limerick, by bus to Ennis, by a second bus to the village of Corofin, and finally by a hired car from the village to the cottage, the month being March, the day misty and windy, the daylight barely holding its own against the shrouds of the sun. When she got out of the hired car and stood under her umbrella on the roadside, cold and stiff, she saw a white box in a field, oblong, one-storied, wet-slated with two blank eyes. It was backed by a low wall through whose lacy chinks she saw the sunset. She saw rocks, she saw a dark lough blown into froth by the wind. She could barely discern the limestone-grey uplands that she was to come to know as the elephant's hide of the Barony of Burren. That night, from their bed, she listened for hours to the rain pattering on the tin roof of the turf-shed.

A couple of days later, during a dry, windy hour, she ventured alone on her first walk. She saw a small village huddled below the corrugated uplands. She followed a slim road. On a low rise she came on a ruined castle with six motionless goats on the tiptop of it, their beards blown by the wind. In the far distance she saw a broom of rain gradually blot out a tiny belfry. She saw two cottages whose smoke streamed sideways like two small ships in a gale vanish under the broom. When she got back to the cottage she went into their bedroom to weep in secret. Nor was she converted in May when the entire expanse of lava became lit up by millions of tiny gentians that brought the blue sky down into every sheltering furrow. She was not even comforted by the one blessed hot spell the Burren enjoyed that August when she could watch scores of small black cows wandering slowly over it to lick the tender grass from its marrowbones. Cows to her had always meant only two white bottles tinkling on her front step in Saint Rita's Villas.

She had nobody to consult except Molly. She did not write to her until the grunting September wind under the door warned her that winter would soon be counting her bones. Even then she wrote only because of a fright she got one frosty night, hard with stars and silence, when she was sitting on one side of the fire gazing into it, and Phil was at his table on the other side bent over the terrible Book. Hearing that vast autumnal silence of the Burren, broken only by the faint hiss of their petrol lamp and an occasional purr from the great fire of burning peat, it suddenly came to her with a pang of regret, as if for one other precious thing she had left behind her in Dublin, that he had never recited the Pome to her since they came to Corofin. She turned to him to ask him to recite it to her, and was startled to find him staring blankly into the globe of the lamp. She stole another glance, and yet another glance. Each time she looked he was still staring fixedly at the white globe. At last, as if he felt her eyes on him, he turned his head towards her, threw down his pen, said, 'I think I'll go for a stroll, it's a fine frosty night for a ramble,' put on his long greatcoat, took his stick and went out.

She waited until his footsteps faded down the ringing road. Then, she dared to peep at the Book. In his minute but beautiful handwriting he had, so far, covered only four pages – all, she gathered, skimming quickly over them, about his youth in Dublin. She also found, pasted inside the front cover, a calendar of dates and events. These she read with as much fear as if she was reading an account of his death in a newspaper:

Philip Ignatius Doyle, M.A., D.Litt. Born in Dublin, February the fourth, 1901. Educated at the Christian Brothers' school in Synge

Street, 1914 to 1918. Studied at Saint Patrick's Training College for teachers, Drumcondra, from 1918 to 1921. I taught school in Drumcondra from 1921 to 1926. I met Failey Quigley there in my last year. He was then aged twenty. Already balding, ingratiating, devious, ambitious, convivial. I attended evening courses at University College, Dublin, for my B.A. and M.A., 1922 to 1927. In my last year there I met Failey again, studying for his B.L. I duly completed my doctoral thesis on 'The Folk High Schools of Denmark.' I became Inspector of Primary Schools in 1928.

She looked a long time at the next three entries:

Met Abby (Abigail) Goggin with Molly (Máire) Goggin at the Gaelic League in Parnell Square. Striking contrast. Molly dark. Abby blue-eyed, Danish hair, the colouring of a young seagull. She sang sweetly in Irish. A small but perfect voice. I married Abby in 1929. Failey married Molly in 1930.

In, she remembered, the University church on Saint Stephen's Green, with Phil as the best man. But that was in their good days when they were all still on warm terms with one another, before Failey went into politics.

She closed the book and returned, shaken, to the fire. He came back from his walk as silently as he left. On the three following nights exactly the same thing happened. She bore with it for a few more days and then she wrote to Molly. This place was getting them both down. The Book was a flop. He had not spoken to her for a week. What in God's name was she going to do?

4

Another week passed and then, to her delight, he told her, grumbling mightily about it, that he had to go to Dublin to clear up some damnfool remnant business in the Department. 'The change will do you good,' she said, but he only huffed and puffed at the very idea. On his return, three days later, she was hurt to notice how much good it had done him, how talkative he was again, full of gossip and guff, relaxed, looking ten years younger. Then the lone walks and the silent nights came back again, unless he had met somebody on his wanderings, even if it was only the breadman, or a tinker, or even a child herding cows – he, who had always been used to travel and company of every kind.

One bright Sunday evening, in the first week of October, he returned from one of those walks, full of excitement because he had come on a few late gentians among the rocks.

'Look!' he cried, holding out the pallid blue flowers. 'Autumn gentians! I never knew they even existed. I came on them by pure chance up there on the hill behind Kilnaboy, Shining in the full moon. Aren't they miraculous?'

She looked indifferently at the pale flowers, and for the first time since they came there she summed up her feelings about everything.

'They make me feel like one myself.'

Startled, he looked at her pallid eyes and at her white head, hearing far away a young girl with gentian eyes and fair hair, singing a fluting love song in Irish. Slowly he laid the few flowers down on the black cover of the Book. He said, 'I must go back to the village, I forgot my tobacco. I'm forgetting everything these days. I'll soon be forgetting my own head,' and went out again.

He did not rightly know where he was going, or what he was remembering, until the little road brought him to the side of a moonlit lough where he paused to rest. There, he remembered that one of the things he had been looking forward to doing in Clare was fishing, and that another was shooting. He had done neither. And yet, when he used to be telling his colleagues in the Department about all the things he would do when he retired he had always boasted that 'that wrist' could drop a dry fly lighter, longer and later than any fisherman he ever met on Corrib or on Mask; and what a marvellous place Clare was for wild duck, planing down on their orange legs to the lakes at evening. He looked about him. What exactly was he remembering? He slashed a ghostly head off a ragweed. What the hell exactly was he trying to write about in his book? Why wasn't it blazing? Why wasn't he getting on to

Failey? And leaning his two hands on the stick, he recalled that absurd talk he had with him three weeks before, in Dublin, about those two teachers in Mullaghabawn East.

'Failey!' he had said. 'I can call you Failey now, not "Minister" as I used to have to. I don't quite know exactly why you asked me to come back up here to talk about these two people. Unless it's just that, as usual, you want to find some pleasant way out of a nasty problem! If that is what you want, there is no way out of it! Because what that report of mine is really about,' tapping the grey folder on the desk, 'is Love. And as an old fellow in Kerry once said to me, all love is just "shteam" condensed by the cold air of marriage.'

Failey had ruffled his grey poll and laughed delightedly.

'Phil! You haven't changed one iota since the first day we got to know one another. Always the same old cynic!'

'I am not a cynic. I am a stoic. Look! All that is wrong with those two stupid and thoroughly worthless people is that they got married before they knew one another. They found out their mistake too late. Live with me and know me, as the old Irish proverb says. This clod Hooligan is forty-one. His fool of a wife is thirty-five. I knew that fellow when he first came to that school at the age of twenty-three. A decent poor hoor of a fellow with no other interest in life bar football and his occasional pint. The first time I knew her she was a junior teacher in Blackrock. She wasn't bad-looking. In fact she was quite good-looking. And all she was interested in was golf. They were perfectly happy with their football and their golf until they fell in love – whatever the hell that means – and got married. Now look at them! He's drinking like a fish. You could cut cheese with her nose. And they hate the living sight of one another.'

Failey had scoffed.

'Come off it, Phil! Married people don't live like that. Squabble? Yes! Have a row? Sure! We all have rows. But married people don't hate one another to that extent, not anyway in Ireland! You know that!'

'I know it's the way with these two people. All marriage ever did for the pair of them was to ruin their lives.'

'It gave them five sturdy children,' Failey pointed out sensibly, and insensitively, to his childless friend.

'I wouldn't know anything about that side of it. How many have you, Failey?'

'Eleven.'

Phil noted how proudly he threw out the figure. That for the Book. 'Our beardless Palmerston, active in only one Department!'

'Phil, what are we going to do with these two unfortunates?'

'It's in my report. Dismiss them. And at once!'

'My God, I can't sack a man of forty-one with five children?'

'It's up to you. It is a question of principle. Or are you more interested in cohabitation than in coeducation?'

(That for the Book, too – a darling phrase.)

Failey put a ministerial look on himself, calculating, would-be wise, his mind plainly as restless as his ten fingers. He got it out in bits:

'I was thinking. Principles are one thing, Phil. Human beings are another. What may be wrong. With those two unfortunate people. Is the place where they're living. Suppose now we could shift them? To some big town? Or even to some place like Galway city? You see, it must be very hard for any city girl, born and bred to the sights and sounds of the streets . . .'

And while he went on expatiating Phil had got so angry at the absurdity of the proposal that it never occurred to him what Failey was aiming at until now, by the glittering lake, savagely whipping the heads off stalk after stalk of ragweed. So mistress Abby had been conspiring against him with this unprincipled botch and boshtoon. And Molly, no doubt, with her!

He whirled for home, a thousand angry snakes writhing in his head, so possessing him with hatred of all three of them that he scarcely noticed the boy cycling away from his cottage gate. He strode down the moonlit path and with a bang flung the door open. Abby's face was twisted up with tears as she handed him the telegram.

'It's Failey,' she wept. 'Killed in a car crash!'

He snatched it from her and read it down to '. . . funeral eleven on Tuesday morning November first to Glasnevin Cemetery.' Glaring at his own dim face in the window, hearing Abby behind him, weepily talking and talking about the old days when they used to be so happy together in Dublin, all he wanted to say was, 'This is the ultimate interference. This is logical, a botch in life and a botch in death.' Quietly he said, 'Ah, well! Another poor devil whose dancing days are done. The Lord be kind to him. This means, I suppose, that we must put on our hats and coats tomorrow morning and go up to Dublin for another miserable jaunt to Glasnevin.' And to get away from her whining he went into the back room, took down his suit of clerical charcoal, removed the mothballs from its pockets and started to brush the dust from his black homburg that he had worn for the interment of so many other public men whom he had neither liked nor admired.

5

The next morning ghost after ghost of mist went sheaving past their crucified window. At every pause on the journey it caressed their ankles, wrists and throats. They went by taxi (late and smelling of fish), by bus (late and damp), by another bus (so prompt that they barely managed to board it), by train (slow), finally by another taxi in Dublin shrouded by the same mist. They did not talk much on the way, yet, by the little that was spoken, each could guess at the unspoken thoughts of the other. Abby had talked again about their young days in Dublin. Once she was so frank as to say expectantly, 'I hope it won't look much changed.' He spoke twice about Failey's latter-day career, drily and ironically. Once he said outright, 'Everything can come out now! All will be revealed.' It was like him at his solitary worst and his sensitive best to insist that they must not stay with Molly. 'The house will be full of his country relatives.' She was disappointed at first, but she liked the small hotel he chose, on the Liffey, near the station and the old North Circular. After supper they called on Molly to pay their respects, and as he always did on such occasions he said all the proper, kindly things. He even said, 'Happy the corpse the rain falls on,' though he made up for it to his conscience the following morning by adding to Abby as the cortège moved slowly through the mist to Glasnevin, 'And miserable the mourners!'

The sky was low, wet and matted. It darkened every headstone, cobwebbed every yew and made the massed umbrellas about him look like barnacles. He had to stand at the graveside in line with Molly, and Abby, Failey's nearest relatives and his family of eleven, ranging from a middle-aged man of about thirty-five down to a young woman in her first twenties. With one glance from under his umbrella he ranked this as a Class B funeral. It was understandable that the President had not come; it was a bad day and he was an old man. But there were only three members of the Cabinet, including the Taoiseach. The leader of the Opposition had managed to rally only two members of his party. The Labour Party was not represented at all. He discounted the six priests, the three Franciscans and the two nuns. Relatives. The general public was small. The usual flock of civil servants, glad to take the day off. He frowned at the tricolour clinging wetly to the coffin. He lifted his eyebrows wearily when the surpliced priest, conducting the burial service from under an umbrella held by a mute, said the last few prayers in Irish – a language that, to his knowledge, Failey had never spoken in his life. He had to lower his umbrella to hide his amusement when he saw, among the wreaths that the gravediggers were now strewing on their wet hummock, a garland of bays. (What scoundrel, what embittered clerk, had the wit to think of that one?) He bowed his head in agony as the Taoiseach began the formal words of farewell.

'...a colleague who did Ireland and me the honour of accepting without demur the arduous duties of a post of the greatest import to our country's future. Yet when he did so, Phelim Patrick Quigley did no more than he had always done, in the same spirit of devotion that, from his earliest years, inspired him to serve and suffer for Ireland. A man who...'

Suffer? The reference, he presumed, could only be to the occasion when Failey, by the greatest stroke of political good luck, had been arrested on suspicion during the Civil War, at the age of twenty, and detained for three nights in the Bridewell. When the oration finished, he glared quickly around to see if there was going to be a firing squad or a bugler sounding the last post. Seeing that there was not, he relaxed; and then wished there had been – it would have made a lovely chapter ending for the Book, which he was at last free to write without quarter.

It was all over. The crowd began to dissolve with a seemly slowness that did not conceal from him their eagerness to re-gather in The Crossed Guns for the usual elegaic hot toddy. He was peeping at his watch, about to drag Abby away to the afternoon train for the west, when he felt her softly pulling his sleeve and whispering that Molly wanted them both to stay with her for a night or two. If she had not known him so well she might have mistaken his fright for anger.

'I will do nothing of the kind!' he was growling down at her. 'Stay alone in a house with two wailing women for two nights? I have no more to say to Molly. Anyway it isn't me she wants, it is you. You can stay if you like, but I am going home.'

'She does want you. She's worried about the future. Failey had some investments. There's the insurance. And the will. The house will have to be sold. All sorts of money matters. And the relatives will be all gone, Phil. She will be left all alone. You must come.'

'She has lawyers. She has a son of thirty-five. Why pick on me? Am I never to be shut of that man?'

'She trusts you. And Failey was always kind to us. You can't refuse her.'

With a groan he surrendered.

'All right. But I'll stay only one night. I want to get back to my Book.'

Abby recoiled.

'Oh, Phil! What a time to be thinking of that!'

After the funeral the feast. They found the house on the Infirmary Road crowded with half a hundred people enjoying, as the old sagas loved to say, 'the freshest of every food and the oldest of every drink'; secular priests, the three Franciscans, country relatives, greying politicians, lots of young people whom he took to be the Dublin friends of the family and a gaggle of civil servants who welcomed him so eagerly that he forgot himself in their cascade of talk, argument and gossip whispered behind palms with sidelong glances towards the politicians. It was four o'clock before the crowd began to thin out. By six all that remained were Molly, Abby, himself, two unmarried daughters and a young man who was obviously courting the older of them. When the young man took her away, the three women began to tidy up the house and prepare the usual Dublin supper of 'Tea and Something' – the Something tonight being the remains of the funeral feast. It was eight o'clock before the remaining daughter went out. To the chapel? Or to meet another young man? Molly and Abby sat reminiscing before the drawing-room fire. By nine o'clock he was deep in gloom.

'Where are those papers, Molly?' he finally asked, glad of any excuse to get away by himself for the rest of the night.

'I'll show you,' she sighed. 'They're all in the engine room. It is what Failey always called his study. Where he did his homework at night. I have the fire lit for you and a bottle of Irish on the table.'

She led him upstairs. In the return room he saw an old roll-top desk, a green-shaded reading lamp on top of it. He saw shelves of books, a table, an old-fashioned mahogany wardrobe, a couch with a plaid rug on it and an armchair by the turf fire. As she closed the long rep curtains he saw raindrops gleaming on the windowpane. The wet wind was still blowing from the west, down the Liffey. Tonight the sea would be covered with white horses.

'Pay no heed to me,' he ordered her. 'You two can go off to bed when ye want to. I'll stay up until I finish this job.'

'Ayeh!' she sighed. 'As poor Failey often did until three in the morning. He was as strong as a bull. If it wasn't for that damned accident he'd have lived to be ninety.'

6

There was no doubt whose room he was in. The wall above the fireplace was covered with black-framed photographs of Failey, massed shoulder to shoulder and head to tail. Failey, with a face like a boy, dressed in cap and gown, holding a scroll. Failey wearing a barrister's wig. Failey in a cutaway coat, holding a grey topper in the crook of his left arm, standing beside Molly in a wedding dress whose train curved in a white stream about her feet. Failey as Parliamentary Secretary to the Minister for Roads and Railways opening a factory. Failey as Minister for R. and R. opening another factory. Failey as Minister for Education opening a new school. Failey grinning on the golf course. Failey addressing Rotary. Failey in a Franciscan robe with a white cincture roped around his belly recalled the press announcement of his death. 'Phelim Patrick Quigley, B.L., T.S.O.F.' Third Order of Saint Francis. To what other order, association or society had he belonged? The Knights of Columbanus? Probably. The Knights of Malta? But you'd have to be at least a doctor to get into them. There were at least a hundred of those black-edged pictures. Vanity? Or just a cool awareness of the value of publicity? The bookshelves were untidy, disorderly and wholly predictable. Rows of the official records of parliamentary debates; books and pamphlets about railroads, canals and aeronautics; paperback thrillers, *A Portrait of the Artist as a Young Man*, books on religion, the odd Yeats, a book entitled *How to Make a Million Dollars a Year*, a rhyming dictionary.

He rolled up the hood of the desk and found what he expected. Chaos. He filled himself a stout glass of malt, lit his pipe, seized a pad of writing paper and set to work. The first pile he made was of the unopened letters, most of them from constituents. He read them all conscientiously: begging letters, abusive letters, grateful letters. It took him an hour to sweep them one by one into the waste-paper basket. He wrote on his pad the word *Investments* and started to search for them. He found only five in all. He humphed as he noted that Failey had not invested a penny in Irish Government Stock or Irish Industrials. He had favoured English gilts and equities. Unaccustomed to such matters, it took him another hour to work out whether Molly should keep or sell them, poorly helped by a three-day-old *Irish Times* that he found on the floor beside the desk. If Molly kept them they would not bring her in £200 a year, though the real wonder was that the man had been able to invest anything with such a long-tailed family and the modest salary of a Minister.

He was just about to pass on from Investments to Insurance when he came on a wallet containing a broker's contract notes of sales and purchases. These showed that, at one time, Failey must have invested much more. Only two weeks before he had sold over £4,000 worth of stock. He looked for and found the bank sheets, and there it was duly credited, and on the same day a corresponding debit of £4,310. He tumbled everything about in his eager search for Failey's chequebook, found it, riffled the stubs, and there was what he was looking for. The sum had been made payable to a well-known Dublin firm of solicitors. But what on earth was it for? Debts? The sum was too large for debts. A property purchase?

Thoughtfully, he wrote down on his pad the word *Insurance* and started to look for the policies. There were two, each for £1,000, each taken out many years ago. He added the sums to Molly's credit. He next wrote down on his pad the word *Property* and started to search for the indentures, if any. He found two. To his relief the first one was for the house. This, at least, would be something of real value for poor old Molly. What Failey had paid for it he had no idea, and he would have to wait until the morning to find out precisely, but he had guessed ever since last February, when he had sold his own house at 26 Saint Rita's Villas, that this place, standing in an acre of land, must be now worth at least £12,000. He wrote down the sum £12,000, followed by a cautious query mark, to Molly's credit, reached for his glass and found it empty.

He rose, stretched himself and looked at his watch. Past midnight. He refilled his glass, went to the curtains and parted them. The windowpanes were still speckled with rain, the sky over the city a sodden pink sponge. He returned to the desk, picked up the second grey document, also headed in large decorative gothic letters with the word INDENTURE, relit his pipe and puffing easily began to read it. Abruptly he laid down his pipe and began to reread. There was no question about it. The document did witness that in consideration of the usual this, that and the other 'the Lessor doth hereby DEMISE unto the Lessee ALL THAT the plot of ground known as 26 Saint Rita's Villas, North Circular Road, in the City of Dublin . . .'

For a while he sat as rigid in his chair, staring as fixedly in front of him, as if he had suddenly died there. Galvanized he whirled to the last page to see the date. Two weeks ago. He grabbed the chequebook again and compared the stub. The dates agreed. Two weeks ago? Molly must have known of it. If Abby had not known of it before the funeral she did now. But why the secrecy?

He strode to the door, opened it and listened. Not a sound from downstairs. The two of them must have gone to bed. He opened the door of the bedroom allotted to Abby and himself, and seeing it empty bethought himself. She would, naturally, be sleeping tonight in the same room as Molly. He moved down the corridor to its door and bent his head to listen. Through the door he could hear a soft whispering, lifted now and then to an audible feminine murmur. He was about to put his hand on the doorknob when he heard the sound of one or the other of them crying. At the same moment he thought of the will. He hurried back to the desk to look for it. Two hours ago he would have blandly assumed that there would, characteristically, be no will. He now knew better. He went carefully through every pigeonhole and drawer again. It was not in any of them. Then he saw what had earlier seemed to him to be a long, slim horizontal panel, slightly protruding along the top of the pigeonholes, eased it forward and there was the buff envelope, duly inscribed *My Will*. He drew out the document. In the usual benignant legal language of all wills everything had been left 'to my dear wife Molly for her own use absolutely'. He added everything up and found that if she sold the house well, she would enjoy an income of about two thousand pounds.

The pictures over the fireplace, the shelves of books, even the old-fashioned furniture suddenly possessed an ominous solidity. He had belittled Failey. This room, this home that he had created, the family he had reared were all about him. The man had been a rotten Minister, but he had been a good husband. To reassure himself he looked again at the massed photographs over the fireplace. He felt humiliated to notice that the wedding photograph hung in the middle of them.

When he came to himself he found that the hour was approaching two o'clock. To be certain that he had performed his task completely he returned to the desk, now tidily in order, and checked off each of its seven small drawers and eight pigeonholes, running his fingers back into their recesses to be sure he had missed nothing. He had missed nothing. The last central compartment had a small door like a tabernacle. It was empty, but as his fingers groped in the rear of it they entered a crevice, and at once a small upright panel to the side of it moved slowly forward a half-inch. He drew it towards him, one of those so-called secret receptacles, that are sometimes to be found in old desks. He pulled it out and turned it upside down. It was empty. He did the same with the opposite crevice of the tabernacle, drew out its second panel, turned it upside down and out of it fell a book. It was a small black book. Inside it was an envelope marked *Private*. On its black cover was pasted a white label bearing the written words:

THE DARK AND FAIR
1930–1935
A Sequence in Quatrains
by
PHELIM PATRICK QUIGLEY, B.L.

He found that it contained a gathering of verses, each one a numbered quatrain, each on a single page. Between embarrassment and pity he took it to the armchair by the sinking fire, threw on a few sods of turf from the turf-basket, relit his pipe and started to read the first verse.

Think not, who reads these tortured lines, I pray,
  Of Dark or Fair. To me they symbolize
Lost dreams of love or none, night after day,
  A dream I dreamed, a forfeit prize.

He turned the leaf indifferently. Unprepared, he felt the knife slip in:

This fool once suffered eyes of midnight hue,
  And gypsy-colored ringlets to betray
A heart that burned for eyes of gentian blue,
  And virgin smiles, and primrose-colored hair.

He tautened too late. He felt his skull crawling as he ran through the third, the fourth and the fifth quatrains to find out for certain who was who in this farrago.

Until, with gypsy smiles and wiles, she wound
  Her hair about my eyes and drew me deep
Into her gypsy flesh where passion crowned
  Desire, and Love cast out could only weep.

He was sweating when he came to the eighth quatrain. He read it several times, reliving every single one of those nights of his betrayal:

Yet, every night as that last train drew out
  For Bray, two girls backward waving, someday,
I swore, I'd hold her in my arms, and mouth
  To mouth on fire, my Fair would whisper, Stay!

Forty years ago. On the platform of Amiens Street Station smelling of midnight dust, fish, steam, petrol. The two of them joking upwards to the two girls in the lighted carriage, holding their hands until the very last moment when the engine shook itself and chugged slowly out. Then two white hands waving back through the steam until train and lights and hands vanished around the curve like falling cards. Out, then, mocking one another's ardour, into the empty streets for the slow walk back to their lodgings on the North Side, and the usual prolonged last talk or argument on the canal bridge, often not parting until two in the morning with cheery backward calls of farewell.

Did she? Ever? Let her hot mouth stay? He had to read on to the thirteenth quatrain before he knew.

At last, the moonlight on the waves' soft sigh,
  We kissed. Then bracken-deep in love we lay,
Until, 'Too late!' I heard her sobbing cry.
  'Last night, in bed, he said, "Our wedding day!"'

The one secret of his life! His one lovely, imperious, flaming passion shared with that lying clod!

'The poor bastard!' he said, and laid the book aside. 'What have his private sins to do with me?'

★

It was only when he found himself standing in the rain on the pavement outside 26 Saint Rita's Villas, peering at the TO LET sign pasted inside the lamplit window that he knew that he was out of control. He was carrying Abby's ridiculous blue umbrella. He was wearing no overcoat. He removed his hat, looked at it and found that he had taken Failey's. He had no key to let him back into the house. He began to return quickly, but after walking for half an hour stopped dead. He was lost in a suburban maze. Not a soul in sight, nor a sound to be heard except the rain spitting into him like arrows. Had he been making for Glasnevin? He listened. A sighing wind down the concrete avenue made him turn in fright. He halted and listened again, and again he heard that sifting sigh. He started to run, gripped himself, and hurried as quickly as he could walk, back on his tracks. He calmed only when he had found his way to the door, shocked to see that he had left it so wide open that the rain was blowing into the hall as if it were a deserted house.

He closed the door silently behind him, and crept carefully up to the engine room, halting at every creak of the old stairs. The fire had melted into grey ash. With the box of firelighters beside the turf-basket, a bundle of Failey's discarded papers and fresh turf he made a blazing fire, and stripped to his skin; he hung the shirt by its sleeves from the mantelpiece, outspread like a crucifix, and sat naked before the fire watching the steam begin to rise from the clothes that he had strewn to dry on the brass fender.

It was then that his uplifted eye saw, peeping down at him over the corner of the mantelpiece, the envelope that he had found in the black book. He snatched it down and ripped it open. It contained two letters. He had at one time smiled at her handwriting for being so simple and childlike. Later he had frowned at it for being quavering and old. But, for years now, everything she said and did had made him think of her as somebody who had never had any proper womanhood between her girlhood and her age. The first letter was dated December 20, 1935, five years after they had married. As he read it, in spite of the fire mottling his shinbones, his whole body began to exude cold sweat.

DEAR FAY,

How kind you were to write to me in my great unhappiness. I have read your letter so many times that I have it all off by heart. I will never forget one word of it as long as I live. I am sure you are right in everything you say about Phil, and there can be nobody living or dead who knows him better. You are right in another thing. He is not an unkind man by nature and he can be very warm, and giving, and loving. But there is something in him, or maybe in me, that brings out the worst in him and turns him into what you call an irate man full of cold principle. But it is all very well for you, Fay, to say that that is what makes him the most honest and reliable civil servant you ever met. You do not have to live with him night and day. God knows I don't ask much. If only he would not be so contemptuous of me. If only he'd make a few allowances for me. If only he would not turn all his anger on to me. The way he is I just can't go on with it. I feel I will have to leave him or have the life crushed out of me. I am terribly sorry Fay to have poured all this over you but I have nobody else to confide in. Molly is so strong and so dominating that whenever I have tried to hint any of this to her she just laughs and tells me to slap back at him. I can't write any more tonight, I am so miserable. God bless you for trying to understand. I pray that you and Molly and the children may have a happy, happy Christmas.

Ever,

ABBY

He tried to remember that Christmas, but it was too long ago. The second letter was dated New Year's Day, 1935.

DEAR FAY,

Thank you and bless you for all you said to me yesterday in Wynne's Hotel. I have thought it over and over and as always I see that you are dead right. I must stick it out. I will always remember specially two things you said. I hope it *is* true that he needs me, though I'll never know what he saw in me to want to marry me at all. The other thing you said was how wonderful he is with the schoolchildren and how tough he is with their teachers. I wish I could have given him children. It might have made him a bit more kind to me. As it is I must look on him now as my only child. I will not bother you any more, Fay. I promise. Not a word to Molly about any of this. And may you and yours all have a very, very happy New Year.

ABBY

The letter fell from his hand, he closed his eyes, crumpled into his armchair and swooned out of the memory of man.

He woke, shivering. It was five o'clock. With a groan he remembered, rose, stiff in all his bones, laid another couple of firelighters into the seed of the ashen fire, the two letters on top of them, then the book of verses, then a pyre of turf, and watched until the flames embraced them all. Then he opened the wardrobe door, found a worn woollen dressing gown, and an overcoat, and put them both on. He went to the window and drew the curtains apart. The rain had stopped. By the city's glow and the presence of a few stars he could see that the clouds were breaking up. Once, for a moment, between their torn edges, he saw the moon, a steaming rag hung there to dry. To the north east the sky was becoming paler. Inside an hour morning would be creeping in across the plain of Swords, over Drumcondra and Glasnevin. After that it would soon be touching the city's spires.

A mile away, up there, he was lying where they had left him, a man he had never known, a life he had failed to share. He did not feel guilty. He felt only the barrier. Of late years he had noticed that his old friends no longer died. He would ask casually after one of them and be told in some surprise, that it must be a year or so since the poor chap had disappeared around some corner. Looking out at the paling sky he felt the pain of loss, the brevity of life and its challenge that never stops. He turned to the couch, lay and wrapped the rug about him.

When he woke again it was ten o'clock, the room filled with blinding sunlight, nearby roofs exuding a faint steam more soft than pity. A Saint Martin's summer? He found the bathroom, gave himself a cold shower, shaved, put on his dried clothes and went slowly downstairs in search of the Dark and the Fair. He found them in the kitchen, two white-haired old ladies talking quietly over their late breakfast. Molly got up to greet him. She was hooped even when she stood.

'Come in, Phil,' she said warmly. 'I hope you got some kind of a sleep on that old couch. Sit down there by Abby and we'll all have a fresh pot of tea. And you are going to eat a good plate of bacon and eggs, Master Philip, and none of your old arguments about it, if you please!'

'I will eat them,' he said obediently and watched her gather the soiled china on a tray. 'Anyway, I deserve them. I've done a good night's work for you. And to be shut of it at once, you are going to be all right, Molly. That is if you can live on fifteen hundred a year, tax-paid. Failey looked after you well.'

'Thank you, Phil. It's a great relief to me.'

As she lifted the tray and turned to go out to the scullery he held her.

'There is one thing I must ask you, Molly. Did you know that Failey had bought our old house on the North Circular?'

She half-turned.

'Yes, of course. He bought it two weeks ago when he saw it was up for sale again. He was going to write to you about it. He told me I should rent it. But he did say that if you and Abby want it you should have first call on it. At,' she added briskly, 'a nominal rent of five pounds a week,' and went out.

Abby was staring at the milk jug. Her left hand was trembling. He laid his hand on it and spoke as slowly and softly as if he were talking to a child.

'Abby! Do you want very much to go back to that house?'

Still looking at the milk jug she whispered, 'Yes.'

'Very well. Let's do it.'

Her hand closed tightly on his. He could see her throat gulping, and then the tears were creeping down her face, and she was sobbing into her palms. She raised her wet face to say, 'Oh, Phil, how soon can we go back there?'

'Right away, I suppose. We should be well settled in by Christmas.'

Molly came bustling in with the teapot.

'You can start on that, the bacon is sizzling, how do you like your eggs, basted or turned?'

'He likes them basted,' Abby said comfortably. 'And he likes two. With a nice little slice of fried bread, and a touch of parsley on it.'

'Ha!' Molly said sourly, but with a grin to take the harm out of it. 'You've spoiled him,' and bustled off again.

When she came in and out again with the toast he felt it to be sure it was not too crisp. 'She makes good toast,' he said and buttered it and began to eat, vaguely aware that Abby was babbling on and on about the house.

'We'll be doing it up,' he heard her saying, 'between now and Christmas. I'll be sitting on one side of the fire making new curtains. And you will be sitting on the other side writing the Book.'

'The what?' he said, startled. 'Oh! That? Pour me out a cup of tea, will you? Milk first. You always forget it. I see she has lump sugar. Why don't we always have lump sugar?'

'You will, Phil,' she said as she poured, forgetting the milk again. 'You'll have the best of everything. And peace, Phil. And calm, Phil. And philosophical content, Phil. And serenity without end.'

He munched silently, looking at the sun in the back garden. Saint Martin? He sniffed at the absurd legend: a soldier-saint who saw from horseback two beggars shivering in the snow, took off his cloak, cut it in two and gave half to one beggar; then looked at the other beggar, took what was left of his cloak, divided it with his sword and gave half to him – so that now all three of them were shivering, until God, in pity, sent back the summer. And people believe things like that can really happen! Staring out he did not hear one word of the childish prattle by his side. He sniffed again. He smelled the rashers frying.

The Talking Trees

There were four of them in the same class at the Red Abbey, all under fifteen. They met every night in Mrs Coffey's sweetshop at the top of the Victoria Road to play the fruit machine, smoke fags and talk about girls. Not that they really talked about them – they just winked, leered, nudged one another, laughed, grunted and groaned about them, or said things like 'See her legs?' 'Yaroosh!' 'Wham!' 'Ouch!' 'Ooof!' or 'If only, if only!' But if anybody said, 'Only what?' they would not have known precisely what. They knew nothing precisely about girls, they wanted to know everything precisely about girls, there was nobody to tell them all the things they wanted to know about girls and what they thought they wanted to do with them. Aching and wanting, not knowing, half guessing, they dreamed of clouds upon clouds of fat, pink, soft, ardent girls billowing towards them across the horizon of their future. They might just as well have been dreaming of pink porpoises moaning at their feet for love.

In the sweetshop the tall glass jars of coloured sweets shone in the bright lights. The one-armed fruit-machine went zing. Now and again girls from Saint Monica's came in to buy sweets, giggle roguishly and over-pointedly ignore them. Mrs Coffey was young, buxom, fairhaired, blue-eyed and very good-looking. They admired her so much that one night when Georgie Watchman whispered to them that she had fine bubs Dick Franks told him curtly not to be so coarse, and Jimmy Sullivan said in his most toploftical voice, 'Georgie Watchman, you should be jolly well ashamed of yourself, you are no gentleman,' and Tommy Gong Gong said nothing but nodded his head as insistently as a ventriloquist's dummy.

Tommy's real name was Tommy Flynn, but he was younger than any of them so that neither he nor they were ever quite sure that he ought to belong to the gang at all. To show it they called him all sorts of nicknames, like Inch because he was so small; Fatty because he was so puppy-fat; Pigeon because he had a chest like a woman; Gong Gong because after long bouts of silence he had a way of suddenly spraying them with wild bursts of talk like a fire alarm attached to a garden sprinkler.

That night all Georgie Watchman did was to make a rude blubberlip noise at Dick Franks. But he never again said anything about Mrs Coffey. They looked up to Dick. He was the oldest of them. He had long eyelashes like a girl, perfect manners, the sweetest smile and the softest voice. He had been to two English boarding schools, Ampleforth and Downside, and in Ireland to three, Clongowes, Castelknock and Rockwell, and been expelled from all five of them. After that his mother had made his father retire from the Indian Civil, come back to the old family house in Cork and, as a last hope, send her darling Dicky to the Red Abbey day-school. He smoked a corn-cob pipe and dressed in droopy plus fours with chequered stockings and red flares, as if he was always just coming from or going to the golf course. He played cricket and tennis, games that no other boy at the Red Abbey could afford to play. They saw him as the typical school-captain they read about in English boys' papers like *The Gem* and *The Magnet*, *The Boys' Own Paper*, *The Captain* and *Chums*, which was where they got all those swanky words like Wham, Ouch, Yaroosh, Ooof and Jolly Well. He was their Tom Brown, their Bob Cherry, their Tom Merry, those heroes who were always leading Greyfriars School or Blackfriars School to victory on the cricket field amid the cap-tossing huzzas of the juniors and the admiring smiles of visiting parents. It never occurred to them that *The Magnet* or *The Gem* would have seen all four of them as perfect models for some such story as *The Cads of Greyfriars*, or *The Bounders of Blackfriars*, low types given to secret smoking in the spinneys, drinking in The Dead Woman's Inn, or cheating at examinations, or, worst crime of all, betting on horses with redfaced bookies' touts down from London, while the rest of the school was practising at the nets – a quartet of rotters fated to be caned ceremoniously in the last chapter before the entire awestruck school, and then whistled off at dead of night back to their heartbroken fathers and mothers.

It could not have occurred to them because these crimes did not exist at the Red Abbey. Smoking? At the Red Abbey any boy who wanted to was free to smoke himself into a galloping consumption so long as he did it off the premises, in the jakes or up the chimney. Betting? Brother Julius was always passing fellows sixpence or even a bob to put on an uncle's or a cousin's horse at Leopardstown or the Curragh. In the memory of man no boy had ever been caned ceremoniously for anything. Fellows were just leathered all day long for not doing their homework, or playing hooky from school, or giving lip, or fighting in class – and they were leathered hard. Two years ago Jimmy Sullivan had been given six swingers on each hand with the sharp edge of a metre-long ruler for pouring the contents of an inkwell over Georgie Watchman's head in the middle of a history lesson about the Trojan Wars, in spite of his wailing explanation that he had only done it because he thought Georgie Watchman was a scut and all Trojans were blacks. Drink? They did not drink only because they were too poor. While, as for what *The Magnet* and *The Gem* really meant by 'betting' – which, they dimly understood, was some sort of depravity that no decent English boy would like to see mentioned in print – hardly a week passed that some brother did not say that a hard problem in algebra, or a leaky pen, or a window that would not open or shut was 'a blooming bugger'.

There was the day when little Brother Angelo gathered half a dozen boys about him at playtime to help him with a crossword puzzle.

'Do any of ye,' he asked, 'know what Notorious Conduct could be in seven letters?'

'Buggery?' Georgie suggested mock-innocently.

'Please be serious!' Angelo said. 'This is about Conduct.'

When the solution turned out to be *Jezebel,* little Angelo threw up his hands, said it must be some queer kind of foreign woman and declared that the whole thing was a blooming bugger. Or there was that other day when old Brother Expeditus started to tell them about the strict lives and simple food of Dominican priests and Trappist monks. When Georgie said, 'No tarts, Brother?' Expeditus had laughed loud and long.

'No, Georgie!' he chuckled. 'No pastries of any kind.'

They might as well have been in school in Arcadia. And every other school about them seemed to be just as hopeless. In fact they might have gone on dreaming of pink porpoises for years if it was not for a small thing that Gong Gong told them one October night in the sweetshop. He sprayed them with the news that his sister Jenny had been thrown out of class that morning in Saint Monica's for turning up with a red ribbon in her hair, a mother-of-pearl brooch at her neck and smelling of scent.

'Ould Sister Eustasia,' he fizzled, 'made her go out in the yard and wash herself under the tap, she said they didn't want any girls in their school who had notions.'

The three gazed at one another, and began at once to discuss all the possible sexy meanings of notions. Georgie had a pocket dictionary. 'An ingenious contrivance'? 'An imperfect conception (*U.S.*)'? 'Small wares'? It did not make sense. Finally they turned to Mrs Coffey. She laughed, nodded towards two giggling girls in the shop who were eating that gummy kind of block toffee that can gag you for half an hour, and said, 'Why don't you ask *them*?' Georgie approached them most politely.

'Pardon me ladies, but do you by any chance happen to have notions?'

The two girls stared at one another with cow's eyes, blushed scarlet and fled from the shop shrieking with laughter. Clearly a notion was very sexy.

'Georgie!' Dick pleaded. 'You're the only one who knows anything. What in heaven's name is it?'

When Georgie had to confess himself stumped they knew at last that their situation was desperate. Up to now Georgie had always been able to produce some sort of answer, right or wrong, to all their questions. He was the one who, to their disgust, told them what he called conraception meant. He was the one who had explained to them that all babies are delivered from the navel of the mother. He was the one who had warned them that if a fellow kissed a bad woman he would get covered by leprosy from head to foot. The son of a Head Constable.

living in the police barracks, he had collected his facts simply by listening as quietly as a mouse to the other four policemen lolling in the dayroom of the barracks with their collars open, reading the sporting pages of *The Freeman's Journal*, slowly creasing their polls and talking about colts, fillies, cows, calves, bulls and bullocks and 'the mysteerious nachure of all faymale wimmen'. He had also gathered a lot of useful stuff by dutiful attendance since the age of eleven at the meetings and marchings of the Protestant Boys' Brigade, and from a devoted study of the Bible. And here he was, stumped by a nun!

Dick lifted his beautiful eyelashes at the three of them, jerked his head and led them out on the pavement.

'I have a plan,' he said quietly. 'I've been thinking of it for some time. Chaps! Why don't we see everything with our own eyes?' And he threw them into excited discussion by mentioning a name. 'Daisy Bolster?'

Always near every school, there is a Daisy Bolster – the fast girl whom everybody has heard about and nobody knows. They had all seen her at a distance. Tall, a bit skinny, long legs, dark eyes, lids heavy as the dimmers of a car lamp, prominent white teeth, and her lower lip always gleaming wet. She could be as old as seventeen. Maybe even eighteen. She wore her hair up. Dick told them that he had met her once at the tennis club with four or five other fellows around her and that she had laughed and winked very boldly all the time. Georgie said that he once heard a fellow in school say, 'She goes with boys.' Gong Gong bubbled that that was true because his sister Jenny told him that a girl named Daisy Bolster had been thrown out of school three years ago for talking to a boy outside the convent gate. At this Georgie flew into a terrible rage.

'You stupid slob!' he roared. 'Don't you know yet that when anybody says a boy and girl are talking to one another it means they're doing you-know-what?'

'I don't know you-know-what,' Gong Gong wailed. 'What what?'

'I heard a fellow say,' Jimmy Sullivan revealed solemnly, 'that she has no father and that her mother is no better than she should be.'

Dick said in approving tones that he had once met another fellow who had heard her telling some very daring stories.

'Do you think she would show us for a quid?'

Before they parted on the pavement that night they were talking not about a girl but about a fable. Once a girl like that gets her name up she always ends up as a myth, and for a generation afterwards, maybe more, it is the myth that persists. 'Do you remember,' some old chap will wheeze, 'that girl Daisy Bolster? She used to live up the Mardyke. We used to say she was fast.' The other old boy will nod knowingly, the two of them will look at one another inquisitively, neither will admit anything, remembering only the long, dark avenue, its dim gas-lamps, the stars hooked in its trees.

Within a month Dick had fixed it. Their only trouble after that was to collect the money and to decide whether Gong Gong should be allowed to come with them.

Dick fixed that, too, at a final special meeting in the sweet-shop. Taking his pipe from between his lips, he looked speculatively at Gong Gong, who looked up at him with eyes big as plums, trembling between the terror of being told he could not come with them and the greater terror of being told that he could.

'Tell me, Gong Gong,' Dick said politely, 'what exactly does your father do?'

'He's a tailor,' Tommy said, blushing a bit at having to confess it, knowing that Jimmy's dad was a bank clerk, that Georgie's was a Head Constable, and that Dick's had been a Commissioner in the Punjab.

'Very fine profession,' Dick said kindly. 'Gentleman's Tailor and Outfitter. I see. Flynn and Company? Or is it Flynn and Sons? Have I seen his emporium?'

'Ah, no!' Tommy said, by now as red as a radish. 'He's not that sort of a tailor at all, he doesn't build suits, ye know, that's a different trade altogether, he works with me mother at home in Tuckey Street, he tucks things in and he lets things out, he's what they call a mender and turner, me brother Turlough had this suit I have on me now before I got it, you can see he's very good at his job, he's a real dab . . .'

Dick let him run on, nodding sympathetically – meaning to

convey to the others that they really could not expect a fellow to know much about girls if his father spent his life mending and turning old clothes in some side alley called Tuckey Street.

'Do you fully realize, Gong Gong, that we are proposing to behold the ultimate female beauty?'

'You mean,' Gong Gong smiled fearfully, 'that she'll only be wearing her nightie?'

Georgie Watchman turned from him in disgust to the fruit-machine. Dick smiled on.

'The thought had not occurred to me,' he said. 'I wonder, Gong Gong, where do you get all those absolutely filthy ideas. If we subscribe seventeen and sixpence, do you think you can contribute half-a-crown?'

'I could feck it, I suppose.'

Dick raised his eyelashes.

'Feck?'

Gong Gong looked shamedly at the tiles.

'I mean steal,' he whispered.

'Don't they give you any pocket money?'

'They give me threepence a week.'

'Well, we have only a week to go. If you can, what was your word, feck half-a-crown, you may come.'

The night chosen was a Saturday – her mother always went to town on Saturdays; the time of meeting, five o'clock exactly; the place, the entrance to the Mardyke Walk.

On any other occasion it would have been a gloomy spot for a rendezvous. For adventure, perfect. A long tree-lined avenue, with, on one side, a few scattered houses and high enclosing walls; on the other side the small canal whose deep dyke had given it its name. Secluded, no traffic allowed inside the gates, complete silence. A place where men came every night to stand with their girls behind the elm trees kissing and whispering for hours. Dick and Georgie were there on the dot of five. Then Jimmy Sullivan came swiftly loping. From where they stood, under a tree just beyond the porter's lodge, trembling with anticipation, they could see clearly for only about a hundred yards up the long tunnel of elms lit by the first stars above the boughs, one tawny window streaming across a dank garden, and beyond that a feeble perspective of pendant lamps fading dimly away into the blue November dusk. Within another half-hour the avenue would be pitch black between those meagre pools of light.

Her instructions had been precise. In separate pairs, at exactly half-past five, away up there beyond the last lamp, where they would be as invisible as cockroaches, they must gather outside her house.

'You won't be able even to see one another,' she had said gleefully to Dick, who had stared coldly at her, wondering how often she had stood behind a tree with some fellow who would not have been able to see her face.

Every light in the house would be out except for the fanlight over the door.

'Ooo!' she had giggled. 'It will be terribly oohey. You won't hear a sound but the branches squeaking. You must come alone to my door. You must leave the other fellows to watch from behind the trees. You must give two short rings. Once, twice. And then give a long ring, and wait.' She had started to whisper the rest, her hands by her sides clawing her dress in her excitement. 'The fanlight will go out if my mother isn't at home. The door will open slowly. You must step into the dark hall. A hand will take your hand. You won't know whose hand it is. It will be like something out of Sherlock Holmes. You will be simply terrified. You won't know what I'm wearing. For all you'll know I might be wearing nothing at all!'

He must leave the door ajar. The others must follow him one by one. After that . . .

It was eleven minutes past five and Gong Gong had not yet come. Already three women had passed up the Mardyke carrying parcels, hurrying home to their warm fires, forerunners of the home-for-tea crowd. When they had passed out of sight Georgie growled, 'When that slob comes I'm going to put my boot up his backside.' Dick, calmly puffing his corncob, gazing wearily up at the stars, laughed tolerantly and said, 'Now Georgie, don't be impatient. We shall see all! We shall at last know all!'

Georgie sighed and decided to be weary too.

'I hope,' he drawled, 'this poor frail isn't going to let us down!'

For three more minutes they waited in silence and then Jimmy Sullivan let out a cry of relief. There was the small figure hastening towards them along the Dyke Parade from one lamppost to another.

'Puffing and panting as usual, I suppose,' Dick chuckled. 'And exactly fourteen minutes late.'

'I hope to God,' Jimmy said, 'he has our pound note. I don't know in hell why you made that slob our treasurer.'

'Because he is poor,' Dick said quietly. 'We would have spent it.'

He came panting up to them, planted a black violin case against the tree and began rummaging in his pockets for the money.

'I'm supposed to be at a music lesson, that's me alibi, me father always wanted to be a musician but he got married instead, he plays the cello, me brother Turlough plays the clarinet, me sister Jenny plays the viola, we have quartets, I sold a Haydn quartet for one and six, I had to borrow sixpence from Jenny, and I fecked the last sixpence from me mother's purse, that's what kept me so late . . .'

They were not listening, staring into the soiled and puckered handkerchief he was unravelling to point out, one by one, a crumpled half-note, two half-crowns, two shillings and a six-penny bit.

'That's all yeers, and here's mine. Six threepenny bits for the quartet. That's one and six. Here's Jenny's five pennies and two ha'pence. That makes two bob. And here's the tanner I just fecked from me mother's purse. That makes my two and six-pence.'

Eagerly he poured the mess into Dick's hands. At the sight of the jumble Dick roared at him.

'I told you, you bloody little fool, to bring a pound note!'

'You told me to bring a pound.'

'I said a pound note. I can't give this dog's breakfast to a girl like Daisy Bolster.'

'You said a pound.'

They all began to squabble. Jimmy Sullivan shoved Gong Gong. Georgie punched him. Dick shoved Georgie. Jimmy defended Georgie with 'We should never have let that slob come with us.' Gong Gong shouted, 'Who's a slob?' and swiped at him. Jimmy shoved him again so that he fell over his violin case, and a man passing home to his tea shouted at them, 'Stop beating that little boy at once!'

Tactfully they cowered. Dick helped Gong Gong to his feet. Georgie dusted him lovingly. Jimmy retrieved his cap, put it back crookedly on his head and patted him kindly. Dick explained in his best Ampleforth accent that they had merely been having 'a trifling discussion', and 'our young friend here tripped over his suitcase'. The man surveyed them dubiously, growled something and went on his way. When he was gone Georgie pulled out his pocketbook, handed a brand-new pound note to Dick and grabbed the dirty jumble of cash. Dick at once said, 'Quick march! Two by two!' and strode off ahead of the others, side by side with Tommy in his crooked cap, lugging his dusty violin case, into the deepening dark.

They passed nobody. They heard nothing. They saw only the few lights in the sparse houses along the left of the Mardyke. On the other side was the silent, railed-in stream. When they came in silence to the wide expanse of the cricket field the sky dropped a blazing veil of stars behind the outfield nets. When they passed the gates of the railed-in public park, locked for the night, darkness returned between the walls to their left and the overgrown laurels glistening behind the tall railings on their right. Here Tommy stopped dead, hooped fearfully towards the laurels.

'What's up with you?' Dick snapped at him.

'I hear a noise, me father told me once how a man murdered a woman in there for her gold watch, he said men do terrible things like that because of bad women, he said that that man was hanged by the neck in Cork Jail, he said that was the last time the black flag flew on top of the jail. Dick! I don't want to go on!'

Dick peered at the phosphorescent dial of his watch, and strode ahead, staring at the next feeble lamp hanging crookedly from its black iron arch. Tommy had to trot to catch up with him.

'We know,' Dick said, 'that she has long legs. Her breasts will be white and small.'

'I won't look!' Tommy moaned.

'Then don't look!'

Panting, otherwise silently, they hurried past the old corrugated iron building that had once been a roller-skating rink and was now empty and abandoned. After the last lamp the night became impenetrable, then her house rose slowly to their left against the starlight. It was square, tall, solid, brick-fronted, three-storied and jet-black against the stars except for its half-moon fanlight. They walked a few yards past it and halted, panting, behind a tree. The only sound was the squeaking of a branch over their heads. Looking backwards, they saw Georgie and Jimmy approaching under the last lamp. Looking forwards, they saw a brightly lit tram, on its way outward from the city, pass the far end of the tunnel, briefly light its maw and black it out again. Beyond that lay wide fields and the silent river. Dick said, 'Tell them to follow me if the fanlight goes out,' and disappeared.

Alone under the tree, backed still by the park, Tommy looked across to the far heights of Sunday's Well dotted with the lights of a thousand suburban houses. He clasped his fiddle case before him like a shield. He had to force himself not to run away towards where another bright tram would rattle him back to the city. Suddenly he saw the fanlight go out. Strings in the air throbbed and faded. Was somebody playing a cello? His father bowed over his cello, jacket off, shirt-sleeves rolled up, entered the Haydn; beside him Jenny waited, chin sideways over the viola, bosom lifted, bow poised, the tendons of her frail wrist hollowed by the lamplight, Turlough facing them lipped a thinner reed. His mother sat shawled by the fire, tapping the beat with her toe. Georgie and Jimmy joined him.

'Where's Dick?' Georgie whispered urgently.

'Did I hear music?' he gasped.

Georgie vanished, and again the strings came and faded. Jimmy whispered. 'Has she a gramophone?' Then they could hear nothing but the faint rattle of the vanished tram. When Jimmy slid away from him, he raced madly up into the darkness, and then stopped halfway to the tunnel's end. He did not have the penny to pay for the tram. He turned and raced as madly back the way he had come, down past her house, down to where the gleam of the laurels hid the murdered woman, and stopped again. He heard a rustling noise. A rat? He looked back, thought of her long legs and her small, white breasts, and found himself walking heavily back to her garden gate, his heart pounding. He entered the path, fumbled for the dark door, pressed against it, felt it slew open under his hand, stepped cautiously into the dark hallway, closed the door, saw nothing, heard nothing, stepped onward and fell clattering on the tiles over his violin case.

A door opened. He saw firelight flicker on shining shinbones and bare knees. Fearfully, his eyes moved upwards. She was wearing nothing but gym knickers. He saw two small birds, white, soft, rosy-tipped. Transfixed by joy he stared and stared at them. Her black hair hung over her narrow shoulders. She laughed down at him with white teeth and wordlessly gestured him to get up and come in. He faltered after her white back and stood inside the door. The only light was from the fire.

Nobody heeded him. Dick stood by the corner of the mantelpiece, one palm flat on it, his other hand holding his trembling corncob. He was peering coldly at her. His eyelashes almost met. Georgie lay sprawled in a chintzy armchair on the other side of the fire wearily flicking the ash from a black cigarette into the fender. Opposite him Jimmy Sullivan sat on the edge of a chair, his elbows on his knees, his eyeballs sticking out as if he had just swallowed something hot, hard and raw. Nobody said a word.

She stood in the centre of the carpet, looking guardedly from one to the other of them out of her hooded eyes, her thumbs inside the elastic of her gym knickers. Slowly she began to press her knickers down over her hips. When Georgie suddenly whispered 'The seventh veil!' he at once wanted to batter him over the head with his fiddle case, to shout at her to stop, to shout at them that they had seen everything, to shout that they must look no more. Instead, he lowered his head so that he saw nothing but her bare toes. Her last covering slid to the carpet. He heard three long gasps, became aware that Dick's pipe had fallen to the floor, that Georgie had started straight up, one fist lifted as if he was going to strike her, and that Jimmy had covered his face with his two hands.

A coal tinkled from the fire to the fender. With averted eyes he went to it, knelt before it, wet his fingers with his spittle as he had often seen his mother do, deftly laid the coal back on the fire and remained so for a moment watching it light up again. Then he sidled back to his violin case, walked out into the hall, flung open the door on the sky of stars and straightway started to race the whole length of the Mardyke from pool to pool of light in three gasping spurts.

After the first spurt he stood gasping until his heart had stopped hammering. He heard a girl laughing softly behind a tree. Just before his second halt he saw ahead of him a man and a woman approaching him arm in arm, but when he came up to where they should have been they too had become invisible. Halted, breathing, listening, he heard their murmuring somewhere in the dark. At his third panting rest he heard an invisible girl say, 'Oh, no, oh no!' and a man's urgent voice say, 'But yes, but yes!' He felt that behind every tree there were kissing lovers, and without stopping he ran the gauntlet between them until he had emerged from the Mardyke among the bright lights of the city. Then, at last, the sweat cooling on his forehead, he was standing outside the shuttered plumber's shop above which they lived. Slowly he climbed the bare stairs to their floor and their door. He paused for a moment to look up through the windows at the stars, opened the door and went in.

Four heads around the supper table turned to look up inquiringly at him. At one end of the table his mother sat wearing her blue apron. At the other end his father sat, in his rolled-up shirt-sleeves as if he had only just laid down the pressing iron. Turlough gulped his food. Jenny was smiling mockingly at him. She had the red ribbon in her hair and the mother-of-pearl brooch at her neck.

'You're bloody late,' his father said crossly. 'What the hell kept you? I hope you came straight home from your lesson. What way did you come? Did you meet anybody or talk to anybody? You know I don't want any loitering at night. I hope you weren't cadeying with any blackguards? Sit down, sir, and eat your supper. Or did your lordship expect us to wait for you? What did you play tonight? What did Professor Hartmann give you to practise for your next lesson?'

He sat in his place. His mother filled his plate and they all ate in silence.

Always the questions! Always talking talking at him! They never let him alone for a minute. His hands sank. She was so lovely. So white. So soft. So pink. His mother said gently, 'You're not eating, Tommy. Are you all right?'

He said, 'Yes, yes, I'm fine, Mother.'

Like birds. Like stars. Like music.

His mother said, 'You are very silent tonight, Tommy. You usually have a lot of talk after you've been to Professor Hartmann. What are you thinking of?'

'They were so beautiful!' he blurted.

'What was so bloody beautiful?' his father rasped. 'What are you blathering about?'

'The stars,' he said hastily.

Jenny laughed. His father frowned. Silence returned.

He knew that he would never again go back to the sweet-shop. They would only want to talk and talk about her. They would want to bring everything out into the light, boasting and smirking about her, taunting him for having run away. He would be happy forever if only he could walk every night of his life up the dark Mardyke, hearing nothing but a girl's laugh from behind a tree, a branch squeaking and the far-off rattle of a lost tram; walk on and on, deeper and deeper into the darkness until he could see nothing but one tall house whose fan-light she would never put out again. The doorbell might ring, but she would not hear it. The door might be answered, but not by her. She would be gone. He had known it ever since he heard her laughing softly by his side as they ran away together, for ever and ever, between those talking trees.

Liars

Before Miss Gogan finished her fifth lunch in the Grand Hotel Villa Serbelloni she had made a dreadful scene in the dining room – and on a Sunday afternoon at that! It was not that there had been anything wrong with the lunch; not in a hotel honoured by the red print of the *Guide Michelin* for its exquisite situation, gardens, decor, food and unbroken silence. It was simply that as she was finishing her usual excellent *scaloppine*, at her usual table, in the corner of the dining room, with her volume of *The Forsyte Saga* open before her – her fork poised over Soames proposing marriage to the reluctant Irene – seven or eight boys and girls in coloured wraps and sandals came crowding in from the lake, sun-bronzed and wet-haired, to occupy a large table at her elbow, laughing and babbling as noisily as if they were still cavorting on the sunblanched beach.

More annoying still, her old waiter who had hitherto been so attentive to her began to neglect her and cosset them, jocosely called them 'my little daughters' and 'my little sons'. It took her fully ten minutes to persuade him to remove her plate. It took him another ten minutes to bring her the fruit dish. And when she had eaten her peach she found herself beckoning and calling to him in vain for her coffee until she became so cross with him that she could not remember the Italian for waiter and began calling him *garsone, waitore* and *monsignore*. In the end she got into such a frenzy of irritation that she seized Aunt Rosa's thirty-year-old phrase book and her own new pocket dictionary, composed and rehearsed a speech of protest, got up, slapped her books closed, walked over to the old man, tapped him on the shoulder and let him have it.

He whirled, wide-eyed, to find the fat little woman with the lovely blue eyes and black eyelashes, the one dressed in red like a robin redbreast, all bosom and bum, announcing (insofar as he could make out at all what she was trying to say) that she had come here from (was it Iceland or Holland?) to search with a skewer (*con fuscellino*) for the peace and the repose, but now, 'Thy fault, O hunter, I go forth alone *abbandonata* to search for a coffeepot in the piazzetta!' Which said, she threw a ferocious, blueblack glare at him – who raised his hands aloft as if to bless her departure – and strode out between the staring diners, most of whom, she observed with chagrin, seemed chiefly interested in her long red cotton dress (bought last week at a sale at Cannocks' in Limerick) that she could feel flapping about her calves at every step like a bloody flag.

The sun in the whirling glass doors blinded her. The heat smote her. Below her lay the piazzetta, shadowless, over-exposed, empty. Taking courage from her anger, she decided that she really would have her coffee there and bravely descended to it. To her relief every one of the little round tables outside the cafe was unoccupied. The only person in sight was a beautiful boy in a white apron, shading his eyes to look at a white steamer slowly crossing from Cadenabbia. Looking at him, so young, so lightly poised on one leg, his hand lifted so gracefully to his brow, she felt Italy returning in all its former plenitude. When, with a start, he came hurrying towards her, she knew again that this must be the most simple, innocent, warm and welcoming country in the whole world.

'Signora?' He smiled eagerly.

The word, so clearly implying that she had long ceased to qualify for the younger title, had irked her a little in the mouths of the waiters and chambermaids of the hotel. Coming from this child it accentuated his youth rather than her age.

'Oh, very well!' she laughed. 'As the song says, "Call me Madam," I suppose, anyway, once you turn forty ...'

'Signora?' he asked again, not understanding a word.

'*Un caffè, per favore.*'

While she waited she stared at the approaching steamer. Why on earth had she made that awful exhibition of herself? It could be nothing to do with the hotel. He was really a very nice poor old waiter. And it could, most certainly, be nothing to do with lovely Bellagio. She looked about her questioningly.

Or could it? The quayside was as silent as it was blank. When she heard the hoot of the steamer, she thought for a moment of crossing back on it to pass an hour in Cadenabbia, but a second hollow hoot extended the same sense of blankness up and down the entire lake from north to south. It would be the same story over there. Every shutter closed. A dog stretched panting in the shade. A boatman asleep beside his boat. She received her answer from a third hollow hoot. 'Pao-o-la,' it said, and she repeated it aloud.

'Who has not rung me since last Friday!'

Unnoticed, her beautiful boy laid her coffee on the table, offered her an unseen smile, retired with an unacknowledged bow. She had snatched up her letter to Aunt Rosa on which she had spent the entire morning, and was lost in the reading of it, very slowly and very carefully, watching now not for the meaning of the words but, as she knew Aunt Rosa would also do, for their tell-tale tone:

Bellagio
Lago di Como
Sunday, June 14th

MY DEAREST AUNT ROSA,

I am sure you got my telegram saying I arrived safely. Now I must tell you all my news. But before I do, I must tell you how wildly grateful I am to you for arranging this wonderful trip for me to your dear, darling Italy. For years and years whenever you spoke of Italy I used to imagine, afterwards, what it must be really like. Now that I have, thanks to you, laid eyes on it I can assure you that it has surpassed my wildest dreams. How right you were! Lake Como is truly a vision of delight. Bellagio is, as you have always said, out of a child's picture book, winding back and up under the bluest sky to the loveliest country walks. Every moment I am enchanted by the magnificent views over the lake, with its dear little white steamers coming and going, offering to transport me to other delights, and its hundreds of darling pink villas dotted like flowers on every hillside. The hotel, the food, the service are beyond description. But I do not need to tell any of this to *you*! I cannot believe that a single thing has changed here since you and poor, dear Sir Julian, may God rest him, came to this very same hotel on your honeymoon thirty-odd years ago. But now I must at once explain to my dear benefactor how it has happened that I am spending the holiday here on Lake Como in this super hotel and not, as you so kindly planned, with Paola Buononcini in the villa at Forte dei Marmi. Well, this is the extraordinary thing that happened, and I can only hope and trust that in the circumstances I have acted just as you would have wished me to act. If I have not done so please write to me at once and I will obey you in every respect.

When I got off the plane at Milan on Tuesday afternoon, there indeed was Paola waiting for me, as you said she would be, as ravishingly elegant and lovely as when she stayed at the Castle last October, wearing pink raw-silk slacks, so tight that I could not imagine either how she got into them or out of them – zipped, do you suppose? – with openwork gold sandals, silver toenails, her fair hair down about her shoulders, looking about seventeen instead of, is it twenty-three? Before she said a word I knew there was something wrong. I could see it in her tragic eyes and the way she kissed me on both cheeks, which she never did in Limerick, and the way she at once began to gesticulate and talk like a machine gun. She told me, half in English, half in Italian, about the terrible *disgrazia* (this, I gather, is the Italians' curious word for an accident) that had happened to their villa in Forte dei Marmi only the night before.

It appears that their villa caught fire in the middle of the night and, though nobody was hurt, her mother had to be taken back at once to Milan suffering badly from shock. So, very apologetically, and sweetly, she really is the sweetest girl, she asked me would I mind if just we two spent the holiday together in this marvellous hotel on Lake Como, where she would be near her mamma in Milan, rather than in some seaside hotel in Forte dei Marmi where she would be very far away from her. Well, I said that I was terribly upset about the loss of the villa, and the shock to her mamma, but that I did not mind the change at all, though I was privately much more worried lest in saying so I might not be acting as you would have wished me to act. Still, looking back at it, I do not really see what else, at that moment, I could have said or done except to take the next plane home, an abrupt action that might well have seemed rather cavalier to the good Buononcinis. Nevertheless, I repeat, if you do not approve of my staying here, please do say so and I will follow your instructions in every particular.

Paola was accompanied by a very tall man, an old friend of the family, one Count Algradi, who had his car waiting outside the airport. In this great, long, white, shining vehicle, called I believe an Alfa-Romeo, like Romeo and Juliet, he at once whirled the pair of us off at a speed which frightened the very life out of me, in through the suburbs of Milan and out and on and up through the lakeside town of Como for my first view of the real Italy. On we drove, over the hills and far away, to this ritzy hotel on the edge of the lake, at the point of a peninsula, surrounded by flowers and gardens, tucked away from all traffic which, Paola told me, can be quite noisy on Sundays and holidays on these narrow roads.

Paola could not, unfortunately, stay with me that night as she had to go back to reassure her mother in Milan. On Wednesday night she rang to say her mother was much better though still so shaken that she, Paola, would not be able to join me for another couple of days and would I be all right by myself until then? Of course, I said yes, and of course I am. I mean how could anybody be otherwise in this exquisite place of peace, joy and total relaxation? She could not, apparently, call me on Thursday but on Friday morning she did ring again to explain that her poor mamma was still feeling a little down, but she, Paola, would ring again on Saturday, and join me as soon as possible ...'

Were those last four words a giveaway? More cold than whatever that Italian phrase was that Paola had used?

It is now Sunday morning and here I am happily sitting in the sun on the hotel terrace awaiting her call. It will, I am sure, come any minute now ...

The steamer bumped against the pier. She sipped her coffee. It had gone cold. Two motorcars came lumbering onto the quay. A few pedestrians disappeared into the shadows of the village. She wondered again if she ought to cross back on the ferry to Cadenabbia. Those roads behind Bellagio were all the same. Besides, it was really the evenings that got her down. Reading Galsworthy in the hotel lounge, while that chinless, chain-smoking young man doodled at the piano. She glanced over the rest of her letter.

So very, very, very grateful .. All my love to my dear cousins ... I do hope the new paying guests are nice, I wish I were there to help ... I wonder would somebody be so very, very, very kind as to water my white jasmine? Unless there has been more rain? My goodness, it was wet the morning I left . . . Endless love to you all.

Your devoted niece,
MARY ANNE

She folded it and put it into its envelope and looked at the address. *Lady Alleyn, Doon Castle, Castledoon, near Croom, Irlanda.* Limerick's long Sunday afternoons. The black eye of a raincloud glowering over the flat plain. So lush. So level. Damp potholes in the avenue. Tree trunks green on the windy side. Every single one of the battlements along the top of the house a bucket of rain. Water her white jasmine? Nobody's shoes would leave green marks on the grey dew of her lawn these mornings. Her twelve-year-old lawn behind the gate-lodge. Where she had lived with old grand-aunt Jenny until that Sunday afternoon last March when the poor, silly old soul sat down on a chair that was not there and broke her skull. She sighed, licked a mauve stamp and walloped it onto the envelope so passionately that she toppled her Galsworthy off the table. A cadaverous elderly man who, unobserved, had seated himself at the next table politely restored it, saying in perfect English, with a ghastly lower-lip smile, 'Your book, Miss Gogan.' She turned to stare at him.

'Good gracious!' she cried, enchanted to meet somebody she knew, and who could talk English. 'If it isn't Count Algradi!'

He was dressed in a metallic pink-grey suit, with big gold links in his long white cuffs. He rose above her, a pink flamingo, took her proffered hand by the fingertips and lowered his lips to the back of it. His splendid grey eyes stared frighteningly at her. He was the thinnest man she had ever seen.

'I am so pleased, Miss Gogan,' he said rapidly, precisely and sweetly, 'that you have not forgotten me.'

He resumed his seat, his panama perched on his pointed knee.

'Of course, I remember you,' she smiled, and involuntarily touched her letter to Aunt Rosa. 'But I do not remember your talking English to me at the airport?'

He smiled another lower-teeth smile.

'I did not talk to you at all, Miss Gogan. Paola Buononcini did all the talking. As she always does. Quite a chatterbox, isn't she? I think I should introduce myself again. My name is Federico Algardi. Not Algradi. But everyone calls me Freddy. My father had an enormous admiration for England. He sent me to an English school at Lausanne. They all called me Freddy there too. I went for two years to the University of Nottingham just before the war. Everyone there called me Freddy. Everyone in Milan knows me as Freddy Algardi. But I can talk Scots, too, ye know. I can recite your great poet Shelley in Scots. Shall I do it for you? *Hael taw thee, bliuthe speerutt! Burrd thaw neverr wurt, With thay baded bobbles winkin' at thay brrum, and thay purple-stained mourth!* Quite good, don't you think? I learned my Scots from the pastor at the Church of Saint James in Cadenabbia. I was there this morning. He is the Reverend Jamie Macandrew, from Aberdeen, an awfully nice fellow, though he does talk an awful lot of rot about hellfire. I am afraid in Nottingham we would have called him a bally ass. Mark you,' he said, and liked the phrase enough to repeat it, 'mark you, he really does believe in hellfire. He almost makes me believe in it.' He laughed another toothy laugh. '"To hell with the Pope!" They taught me how to say that in Nottingham. When I came home and said it to my mamma she was absolutely enchanted. Ye see, my mamma believed strongly in hellfire and she loathed all the popes. They taught me to say it because, like all the English, they think that all Italians are Catholics. It's not true, ye know, I'm not a Catholic. I'm a kind of Protestant. Actually I'm a Waldensian. Ye see, my mamma was not a Milanese. She came from Torino, a great stronghold of the Waldensians. The Scots of Italy, a severe people. Born Manichaeans. The persecuted devoted to persecution. My mamma was a tremendous persecutor. She persecuted me for years and years. Oh, my dear Miss Gogan, I cannot tell you how pleased I am to meet a lady from England. I adore Englishwomen.'

'But, Count Algardi,' she demurred. 'I am Irish!'

His bony fingers flashed gold.

'Same thing! Scots, English, Welsh, Irish. All British.'

He was nut-brown from the sun and, on a second glance, not

so bad-looking. In fact, with those greying wings over his ears, he looked quite distinguished, even if he was as thin as a pencil. Aunt Rosa had warned her that all Italian counts are rakes. ('A lot of bad hats,' she had said, remembering Italy under Mussolini. 'Watch out for them, even if you are forty-one. All the more so because you look it.')

'Oh, dear!' he said, and put his bony hand to his mouth, remembering his joke about the pope. 'If Irish, then Catholic? I've made an awful bally bloomer, what, what?'

'Count Algardi,' she said primly, 'all the Irish are not British. And like the Italians, not all the Irish are Catholics. I am a member of the Church of Ireland.'

'Please explain to me Church of Ireland.'

She explained feebly. He waved his wrist again.

'You mean the Church of England in Ireland. I am so relieved. My father greatly admired the Church of England. So do I! In fact, when I was in Nottingham I thought of joining the Church of England, but my mamma put her foot down. She said it was too lax. I have always regretted that I obeyed her. But, I have spent my life regretting that I ever obeyed her in anything. She really *was* an old tyrant.'

He sighed, regretting, and she, feeling also at a loss, stared sidelong at him over imaginary spectacles. Bad counts she could understand. Were there also mad counts? He roused himself from his gloom.

'Mark you, I know a lot about Ireland. The Irish Sweepstakes. Your great patriot De Valera. Your great English writers, Giose, Occasi, Becchetta. How lovely that poem by your great poet Giatsa! *I will rise up and go now far away to Ginnitsfrié.* Miss Gogan, I adore Ireland! The land of ghosts and goblins, of castles and kilts, of murderous queens and murdered kings. Macbeth!'

Miss Gogan decided to take him in hand.

'Count Algardi,' she said. 'What is your news of Paola Buononcini?'

He shifted his chair closer to her table.

'Signorina Gogan, I want very much to talk to you about dear Paola. In fact I badly need your advice about dear Paola. In fact I would like to talk with you about many things. I have a suggestion to make to you. Would you honour me by joining me for dinner tonight? I could collect you at your hotel at six o'clock, we could cross over to Cadenabbia on the ferry, and I would drive you from there to dinner at the Villa d'Este. It is a hotel but it is not a hotel. It is a house that is not a house. It is the most delightful mansion in Europe south of the Alps. I promise to have you back in your hotel by ten o'clock sharp. Please, Miss Gogan, I do so need your help. And your advice. Please join me for dinner.'

She looked into his pleading grey eyes. She thought of those boring hill roads that she had walked and walked. She thought of those empty hours after dinner.

'Thank you, Count,' she said sedately. 'I should be most pleased to join you for dinner.'

'Splendid!' he cried joyfully. 'Until six, then. At your hotel' – and lifted her hand again by the fingertips, bowed over it, and, with long, swift heron steps stooped rapidly away, folded himself into his white car and whirled from the empty quay.

The lake was rippled like a fish by the prow of the steamer. The mountains wavered in the water. She had never met a real count before. Rapidly she changed that. She had never met any sort of count before. Nobody had ever kissed her hand before. Nobody had ever asked her advice about anything, except about such things as whether the paying guests could be fobbed off with liver and bacon. Bad counts? Aunt Rosa must have been joking. Anyway, Aunt Rosa did not have to know every damn thing. She became aware that her beautiful boy was hovering, a bottle in one hand, in the other a tiny glass.

'*Una Strega, signorina?*' (Signorina!) '*Complimenti dello Padrone.*'

She glanced where he was glancing, behind him. The portly *padrone* was bowing to her from the door of his café. Bad or mad, the count apparently counted.

'*Grazie,*' she whispered, wondering as she watched him pour out the golden liquor what a Strega was, and was she doing something absolutely awful again? Guardedly she sipped the sweet liqueur. She stayed there quite a while gazing happily around her. Once she slipped her bookmarker under the flap of her letter to add a postscript, paused and thought better of it.

If Limerick only knew! She tossed back her liqueur, and tossed her head. To hell with them! Let them know! She rose, turned and bowed towards the watching *padrone* and the watching boy beside him, and walked back slowly to the Grand Hotel Villa Serbelloni. On the way she deftly consigned her conscience to the red letterbox fixed to the wall of the shuttered tobacconist. To her relief there was no telephone call from Paola.

He came on the first stroke of the angelus, looking, she thought, like a broken thermometer with his white hair, his black dinner jacket, white front, black tie, white socks. She, after two hours of trying on and casting off every rag she possessed, had settled for her shortest frock – black satin, with great, walloping hand-painted roses, a light shawl of pink wool, an evening bag in silvered calf, a trifle cracked, green evening shoes with red Spanish heels. He looked her over, said, 'You look marvellous! I adore English clothes,' and bowed her into his car. There, seated beside her, on the steamer, he at once began to gabble in his rapid way about the vanity of human wishes.

'Today,' he said, 'the air was so dry you could see a golf ball two hundred yards away. The Reverend Macandrew was very good about that this morning. He said, "Life is like a man's breath on a wintry day, appearrring and vonishing. It reminds him of his mortality. Listen," he said to us, "to what the summer says to us. Last week we had a showurr of rain. Now the earth is as dry as snuff. Our life is like the rrain that the earrth cannot hold. It vonishes into the sky. All things tend upwarrds. Here under the great sunlight of Italy we may dream of a life that will last for everrr, but the lakes are more wise. They dream of the sky." '

She agreed that it was a verra, verra beautiful thought. 'But a bit melancholy?' He startled her by saying that all life is melancholy, bumped off the ferry and began to drive so fast past countless other roaring cars, along a road suitable only for cows in single file, that all conversation was out of the question. He tore within inches of pink villa walls whose hanging bougainvillea swayed in their wind at their shoulders and whose plaster had been scored by the axles of generations of previous roaring drivers. She devoutly hoped that they had all long since evaporated into the sky. She looked sideways at him. He was beaming wildly ahead of him. There could be no doubt about it. The man was as mad as a brush. After that she did not dare open her eyes again until she felt the car slowing on the gravel of what she hoped was his Villa d'Este. When she glared at him she found him gazing at her in happy self-admiration and thought of the drive back, through the night, along those awful donkey-roads. The next moment she forgot everything. He had led her, tottering on her fears, through the foyer out to the terrace. Seeing her delight, he pressed her bare arm. This, also, nobody had ever done to her before. She liked it.

'But this,' she cried, 'knocks the Villa Serbelloni into a cocked hat. This must be the most beautiful place in the whole world. This must be Italy at its very, very, very . . .'

'At its verra, verra, verra?' he laughed, and in her relief she laughed back at him.

'At its verra, verra, verra best!'

It was an opinion she was to abandon heartlessly two days later in favour of a smelly hatbox of a place they discovered halfway to Lugano, a fisherman's trattoria where they ate the freshest of sprats and drank horripilous draughts of a nameless wine under an occluded sky whose low clouds sliced the tops of the mountains. A shutter kept banging in the wind. An invisible cat lapped the shore. At its edge there stood the most romantic figure she had ever seen, a young man in black knee gaiters, a black-brimmed hat and a black cloak. While they ate the young man stood there unstirring.

'Do you think he is a poet?' she asked.

He said that he might be a spy for the Swiss customs. It would not have surprised her if the spy had broken out into an aria from *Il Trovatore*.

He released her arm, to her regret. She touched it where he had held it.

'Now for an aperitif! While we watch the shadows creeping over the lake, and the lights coming up across there in Belvio, and the stars envying us from the mountains.'

By her second martini Miss Gogan felt so much at her ease in Zion that she dared to chide him for his driving.

'Count!' she begged. 'Would yeh tell me wan thing and tell me no more, do you always drive as fast as that? Some day you'll break your blooming neck, so ye will! I'm sure it's very bad for yer nerves.'

'*Noi altri Italiani,*' he said proudly, 'have no nerves. It is why we drive like angels, fight like devils, climb like goats, die like heroes and live without a thought for tomorrow. Besides,' he added casually, 'driving is my business. I sell racing cars.'

'Go along with you! Is that really true? A count? Selling motor cars?'

'My dear signorina, counts, as we would have said at Nottingham, are ten a penny these days. We all have to work,' and he nodded towards the affluent-looking gentlemen seated around them under the vines with their low-backed bulbous wives.

'They look very rich,' she said shyly. 'Look at the pearls. They must have paid hundreds of pounds for those evening dresses.'

'Don't let them impress you,' he laughed. 'That is why all these men have to work. And for those,' he added, nodding towards a frieze of golden youth in bottomy bikinis and coloured wraps strolling against the balustrade of the terrace into the hotel. 'But don't let us waste our time talking about these silly people. I want to talk about you. First of all please tell me your first name.'

'Mary Anne.'

'Marianna! How beautiful! The Madonna and Santa Anna all in one. I have a better idea still, let me talk to you about you. I will tell you all about yourself. You are Marianna Gogan. You live with your dear aunt, Lady Rose Alleyn, the widow of the late Sir George Alleyn, in an ancient castle called Doon Castle. Yes?'

She cocked a wary eye at him.

'You mean,' he laughed, 'who told me? Paola. While we were waiting for you at the airport on Tuesday.'

(How much else, she wondered, did that little monkey tell him?)

'But, you see, our dear Paola is such a dreadful liar I never know how much to believe from her. Let me go on. Your ancient castle stands behind high walls and iron gates in the middle of a great, green rolling plain . . .'

'Not so rolling!'

'. . . dark with woods that are full of foxes, stags, hares and boars specially preserved for the hunt. Yes?'

'Did Paola tell you all that too?'

'She did not enlarge, but I have second sight. Like my mother. But I am right about the woods? Yes?'

She saw the rusty gates that were never shut, the gapped walls that were never mended, the big house at the end of the avenue against the wet sunset, old dotty grandaunt Jenny clucking like a hen after her pet tortoise under the bushes, and, for no reason, she wondered who was now carrying the bath-water upstairs in the tall tin containers clad in red padded wickerwork to be poured by astonished American P.G.'s into brown sitbaths.

'Well,' she temporized, 'it is all certainly very green around Doon Castle.'

'You see!' he cried happily. 'I do have second sight! Now! Your castle. It is so very old that it is covered with ivy. It has turrets and battlements. From its highest turret a flag flies in the wind of every Saint George's Day. And it is lighted only by tiny gothic windows, yes?'

She wove her fingers. A flag, my bottom! And what the hell does he want turrets and battlements for? The next thing he will want is a belfry. He ought to go and live there like a bat. She emptied her glass, he clicked his fingers and one of the white-jacketed waiters immediately refilled it. Old? Doon Castle? *Doon* is the Irish for a fort, and wherever that old thing was it must be ancient.

'Doon Castle,' she smiled at him, 'is indubitably very ancient.'

He creaked back in his wickerwork armchair and gazed up at the vine trellis.

'There,' he intoned dreamily, 'I see young Marianna Gogan, in pig's tails, leaning out of a gothic window in the early morning, awakened by the horn of the huntsman. You are wearing a pink peignoir. You are looking out of your wide, blue eyes down at the line of huntsmen in red coats, the hounds baying before them, the red fox streaking ahead of them across the dewy fields. But then,' he raced on, his hand on hers to silence her, 'as you grow older I see you among the huntsmen, riding sidesaddle, in your long black skirt, wearing your tall black hat, and at one of the mighty jumps your hat flies off on its string and your black hair floats behind you like a thundercloud. Am I right? Yes?'

She gulped half her third martini. 'Christ!' she moaned to herself (long since infected by all the more colourful vices of Catholicism). 'If he only got one look at the East Limericks! The Master would have a red coat. And I know Corney Costigan the vet has one because he bought all Sir George's old cast-offs ten years ago. And I did see Father Binchy one time in a black riding coat with a cravat. And some of the youngsters would have jodhpurs and hunting caps. But if he saw the farmers' sons! Leggings and beret, that's all they'd rise to. And as for the ragtag and bobtail . . .'

But he was galloping on and on again, breathless, to the kill, while she was seeing the old rooky-rawky house in Dublin where she might still be living if her mammy and pappy had not died, and if Sir Julian had not died, and if Aunt Rosa had not had to take in P.G.'s, and get somebody to look after grand-aunt Jenny in the gate lodge.

'When I was in Nottingham,' he was sighing, and she was wishing to God he had never left it, 'I once drove over to Melton Mowbray with a fellow named Ranjit Singh to see the hunt. The car broke down. We never saw it. But I have seen it on television, and in the movies. Didn't you love *Tom Jones*?'

She threw back the second half of her martini.

'Count Algardi! *Please* talk to me about Paola Buononcini.'

'Later! At dinner. Let us have a sherry this time. I forgot that in England you always take sherry before dinner. *Xeres*, ye know, is the Italian for sherry, but nobody ever says it, Domenico! *Due* sherry. *Molto secco!* You remember your Homer?' he asked her. 'How Helen threw a drug into the wine and they forgot all their sorrows. As your great Shakespeare says, "Let our joy be unconfined."'

'Count Algardi,' she giggled. 'I think I'm a bit tiddly already. Look't! Leave us be talking about you thish time. Tell me every single bluddy thing about yourself!'

'Everything? I can tell you that in one sentence. I am a poor, half-crazy fellow who sells cars, dreams dreams and wishes he had a glorious youth like you, and,' he added gloomily, 're-members his own.'

But to remember is also to forget. Her memories of the rest of that night would be as gapped as her memories of the nights that followed it. She would never remember how she got to the dinner table. She would know only that she found herself under a red and white marquee, crowded with diners, surrounded by boxes of paw-pink begonias, scarlet zinnias, purple lobelias and white geraniums, under great billowing loops of nasturtiums. On every table a small pink lamp gleamed on the silver, the glass, the napery. The shadows had by then climbed to the far tip of Monte Beletto, twilight had become dusk, one vast star sat in a hollow between two peaks and across the lake a steamer slowly carried past them a cargo of fairy lights and faint music. But she would remember that the ink-blue night and the skin-pale wine so fumed in her head that whenever a white-haired man in a black tie passed their table with a bare-backed lady and nodded and smiled at him she nodded and smiled back boozily at them, and that presently she was calling him Freddy, and he, with equal amiability, was calling her Marianna. Nothing else stayed with her except the moment when he uttered the name Paola. He did it just after he had risen from his chair – for nobody else had he done this – and bowed deeply to a powerfully built lady with blued hair, and to a gentleman of equal size with a tri-coloured button in the lapel of his dinner jacket.

'They,' he whispered to her over his glass of Soave, the lamplight below his nose hollowing his cheeks, 'are the father and mother of Paola Buononcini.'

Startled sober, she stared at him.

'But that is impossible! Her mother is ill in Milan. Freddy! Tell me at once. Where exactly is Paola?'

Feebly he raised his elbows and his eyebrows.

'In Forte dei Marmi.'

'You mean she has been lying to me?'

He laid his lean hand on her chubby hand.

'Marianna! You do not understand Paola. I have known her for years. I have been devoted to her since she was sixteen. And I am not sure that I even still understand her. You see, you

British . . .' (She let it pass with an exasperated breath.) '. . . have all the honesty, truthfulness and straightness of your noble race. Your yes means yes, and your no means no. With *la bella* Paola yes means perhaps, and no means maybe. Paola is young, willful, selfish, greedy for life. She never decides what she wants until the last minute. At Linate airport, five minutes before your plane arrived, she suddenly left me, telephoned Bellagio, reserved a room for you, came back and told me that I must stay here and look after you for ten days.'

She could hardly speak for rage and shame.

'Are you telling me that the villa was never burned?'

He shook his head sadly.

'Oh! I know. She has always done it. She uses me. She uses everybody. You and I are in the same boat. She has ditched the pair of us. After all, I too was supposed to have gone to Forte dei Marmi. I was to have driven the three of us down there that Tuesday afternoon and stayed for a fortnight. My holidays.'

'I shall take the next plane home,' she said instantly.

His hand tightened on her hand.

'Marianna, please don't be angry with Paola.'

'Angry with her? I could kill the little bitch.'

'No, no! I have as much reason to be cross with her. But I am grateful to her. Because she made me meet you. Besides, she was right about Forte. What is Forte but miles upon miles of coloured *cabane* and umbrellas? Young people shouting, laughing, babbling and flirting all day long, sunbathing or sleeping half the day, dancing or playing canasta half the night. You would have felt out of everything. Paola would not have known what to do with you. Anyway, she probably has a young man there.'

'Then why did she invite me?'

At that he curled.

'Well . . . She didn't really, you know.'

'But Aunt Rosa told me . . .'

'If Paola was telling me the truth, she really invited your cousin, Geraldine. But your cousin could not come. Paola said something about a young American. So, Lady Alleyn suggested you.'

She covered her face in her hands, then slowly parted them and looked at him.

'I see,' she said quietly, 'I was second best – and not wanted. And Aunt Rosa fixed nothing for me. I shall take the plane home tomorrow.'

To her horror, he straightway began to sob like a child who has been struck. He clutched her hands.

'Marianna,' he wailed, while her eyes darted around to see how many people were noticing. 'Please, do not leave me. If you go away, what shall I do without you?'

'You mean I'm to be second best even for that bitch Paola?'

Why, in God's name, had she ever had anything to do with him? With any of them? Filthy Italians! All liars! The whole damned pack of them, all liars. Wops!

'If you go away I'll drink like a fish all day long. I'll do terrible things. I'll drown myself in the lake if you abandon me. I was so happy to meet you again. I came to Bellagio this afternoon solely to meet you. I was looking forward to being your guide, to showing you everything, little villages, little lakes, hidden corners that no foreigner ever sees. Everybody on the Lakes knows me. They are all my dear friends. I owe money to all of them. I owe thousands upon thousands of lire to the old pirate who runs the restaurant on the island of Comacino. We can lunch there every day. I owe millions to the casino at Campione. We will gamble there together and make pots of money. We will visit the Prince Borromeo on Isola Bella – my father was a great business friend of his. He often said it to me, "I will never, simply *never* forget your father!" We will eat in little *trattorie* around the lakes where I owe nothing and they'll only be delighted to let me run up enormous bills. Marianna! Don't abandon me!'

Her rage sank to the bottom of a sea of pity.

'But if Aunt Rosa finds out that Paola never joined me, what will I do? I'd be disgraced in Limerick if they got one word of the wind of all this.'

'Seal your mouth like a fish. Don't tell anybody. If you knew the things I've done that I never told to anybody. Not even to my own mother.'

They argued and argued, though again about what she would

never remember, except only that, there among the pink lights, the scurrying waiters, the elegant diners, the flowers, his eyes as melancholy and his face as long as a wet hake's, she found herself blurting out a terrible thing.

'Freddy! Why are you making yourself out to be a wicked man? Are you a bad man? Aunt Rosa says all Italian counts are bad men.'

He blenched. She curled. Then, for the first time since they had met, he threw himself back and laughed with his whole mouth, and in her relief at his relief she started to weep for the pair of them.

'Your Aunt Rosa!' he laughed, 'she must be just like all the other grownups I've ever known – my mother, my father, the Reverend Macandrew . . .'

'You mean,' she said, 'she is a bally ass? Oh, Freddy, you are a scream! I always thought that about Aunt Rosa but I never had the courage before to say it' – at which he knew that she would stay. He deftly halted the scurrying wine waiter.

'Sesto! Champagne! The Bollinger. Forty-seven.'

With a single flourishing gesture the young man blessed their happiness and saluted the champagne. 'The first champagne, signorina,' he whispered to her, for there was a table of Germans near them, 'that the Germans did not drink,' and hastened away to serve them.

'He likes us!' she cried.

'He likes you!'

'Me?' eyes wide, looking around her.

'And why not?' he asked haughtily.

'All these elegant women! And fat me?'

'Pfoo! Bought elegance. But you are genuine, you are true, you are the real thing,' and took both her hands. 'Oh! My dear, dear Marianna! We are going to have the time of our lives.'

They were the last to leave the marquee. Over their brandies he spoke with a sad dignity.

'You asked me, Marianna, if I am a bad man. I am.'

'I refuse to believe it,' she cried passionately. 'I think you're a grand fellow.'

'I am bad,' he insisted. 'And growing old in my badness! How old do you think I am?'

'I am thirty-five,' she said. 'If not more!'

'I am a hundred. I go back too far. I must tell you that my grandmamma was a Princess Levashov. One of those mad Russian revolutionaries who fled to Switzerland in the sixties and led such wild lives there that she ran away from them all to live in the Vaud and become a Waldensian. From one craziness to another. She had only one child. My mamma. In Torino my mamma met my papa. She, too, had only one child. I was not born until they had been married for six years, and I swear that she never once slept with my papa before that, and I swear that after I was born she never again let him make love to her. She was a monster! A woman who hated and despised everything to do with the body and with pleasure. Shall I tell you what she did to me when I was fifteen?'

Over the pink lamp he whispered it to her. By its underlight he looked like Mephistopheles.

'It was Easter. She found out through her spies that I was going out every night with the girl who sold cigarettes in the railway station in Milan. She went down into our garden and she cut two of her loveliest madonna lilies. She took her paint box and she daubed black paint all over one of the white chalices, and daubed a hideous red paint all over its golden pistil. She put the two flowers into a vase in my bedroom, and, pointing at them with her bony finger, she said, "That candid lily was you before you met that slut. This horrible thing is what you are now!" She left them in my bedroom for a month. I can still smell their stink.'

She took his hand in both her hands and her eyes filled with pity for him.

'Poor little boy! But, Freddy, you must have had lots of nice girls since then?'

'Only the kind I dare not talk about. Even while I longed only for girls who were pure, and sweet, and innocent and *oneste*. Seven years ago when I first met Paola she was sweet, pure and innocent. Or was she? How do I know? Now she is greedy, thinks only of herself, lies like a trooper and makes a fool of me all the time. Yet, I never once blamed her. I blamed only this corrupt south where we live. Until last Tuesday at the airport when I saw her deceiving you, a trusting, truthful, honourable, straightforward, candid, open woman from the honest north. The scales fell from my eyes. I realized then that all I long for comes only with the years.'

She did the only thing she could do. She closed her eyes and uttered a soft ancestral moan.

'Freddy!' she whispered. 'I'm dhronk! Take me home.'

She woke at ten o'clock to insistent tom-toms, in her head and from the telephone. It was Freddy. She confided about her head.

'I will attend to that. And I have fixed your appointment with Toni for half-past eleven.'

'With Toni? Who is Toni?'

'I told you about him last night. Have you forgotten? You asked me about a hairdresser. He is the best *parruchiere* on the Lakes. You will find him in Bellagio, near the church. He is my second cousin. And you asked me, too, about a boutique, though why I cannot imagine; you dress so beautifully. You will find one two doors away from Toni's, called La Fiorella. She is my uncle's sister. Good-bye, dear Marianna. I will call for you at half-past twelve.'

She fell on her pillow with a groan, dedicating her life to cold water, total abstinence and, even if he was an R.C., Father Theobald Mathew, Ireland's apostle of temperance – as her papa used to do long ago in Dublin whenever he woke up after a bad skite. Five minutes later a young waiter knocked and entered. He bore on a silver tray a glass of brown liquid that looked like Mother Siegel's Syrup.

'Compliments of Count Algardi, signorina. Throw it back.'

She did so and he laughed amiably at her face of disgust, assured her with all the sympathy of one who had in his time also paid wages to Bacchus, that she would feel fine within three minutes, and retired with a nod of comradely approval. And, indeed, by the time she had risen, reeled around for a bit, vomited, bathed and vomited again, she did feel better; so much so that when she fared out into the sunshot village in search of his Toni and his Fiorella she was in a state of happy expectation. She saw, blazing in the window of the boutique, a frock so brilliant that it would have seduced a parakeet. Without hesitation she went in, spent half her pocket money on it, and emerged in it feeling half-naked, depraved, a fool and utterly delighted. Two doors on there was Toni, ready and waiting for her, as hairy, tiny and garrulous as a Yorkshire terrier. He conducted her to a throne, swished pink curtains about her and began to walk around her as if she were a horse, prattling saucily to her about the superiority of all northern Italians to the rest of the entire world in matters of hairdressing and of love.

'We are as hotta as Siciliani. But more *intelligente*. I love plenty. I have five kids. Three masculine, two feminine. Siciliani not *intelligente*. Millions of kids!'

Whereupon he fell into a gloomy silence, clicked his fingers to summon two pink-robed handmaidens, pointed to her and spread his hands in despair. At once the three of them began to argue passionately about her face. As suddenly he switched off their torrent and began to snip and snap. One of the handmaidens stripped her of her stockings, and sat by her feet to manicure her toes and her fingers. The other came and went with trays of powders, creams and golden lipsticks which she matched and rematched to her skin, all the while (or so it sounded) cursing softly under her breath. The rising heat crept through the open door. Drowsing smells invaded her. Far away she heard the drone of a buzzbike. A distant steamer cock-crowed. Voices from the village carried on the thin air. 'Air,' she begged, 'can I have some air?' and they swished back the curtains and there was the wide, metallic light of Italy, powerful, penetrating, pitiless and inviting. Part of her said, 'What am I doing this for?' Part said, 'What can they do for me?' Part said, 'How much is this going to cost?' Part said, 'Are we both out of our minds?' Part said, 'What does he see in me?' Part said, 'Poor Freddy!' And part of her said, 'He may be mad, but I do like him.'

She blew bubbles into the washbasin. As she surfaced, a church bell rang away the half hour. Anaesthetized under the dryer, she was barely aware of fingers touching, drying, dabbing her, and those soft murmuring curses going on all the time. She felt the dryer being lifted and Toni behind her again. Then, just as the church bell was striking the angelus Toni was presenting her with a hand mirror and slowly twirling her throne so that she could see herself from every angle, the girls exclaiming at one another's art, and embracing one another in delight, while she thought, 'Sacred Heart of Jesus! I look like a whore!' She was coffee-brown. Her eyelids were as blue as the lake. Her hair was a blue-black helmet. She had eyelashes a yard long. Her mouth was as big as a letterbox. She beamed at them, clapped her paws, babbled thanks and began to rummage in her handbag, at which Toni gave her the Fascist salute with his right hand and machine-gunned her with a hundred no's.

'The friend of my best friend! *Impossible!* In the winter I work in Milano. Freddy send me every woman he know.' (Oh, does he?) 'But,' waving his hand royally to the two girls, 'if you wish . . .'

Fishing for two modest notes she gave each girl a thousand lire. They almost palanquined her to the door. There, one of them suspended her stockings above a waste basket, mimicked 'Yes?' with her painted eyebrows, displayed her own pretty, coffee-dyed legs, and smilingly taking her answer for an 'Oh, yes!' discarded her best Cantreces. (Three and sixpence in Cannocks'! And brand new!) More showers of thanks, smiles, wavings and farewells pursued her as she went scurrying back to her hotel, her handbag to her nose like a yashmak, her other hand feeling her bare thighs, hastening to rub all this stuff off before Freddy saw her. For, in the newfound wisdom of an admired woman, she knew that this could not possibly be what he wanted at all. Unless he really was a bad man? Before her mirror she ruffled her hair, wiped her mouth, and did what she could with the blue eyelids and the coffee face. She hesitated a long time over the beautiful eyelashes. She finally peeled them off, carefully trimmed them with her nail scissors, stuck them back again and approved. To finish, she started to draw on a fresh pair of stockings and fell back in her chair red with shame. They had painted her *all* the way up. The telephone rang.

'Signorina Gogan? Count Algardi has arrived.'

With a groan she abandoned her stockings and her modesty, slipped on her shoes, covered her naked back with her auntie shawl and went forth to meet him, smilingly holding her hand straight out from her shoulder in the hope that when he bowed over it he would not see her legs. He gave her one quick all-over glance.

'Perfect! As Cicero says, when unadorned the most adorned. But, of course,' he added as he bestowed her into his car, 'it is one of the most extraordinary things about women – I once waited two hours outside a *parruchiere* for Paola and when she came out she was exactly the same as when she went in.'

'Perhaps,' she said tartly, 'you did not see her. You didn't notice my new frock,' she pouted, thinking with annoyance of all the money she had paid for it. 'Freddy, I don't think you see me at all! Or do you?'

'Your frock is wonderful,' he said, giving it a casual look as, with three fingers on the wheel, he halted within inches of the edge of the dock. 'As for seeing you? The Reverend Macandrew said a beautiful thing a few weeks ago. "Love, my dear bretherrn," he said to us, "is a secret that grows within the soul." '

She looked hopelessly over the lake. *More* guff? Her look changed to a quick apprehension as he went on.

' "But, dear bretherrrn, the body is love's open book." Now that we are friends, Marianna, we shall have no secrets from one another.'

From that moment on she never looked forward. A woman without a past can read only the present. A woman with no future must ignore it. Even the sun conspired against foresight. Its heat shrivelled the pages of her calendar. Like a moth under a glazed dome of breathless air, wine-fumy and sticky, she began to move slower and slower. Each morning she woke later, stretched out an arm reluctantly for the telephone, breakfasted in bed, bathed as languidly as an odalisque, had to struggle against the temptation to roll back into bed again. She spent hours over a face that, in Limerick, she would have washed in three minutes out of a basin of rainwater from the barrel outside her door. She never wore stockings again. She left her clothes strewn around the bedroom floor. She lost her *Forsyte Saga*. Only once did she manage to squeeze out five lines to Aunt Rosa (who never wrote) telling her about the sweetness and kindness of Paola Buononcini (who never rang), taking her everywhere, showing her everything.

Every noon she kept Freddy waiting when he called to whirl her off to a long, guffy lunch, after it whirling her back to the Grand Hotel Villa Serbelloni for her siesta, during which he, in his panama hat, would snore in a deckchair directly under her window. They drank afternoon tea on so many different terraces that their names became a jumble in her memory – Stresa, Cannobio, Lugano, Varese, Bellano . . . Having eaten, between them, as many pastries as six children of fourteen, he would drive on to some other terrace for their aperitif; and on to a third for dinner, which always finished so late – especially if there were dancing; he was like a stork waltzing with a robin – that she was never in bed until long after midnight.

Debauched by pity, corrupted by kindness, demoralized by all the deceits he forced on her, she had no desire but to please him, to be his friend, nurse, slave, handmaiden, ayah, confidante, governess, scheherazade, or – her own words, spoken silently one exasperated night through the wide-open windows of her bedroom to the gigantic stars – whatever in God's name it was that this poor, good, kind, dignified, dotty, deceived man wanted her to be or to do. For him she only wanted one thing: to fatten him – whence those piles of pastries that served only to fatten her. From him she wanted only one small thing: that he might kiss her just once before they parted forever.

As the days and the nights peeled away and she could not do the first and he apparently had no desire to do the second, she became so frustrated and bewildered – could he be what they call impotent? – that she led him, one night after dinner, up into the dark gardens behind the Villa d'Este, hoping that the stars, the dark and the view might inspire him to do something else beside talk to her. Whereupon, as they sat on a stone bench among the plumes of the cypresses, under a statue that was more shade than stone, a fountain more whisper than water, the light across the lake quivering in the warm air like the fireflies at their feet, dance music thrumming far below them, she became terrified to recall how, in her teens, in their basement kitchen in Dublin, their old servant Molly Power had told her, screaming with laughter, about the night in her own teens when her fellow took her up into the dark of Killiney Hill, and made her lie among the furze and take off every stitch of her clothes so that he could have a good look at her. ('And the blooming furze sticking into me bottom like needles!') Heart pounding, she waited. At last he touched her hand.

'Look, Marianna, how the stars lie in the laps of the mountains like little babies! See how the night passes. So our life passes. As the Reverend Macandrew says, only truth, like love, lasts forever.'

Then he led her gently back, down to the lakeside, to sit and talk some more on the terrace, while she felt as wicked as if she had been trying to seduce a vicar and as exhausted as if she had succeeded.

So far as she could see he appeared to want nothing at all but to take her life in exchange for his. But what was his life? There were mornings when, breakfasting drowsily, she doubted everything about him. How did she know he was even a count? Paola could have lied about that. But unless everybody else, in the Villa d'Este, the Villa Serbelloni, on the Isola Comacina, in all the other grand places he took her to were also taking part in a conspiracy to deceive her ... Poor and odd he might be. He *was* Count Algardi. But all this talk about his miserable youth? If she even knew where he lived. If, instead of wandering with her around these lakes he was walking with her around Milan, showing her where he lived, and worked; the house where he grew up as a boy; where he went to school; the garden where his mamma cut the lilies.

She thought of writing to Paola Buononcini. 'Dear Paola, I know that this must sound a curious request that I am about to make to you. Yet, you are a woman of the world who knows the hearts of men, and you will, I am sure, sympathize with the strange predicament of an older woman who ...' Who what? 'Dear Paola, I feel myself impelled to thank you with all the sincerity of my heart for so generously sharing with me the friendship of your charming friend, Freddy Algardi, who ...' Who what? Who nothing! 'Yet, I must also confide to you that in my heart I find him ...' She could see Paola showing the letter around among her gang in Forte dei Marmi. They would crowd over her shoulder. They would roll on the sand laughing themselves sick over her. She thought of calling on Toni. But Toni was related to him, and indebted to him, and there, in terror, she suddenly felt the ultimate isolation of every traveller who, no matter how well he may speak a foreign tongue, can be defeated by the movement of a thumb.

She tried to probe and trap him.

'Freddy, have you written to Paola?'

'Why should I?'

'Have you rung her? Has she rung you?'

He smiled. A shoulder stirred. An eyelid moved.

'Why should she? She has fixed everything the way she wants it. Or so she thinks.'

'Did you always dance as well as this, Freddy?'

'My mamma disapproved of dancing. I had to take lessons secretly. Even when I was thirty I still had to steal out to dancehalls. I never dared go to invitation dances. Her spies would have told her at once.'

'Were they nice dancehalls?'

'Nice? They were rough, gay, noisy places. Nice?' A hand stirred. '*Popolare*. Away out beyond the cemeteries. I used to wear an old trenchcoat and a cap, and go there on the tramway, through the fog. She drove me to such places. It was her own fault. But you? Ah, you! You went to Hunt Balls! Yes?'

'Of course! Every year. Twice a year sometimes.'

'With pipers? And harpers? I can see the whirling kilts. The tartan shawls flying. And other dances? Tell me about them all!'

'You mean Harvest Home dances? And there were Birthday dances, too. And there were the Pony Club dances. And we always had Coming of Age dances, with all the tenantry lighting great bonfires down the avenue. Freddy! Are there brothels in Milan?'

'What a question!'

'But are there?'

'By the score! Or so I would guess.'

She was afraid to pursue the subject.

'Did you ever get drunk, Freddy?'

'That reminds me. What exactly does go into a stirrup cup?'

'Mulled wine. Freddy, you must have enjoyed something! The opera? Used you to take your girl friend to the opera?'

'A girl? To the opera? Alone? In Milan? My dear Marianna, nobody is ever alone in Milan! We went to the opera *en famille*, and only on opening nights, and only to certain operas of which my mamma approved. And while I was doing that, bored to death, think of what you were doing! Wandering with a lantern through your dark fields, spying on elves, goblins, ghosts and fairies. Oh, please tell me all about them, Marianna.'

'Well, it is more in the mornings, you know, that one sees the fairies. Ghosts only at night. Banshees at any time. Elves, very rarely.'

'Tell me!'

Indulgently, she led him by the hand on summer mornings, at sunrise, over the dew-grey grass to pick newborn mushrooms and watch the leprechauns running away in all directions. She told him every fairy story she had ever read. He listened with her to the dogs at dawn, baying death-warnings, to ghostly whisperings winding down the chimneys on stormy nights. He straightway demanded brigands. She drew the line at that. Instead, she let him see the I.R.A. peeping from behind every tree. Weakly, since he insisted so strongly on it, she allowed them a dirk or two.

'Freddy, there is one thing I'd love to do with you – visit your mamma's grave in Milan.'

'My mamma is buried in Turin.'

'Your father's grave?'

'He was drowned while sailing off Genoa. The body was never recovered.'

She gave it up. She felt, if not happiest, most content, or at least most relieved, when they did not talk at all; seasoned comrades who only needed a glance or a smile to feel the pulse in one another's veins: as when they saw the crescent moon, whose fullness they knew they would not share, look tenderly at itself in the mirror of Orta; or when they stood hand in hand before an orange sun slowly drowning into the mist of Mergozzo; though she did mock him amiably for showing her such expansive lakes and, out of Italian vainglory calling them small.

'You should see my little loch at Doon Castle! It is hardly big enough for the coots to swim about without bumping one another. I swim there in my pelt every morning.' Just for that, he roused her very early on the morning of their last day, drove her up into the Val Tellina and on and up to the Val del Bitto as far as the village of Gerola Alta. There he left the car and bullied her into panting and puffing, protesting every foot of the way, for another thousand feet to a dammed loch on the northern base of a mountain that he called the Three Men. As they lay there, beside one another, after eating the sandwiches and drinking the white wine that he had brought in an Alitalia carry-all, gazing either into one another's eyes or beyond one another's shoulder at the serrated snow-tipped Alps, her heart burned with happiness that he should have gone to so much trouble to share his lakes with her down even to this last, lost, tiny loch. She became even more happy and more fond of him when he boasted that there was not a pass in Lombardy that he had not climbed on foot when he had been young enough to do it – this at least the poor, unhappy boy had wrested from his miserable youth. They stood up, arms about waists, while he indicated, far and wide, some of the ways that he had gone. Just then a drone in the sky made her lift her swimming eyes to a plane that might be her plane tomorrow, which made him look down at her, say, 'Now your blue lakes tend upwarrrds,' and kissed her parted lips. At once her arms snapped tight about his neck, gripping him close until their mouths had to part for air. 'Again!' she implored, her hand pressing him by his poll into so wild and prolonged a kiss that he became lost to everything until she released him with a gasp. He then saw she had shaken out her black hair and that her unzipped parakeet frock was shivering to the ground.

'Marianna! What on earth are you doing?'

'The heat! The sun! The wind!' and dragged his hands by the wrists about her bare waist. 'My darling, I want to take off everything for you!'

And even before he had disengaged himself she had unfastened her brassiere, dragged down one strap and exposed one bursting nippled breast.

'Marianna!' he cried, his joined palms jigging in imploration. 'Not now! Not yet! Not here! We must wait until we get Aunt Rosa's permission. When I come to Ireland next month!'

In the silence – even the high drone of the plane had faded – she felt a cold wisp of fog creeping about her thighs. She drew back from him, her arms across her bosom, her eyes staring up at him like a terrified Magdalen.

'What did you say?' she whispered. 'Until you come to *Ireland*? To ask Aunt Rosa *what*?'

Solicitously he knelt to draw up her fallen frock about her hips.

'Aunt Rosa is your guardian, Marianna. I must naturally ask her permission to marry you.'

'To . . . Did you say to marry me?'

'Dress, my darling, there's a sudden fog coming.' And when they both looked about them every hollow was a white lake and the whole plain back to Milan a grey sea. 'You must have known, Marianna! I have been thinking of nothing else since the first moment I saw you!'

'You must be out of your mind, Freddy, I could never marry you. It would be . . . It would be . . . It would be most unsuitable, it would be ridiculous, it would be impossible in every way. Me? You? Ireland? I am an old, middle-aged woman. O God, I didn't even tell you the truth about that. I'm forty-one, Freddy. And I have nothing.'

Embarrassed, horrified, ashamed, weeping, she began to dress, and tie up her hair into a knot because she had lost all her hairpins. He lifted his arms to the sky.

'And what have I? I live down there,' throwing one arm back across the plain, 'in three rooms with my mamma's old sister Tanta Giuletta. I am so poor I eat pasta twice a day. I wash my own shirts. I press my own trousers. I go shopping with a little basket. I say to the butcher, "Give me some cheap meat for my little dog", and he knows well that I have no little dog, but because he has known me for years he throws in a good piece of meat for myself and Tanta Giuletta. If you marry me you would live with us. And after all, old Tanta Giuletta can't live forever. I would be happy with you if we lived in a cave. We could make such a lovely world together. We would imagine our world so beautifully that everybody who knew us would think that any other sort of world is a lie.'

She turned her back on him. She looked at the Alps, cold, pure, lofty, remote. She spoke quietly to them.

'I told you lies. I don't live the way I told you I live. I made it all up. I deceived you in everything.'

Behind her back he spoke just as quietly.

'You deceived me in nothing. I know all about you. Paola told me. All mothers are spies. Her mother wrote to her about us. Paola is a bitch in the manger. Even when she doesn't want a thing or a person for herself she hates anybody else to have it. She wrote to me five days ago, a mean, bitchy, jealous letter. About Castle Doon, and the paying guests, and you living in the gate lodge.'

'A penniless retainer?'

'She did not use the word. She wrote in Italian. She said *una stipendiata*.'

She turned on him, blazing.

'Then why did you drag me down like that? Why did you go on making me tell you those stupid, stupid, stupid lies?'

His hands pleaded.

'They were not lies, Marianna. It was just a game we began to play that first night in the Villa d'Este. You were so shy, and so innocent, and so lovely – and all those puffed-up, snobby Milanese about us, bloody Fascisti the whole lot of them – I knew them, my father knew them – and you and I worth a thousand of them. It was my way of telling you what we both really are. Then I went on with it to make our holiday more fun.'

The veined nose, the baggy eyes, the hollow cheeks and stooped back of a defeated old man. His white hair blew across his forehead like dust. She touched his hanging hand. Hopelessly she shook her head.

'Let's go down, Freddy. I must pack. Thank you for everything. You gave me a lovely time. But you made one mistake. You gave me the last thing on earth that I want from anybody. You pitied me.'

And ran through the mist down the path to Gerola farther and farther from his wild, beseeching cries to come back to him, to wait for him, to come back to him, to come back. He must have stumbled as he leaped after her, for it was a long time before he appeared beside his white car, his beginning and his end. His trousers were torn, there was dried blood on his cheek, his right hand was wrapped in his silk handkerchief. In the silence of a fallen tower they drove back to the hotel, where, as he scrambled from the car, he called after her that he would come for her at eight o'clock.

'Our last dinner, Marianna!'

When he came he was handed a note from her saying that she was too upset to join him. All he could do was to leave a note for her saying that he would call for her at eleven in the morning to drive her to the airport. When he did come, the majordomo had to tell him, sympathetically, that she had taken the seven o'clock steamer for Cadenabbia; from there, one presumed, gone by bus to Milan. Freddy glanced at his lean wrist. He could still catch up with her. He descended to the *piazzetta* for a coffee. He had his pride.

For months she expected that he would write, was relieved when he did not, half-hoped for a Christmas card and was again glad that he sent none. She had almost succeeded in putting him out of her mind when, one May morning at the family breakfast table, she heard Aunt Rosa utter an exclamation of surprise and looked up to see her beaming over her half-moon glasses and holding up a big gilt-edged card for them all to see.

'A wedding! And guess who? Our little Paola Buononcini.' (Mary Anne felt her heart go burp.) '*To*,' Aunt Rosa read out, '*il conte Federico Amadeo Emmanuele Levashov-Algardi*.' She turned eagerly to her niece. 'Mary Anne, surely you wrote to me last June that when you met Paola she was with a Count Something-or-other. Could he be the same man? But you said he was an old man. Or did you? What was his name?'

'Count Federico Algardi. I said he was an old friend of the family.'

'What an extraordinary coincidence! Was he, in fact, old? What was he like? Tell us all about him. Is he very rich? If I know anything about Paola Buononcini he must be stinking rich. Or else his pedigree must go back to Romulus and Remus.'

'No, he is not old. Though he is not young, either. He is very handsome, and very dashing. He could be forty-five. I took it that he was very wealthy. He drove an immense white car. An Alfa-Romeo, I think it was. But he did not speak at all. It was at the airport and he just drove us to the Hotel Serbelloni. After that he vanished.'

'Mary Anne, how tiresome of you! You never do notice anybody.' She looked again at the card. 'Well, well, so our little Paola is about to become a countess.'

She glanced at Geraldine, sighed, spread her ringed fingers and, with a long accusatory look, passed the card to her. And this, Mary Anne thought, staring sidewards at his printed name, is the man who once dreamed of innocence, and purity, and honesty and true love. She cradled her teacup in her palms and looked across its rim at the snow-tipped Alps, the sun burning the valleys to dust, the blue lakes dreaming of the sky. He had whispered, 'Now your blue lakes tend upwarrrds,' and kissed her. She closed her eyes and smiled.

'I see,' Aunt Rosa said brightly to Geraldine, 'that she is going to be married next month.'

'Sweating,' Geraldine laughed coarsely, 'like a June bride.'

She opened her eyes wide. Another Paola? Jealous, greedy and envious, and in that second she understood it all. His kiss had been his one, last feeble cry for help. She hesitated. Then, imperceptibly, her head shook. It would not have been honest, and it would not have worked. But nothing he had ever done ever had worked. Nothing ever would work. However! He'd had something. They had both had something. Something precious, brief and almost true that, she felt proudly certain, neither of them would ever forget.

Feed My Lambs

It is about eleven o'clock of a sunny September morning in late September. The unfrequented road that crosses the level bog-land from skyline to skyline passes on its way a few beech trees, a white cottage fronted by a small garden still bright with roses and snapdragons, a cobbled path and a small wooden gate bearing, in white celluloid letters, the name *Pic du Jer*. In the vast emptiness of the bog these unexpected and inexplicable beech trees, the pretty cottage, the tiny garden, the cobbled path suggest only a dream in the mind of some-body who, a long time back, thought better of it, or died, or gave up the struggle with the bog.

A young woman in an apron as blue as the sky is sweeping a few fallen beech leaves along the cobbles. She is bosomy, about thirty, with amber hair, and eyelids as big as the two half-domes of an eggshell. Looking idly towards the west she ob-serves, far away, a flash of sunlight. She gives it one thoughtful glance and resumes her sweeping. Whoever the motorist is, he will come and go as slowly as a dot of light emerging from one mirror and as slowly dwindling into another. The bog is as immense as it is flat. It swallows everything.

Pic du Jer? A mountain peak? Asked why, Rita Lamb always says, in her usual saucy, self-mocking way, one quizzical eye-brow cocked: 'Yerrah, it's an old mountain near Lourdes. You go up it in the funicular. It's where I climbed to the pic of my career. It's where I met Jer.' If she admitted that she really met Jer at the foot of the peak, in the waiting funicular, it would spoil the joke. It would be no joke at all if she said, 'It's where I met Father Tom.'

Under the final whisk of her broom the leaves rustle out through the garden gate. She looks again. The car is half a mile away. Her hands tighten on the broom handle. The cups of her eyelids soar, she runs indoors, tearing off her blue apron, looks at herself in the mirror, punches the cushions of her minute parlour, looks into the sideboard to be sure there is a bottle or two there, and is out at the gate again just in time to greet Father Tom with a delighted grin. He has never failed her. He drops in at least three or four times a year, either on his way up to Dublin or on his way back to his parish on the far side of the Shannon. She takes his overcoat, indicates the settee, and begins to make his usual drink, Irish coffee.

'Now!' she says pertly as a parrot. 'What's y'r news? Tell me everything.'

'I'll tell you one thing, Rita,' he laughs. 'You haven't changed one iota since the first day I met you.'

That day, waiting for the funicular to start, the four of them had got talking at once: the two priests, herself and Jer. The older priest – rosy, bony and bald, easygoing and poorly dressed, his waistcoat flecked brown from his scented snuff – simply leaned across and took her paperback from her hand: Franz Werfel's *Song of Bernadette*.

'Not bad,' he conceded, 'For a modern novel. Tell me, my child, did you ever read a novel by Canon Sheehan called *My New Curate*?'

At this, the young priest had pulled down his elegant white cuffs, and all in one breath laughed, groaned, sighed and said, 'Here we go again. Poor old Tom Timlin off to the guillotine once more.'

'Indeed and I did read it,' Rita gushed. 'I think I've read every single thing Canon Sheehan wrote.'

Father Jordan patted her knee.

'Good girl! Most of ye read nothing nowadays but dirty books like the one his reverence here gave me the other day by some young trollop named ... What was this her name is, Father Timlin?'

'Miss Edna O'Brien,' the young priest said, his natural courtesy qualified by an over-patient smile.

'A fine Irish name! It was the only decent thing about her rotten book. I nearly shoved it behind the fire it made me so mad! Upon my word, Father, I don't know for the life of me what you want to be reading books like that for.'

Father Tom folded the crease of his trousers over his knee and observed urbanely that it is one's duty to know what young people are thinking nowadays.

'After all, one belongs to one's contemporaries, Father Jordan, as Simone de Beauvoir puts it.'

'I read her, too!' Rita exclaimed, and blushed wildly, suddenly remembering the picture of a completely naked woman on the cover of her contraband copy of *The Second Sex*, and how its first chapter was all about the machinery of the inside of a woman and the outside of a man. 'I forget now what book by her it was that I read. I think it was a travel book about France.'

'You probably read *The Second Sex*,' Father Tom said dryly. 'Quite an interesting study. It's a pity she has no sense of humour. Sex can be funny, too.'

The old man threw him a cold look. 'In this excellent novel by the late Canon Sheehan,' he persisted, 'there is a poor old parish priest like myself who has the life plagued out of him by his new curate.'

'I remember the two of them well,' said Rita, patting his knee as approvingly as he had patted hers, 'and, do you know, I felt very sorry for the pair of them.'

'The part I love,' he said with relish, 'is where this poor old P.P. walks in one day into his curate's room and finds him, if you please, playing the piano and singing some sloppy German love song about "Roselein, Roselein, Roselein buck – Roselein auf dem heiden"? Wasn't that how the song went, Father?'

Father Tom coughed and said that, yes, it was, indeed, something on those lines.

'Well! Father Timlin here is *my* new curate and he has me plagued out with Italian. Always playing Italian operas on the gramophone. In Italian if you please! Always throwing around words like *Giovannismo*, and *ecumenismo*, and *aggiornamento*, and what's that other word you have, Father, that sounds like an Italian racing car?'

'*La gioventù!*' Father Timlin cried eagerly, and threw his hands out to the two young people seated opposite them. 'And here we have them! Youth at the helm!'

The old priest winked at them.

'He is ancient, you see. He is twenty-six.'

'Ah!' Father Tom said enthusiastically. 'There's nothing like youth. Married or engaged?' he asked.

Rita and the young man beside her looked at one another. He observed that she had eyes as big as a cow, eyelids as sleepy as a cow, soft hair the colour of a Jersey cow and that she was very well made around the brisket. She liked his grin, his white teeth and his warm voice as he answered, 'We are not even acquainted yet, Father. We just met this minute.'

Father Jordan roared with delight.

'There you are,' he nudged his curate. 'Crashing in as usual!'

'Only anticipating, maybe,' the young priest said, unabashed, and they all introduced themselves. Father Malachy Jordan, P.P., and Father Tom Timlin, C.C., from the parish of Annabwee in the County Galway; Jerry Lamb, farmer and butcher, from Barron in the County Kildare; and Rita Lyons, schoolmistress, from Doon in the County Westmeath; at which point the funicular gave a jolt and they started to climb.

'Talking of marriages,' said Father Tom, paying no attention at all to the descending landscape, 'I suppose ye know that Lourdes is a great place for matchmaking? The best Catholic families in France come here with their children. We have a count, and a prince, and their wives and children in our hotel. The idea is that the best young people in France meet, and if they like one another . . . well, you never know your luck.'

Jerry Lamb chuckled.

'It would be one of the unrecorded miracles of Lourdes if I met a princess here and took a shine to her – and she to me!'

Father Tom waved his hand with a man-of-the-world air.

'It would be no miracle at all! We get all kinds in Lourdes. All sorts and sizes come here to see the pilgrimages, Buddhists, Jews, Muslims, Communists, atheists, everybody!'

Rita turned sideways to consider Mr Lamb.

'Wouldn't that be a good joke,' she said, 'if your Catholic princess met a Communist who was a roaring atheist and took a shine to him?'

The old priest's palms applauded silently, but the young priest was unquashable.

'It might be an excellent thing for them both. She might convert him and he might broaden her.'

'Ha!' said his P.P. sourly. 'She might! And so might a mouse! And supposing they did get married? A mixed marriage! And what about the children? If they had any children!'

Father Tom smiled benevolently.

'Ah, now, Father, you must admit that since the *Concilio* the attitude of the church to mixed marriages has greatly relaxed. And as for the question of having children, that will come too. Do you believe in large families, Mr. Lamb?' he asked their butcher.

'I wouldn't be averse to two or three. Or at most four.'

'Two or three?' Father Jordan said sadly. 'I was the youngest of twelve. Brought up on a scrawny thirty-five-acre farm west of Ballinasloe. An acre to the cow, they say, and three acres to the child, we cut it fine.'

'I was the youngest of six myself,' from Father Tom.

'Ai, ai, ai!' Father Jordan sighed. 'I suppose this is your *aggiornamento*.' He gazed into a distant valley. 'My mother was one of fifteen. Twelve of us. Six of you. Mr Lamb here would like three. And if you have three I suppose they will want one apiece. We progress!'

'What I'd like,' Rita said, looking pensively out over the distant Pyrénées, 'would be to have a boy and a girl.'

'Two?' Father Tom asked her amiably. 'Four?' he asked Jerry Lamb. 'Why don't ye split the difference and make it three?' – at which Father Jordan asked him if he was getting a percentage on this, and all four of them laughed, and the funicular stopped and all the passengers except Rita looked down.

'Maybe they want us to enjoy the view?' Jer suggested.

'My sister Joanie has seven children,' Rita said to the sky. 'She is married to a clerk. He gets eleven pounds a week. Seven children. And they are only married seven years.'

'Fine!' Father Jordan said to the valley. 'Splendid! A proud and happy mother!'

Rita's mouth tightened. Father Tom was watching her closely.

'*Is* she happy?' he asked, stressing quietly.

'Tell me, Father,' Rita said to him, 'what's all this about the Pill?'

'It is forbidden,' the old priest said shortly.

'Well, now,' the young priest temporized, 'it is certainly not authorized. But it is still under discussion. I hope,' he added, looking around at the crowded carriage, 'we're not stuck forever?'

'Are we stuck?' Father Jordan asked an old Frenchwoman across the aisle from him, and her husband turned back from where he was looking up the peak to say that the one coming down was stuck too. Jer and the old priest crossed over to look out. Father Tom was left with Rita. She was staring moodily at the sky. He leaned forward, elbows on thighs.

'You are very silent, Rita.'

She said nothing.

'What is on your mind?'

'Nothing.'

'There is something. What is it?'

Struck by the kindness in his voice, she slewed her eyes towards him, and for the first time took stock of him. He had sandy hair; his eyelashes were golden fair; his eyes were as bright blue as a Siamese cat's; he reminded her of her brother who was a sailor. She hesitated. Then she spoke very softly: 'I was remembering why I came to Lourdes.'

'Why did you?'

'Everybody comes to Lourdes to pray for something. I prayed that my sister Joanie won't have any more children. And if I ever get married that I'll only have two.'

He looked at her mischievously. She was to become familiar with that mischievous, mocking way of his – his way of calming her, of calling her to use her common sense.

'When I was young, Rita, I had a small sister who was mad about a sort of sweet called bull's-eyes. The nuns told her one day to pray to the Blessed Virgin to break her of the habit.'

'And did she?' Rita asked with interest.

'She got a terrible pain in her stomach one day and that cured her. Rita! Which are you? Dying to be married, or afraid to be married?'

'I don't want to have a child every year for the rest of my blooming life.'

He smiled at her. She looked away, annoyed.

'Father, you're like every priest. Ye know all about theology and ye know nothing about feelings. Would you like to have a child every year of your life?'

'Not unless I was a rabbit. Still, nathless, and howbeit, and quid pro quo, and all things being carefully considered, and so on, you would like to get married?'

'I'm human.'

'I should hope so, if that means that you are a normal woman with the normal longings and desires of a woman.'

She faced him crossly, at a disadvantage. If he had been a man she could tell him!

'How do I know what I am?'

'Everybody knows what he is. You've had boy friends, haven't you?'

'Yes.' Then she said coldly, 'Am I going to confession to you?'

'Oh, come off it, girl! This talk about confession that women go on with! Why wouldn't you have boy friends? Anyway, nobody confesses any more to a priest. The priest today is only a kind of spiritual telephone operator. To what part of the otherworld do you want a trunk call today, madam? For all faults inquiries and difficulties kindly dial Tom Timlin, C.C.'

She laughed.

'But you listen in!' she pointed out.

'And interpret now and again. And add up the charges. Come now, Rita! Face up to yourself.' He chuckled at her. '*Vide, visse, amò*. She saw, she lived, she loved. You embraced. You kissed. And you hated it like poison!'

'I did not!' she said furiously. 'I liked it.'

'As *il buon Dio* intended you to. "So long as things are," Saint Augustine said, and he was a tough man, "they are good." Kissing is like Guinness, Rita. It's good for you. The *osculum* . . .'

'The what?'

'The kiss on the cheek.'

His eyes were mocking her again. She waved an airy hand.

'The *basium*. On the lips.'

Even more jauntily, she waved the other hand.

'The *suavium*?' and he shrugged.

She waved both her hands and was enraged with herself for blushing; and more enraged when he laughed delightedly.

Jer turned back to them and shouted, 'I think it is a life sentence!'

'Anyway,' she protested, 'that's all damn fine,' not quite knowing what was fine, 'but seven kids in seven years? Eight in eight? Nine in nine?'

He glanced across the carriage to where Father Jordan and Jerry Lamb were now trying out their French on the old French lady and her husband.

'You can only do your best, Rita,' he said gently. 'When any man or woman comes to me with your problem all I ever say is, "You can only do your best." If I was speaking as your spiritual telephone operator I'd always say, "He is saying, you can only do your best." '

She glared down at the huddled red roofs of Lourdes until he thought she was going to throw herself out. Then she breathed out a long sigh of exasperation.

'These last three days,' she said, 'I was so happy down there.'

He gave her a melancholy laugh. He looked down at the basketful of roofs.

'Ai! Ai! – as Father Jordan says. Such a mixture! The lovely and the tawdry, sincerity and sentimentality, lies and truth, God and Mammon. It would remind you of life! And here we are now like Mahomet's coffin slung halfway between ... Where was it slung? I always imagine it was held up between walls of magnetic forces. Impossible?' He paused. 'You mustn't be afraid, Rita.' She kept staring sulkily down at the roofs. 'No woman can do more than her best.' This time he was silent a long while. 'I'd say that to you anytime, anywhere.'

He watched her. She got the point. She smiled at him:

'I have a car. Sometimes I might pay you a visit.'

'Do!'

'But you will never know.'

'I will never know. All I will hear will be a voice. It will come and go. Like a bird singing in flight.'

The carriage jolted a little, started to move, and the whole carriage cheered and laughed. Father Jordan and Jer rejoined them.

'E pur si muove!' Father Tom cried. 'Galileo. The world does

go around the sun. Though I'm not sure Father Jordan entirely believes it. George Bernard Shaw,' he went on, 'once said that in Ireland we still believe that the world, if not exactly flat, is only very slightly removed from the spherical.'

They all chuckled and began to discuss such important things as whether they could get a cool refreshing drink on top of the mountain.

From the peak they gazed far and wide about them, silenced by the gleaming wings of the Hautes Pyrénées, still snow-covered, and the eyes of the lakes in the far valleys, and Father Tom, who knew his Lourdes, pointed out famous peaks like the Pic du Midi de Bigorre that local mountaineers had mastered at the risk of their lives.

'Glory be to God,' said Father Jordan, 'but it's a hard country! Is it good for anything at all?'

'Sheep,' said Jer. 'And I bet you there's fine grazing up there for the cattle in the summertime.'

'I read in the paper this morning,' said Father Tom, 'that the shepherds are complaining that the wolves aren't being shot.'

'Feed my lambs,' said the old priest, and the two of them drifted around, and Rita and Jer went in search of a beer.

Sitting on a rough bench a little apart from the other tourists, she amused him by telling him what it is like to teach in a nun's school, and he entertained her by telling her what it is like to be a farmer-butcher in a small village in the middle of a bog as flat as a a slate. When Father Tom and Father Jordan came by, the old man looked as if he were going to join them, but the curate took him firmly by the arm and pointed off into the distance and drew him away around the corner. Presently Mr Lamb was asking Miss Lyons if she had ever been to Biarritz and when she said no, Mr Lamb said he was going by bus the day after tomorrow, and Miss Lyons said she had wondered if she ought not to visit it someday.

'Yerrah, why don't you? You earned it. If you like you could come with me. I'm all on my own.'

'But, Mr Lamb,' she said, floating her eggshell eyelids wide open, 'we are hardly acquainted!' – and when his laugh showed his splendid teeth she laughed too, and he went on laughing because she looked so happy, and had such big droopy eyelids and was so well made around the brisket.

Father Tom advanced his empty glass of Irish coffee to Rita sideways along the settee, laughed and clinked it with hers.

'So there you have it! That's all my news. Nothing at all since July. I'm the same old three-and-fourpence I always was and always will be.'

She looked at him affectionately.

'We have no news either! Jer goes on with his butchering. I go on with my sweeping. If you are worth three-and-fourpence, then between the three of us we're worth exactly ten bob.'

She took up the empty glasses, the bottle, the cream and the percolator and started to tidy them on the small dining table by the window. He looked appreciatively at her straight back and her trim legs.

'Rita!'

She turned, observed him and cocked an alert eye.

'You look as if you are about to give birth to a profound thought?'

'Divil a profound thought! It's just that ever since I came within sight of this little cottage of yours this morning I was thinking how you once said to me, five years ago, "I have a car." And you have never once paid me a visit?'

She came back and sat on the settee.

'You are a low scoundrel, Father Tom. You only thought of that just half an hour ago? And in all those five years you never once thought of it before? The truth isn't in you.'

'Well, I admit I did give it a passing thought now and again. I'm not probing, Rita!'

'You are. And I don't mind. Sure we're always probing one another. When we have no news it's all we ever do.'

'Why didn't you?'

'Do you really want to know? I'll tell you. But I think you will be sorry you asked me. One reason I didn't visit you was because I had no need to. I had nothing to tell you. Or to tell any other priest. Now you know!'

Her left hand lay supine on the settee near his. He laid his right hand on her palm. The palm slowly closed on his fingers.

'Poor Rita! I guessed it must be that way. I'm afraid your family hasn't had much luck with Our Lady?'

'Not with three more babies for my sister, and none for me.'

'And poor Jer, too!'

'Oh, he's accepted it now. At first, he minded an awful lot.'

'What was the other reason?'

She looked down at their two hands. She gave him a long silent look – so long that he peered questioningly at her. She leaned over a little and castled her right hand on his.

'Did it ever occur to you, Father,' she said, 'that from the first day we met you called me Rita? Because you're a priest and that made it all right – for you. But I have never once called you Tom. Because I'm a woman, and that mightn't be quite so safe – for me. I love it when you drop in here, Father, and pop off again after an hour or so. I love the chat. I love the way I can say anything I like to you. I love the way you say anything you like to me. I love all the things we argue about. I look forward to it for weeks. I think about it for weeks after you've gone. And that's not just because it's lonely out here on this empty old bog. Now and again friends of Jerry's drop in, and I like them to call too, but I never think of them when they're gone, and if they never came again I wouldn't miss them. I love you to come because you are you. Still, so far, I've always managed to remember that you are a priest and I am a married woman. The other reason I did not visit you is because if I started meeting you outside of here it would be very different. It would be admitting to myself that I am fond of you as a man.'

His golden eyelashes fell. She removed her hand. He laid his on his knee.

'Well?' she asked tartly. 'What's wrong with you? Am I to be the only one to tell the truth today? Or did none of this ever occur to you?'

'You are a wonderful woman, Rita! You are the most honest being I have ever met.'

'Is that all you can say to me?'

'It is all I dare say to you. What the hell is the good of

anybody saying anything if he can do nothing about it? What would you want me to say? That I love you? When neither you nor I can ever prove it!'

She shook her amber head at him.

'Well, there's the cat out of the bag at last! Tom! You should never have been a priest. The first day I met you I knew it.'

'Why didn't you say so then?'

'Would it have made any difference?'

He jumped up, walked away from her, whirled and cried, 'I don't know! I was younger then!'

She rose and went over so close to him that he could hear her breathing.

'And now,' she taunted, 'you are a feeble old man?'

He flung his arms around her and kissed her on the mouth. She held his kiss. Then she drew away from him and laid her finger gently but imperatively on his mouth.

'The *basium*?' she mocked. 'You've come a long way in five years, Tom.'

'Do you realize you are the first girl I ever kissed!'

'I do. And I'm the last. You can never come here again.'

He walked away from her and looked angrily at her.

'Is that what you wanted, talking the way you did on that settee?'

'I merely answered your question. I warned you that you might be sorry. You asked for the truth. And you put an end to our story.'

'You didn't have to answer me!'

'I had to. Because immediately you asked me I knew what I'd never let myself know before. And I knew that we both knew it. And I knew something else too. That if it didn't end one day we would explode, and then we'd be torturing one another for the rest of our lives.'

He stared wildly around him.

'There is no sense nor meaning to this. It doesn't hang together. All I ever wanted was a bit of friendship. A bit of companionship. There's nobody else in the world I can talk to but you. That day I first met you I knew that here was somebody at last that I could talk to. Maybe that I could help. That I'd be a better priest if I could . . .'

'Tom! It's long ago that I told you that you knew all about theology and all that stuff, and nothing about feelings. Now you know better! This is what love is like.'

He glared at her in misery and longing. Then, suddenly, he calmed, and then as suddenly he broke into a long peal of laughter, at himself, at both of them, at the whole of life.

'Honest to God, Rita! You're worth fifty priests. You're worth a thousand of us. And I that began it all by trying to educate the simple, ignorant little schoolteacher! Well, I may have learned slow, but you learned damn fast. Where the hell, Rita, did you learn all you know?'

'Where every woman learns everything. In bed. Am I shocking you? Because if I am, then you really are getting very old.'

He considered her answer bitterly.

'The one classroom no priest ever visits. And I suppose the only one that ever tells anyone anything about the nature of love. So! That's it. I'm never to see you again?'

'Why not? I will go my way. You will go yours. If I live I will become an old woman. If you live you will become an old, old parish priest like poor old Father Malachy Jordan.'

'My God! If Father Jordan was alive today and knew about you and me he'd break his heart laughing at me for a botch of a priest and a fool of a man!'

She flashed out angrily at him. He had never seen her so angry.

'Stop that, Tom! Stop it at once! Never say that again! Never think it! I liked you that day in Lourdes because you were honest with me. I grew fond of you, I fell in love with you if you want the whole bloody truth, because you went on being honest with me. You will always be honest. And you will always be a better priest than old Jordan ever was because you will always remember that, if it was only for one minute of your life, you loved your woman and kissed her. When you run yourself down you are only cheapening yourself and cheapening me. I won't have that! I'm not sorry for anything we've done. I'm proud of it.'

Far away a bell gently, faintly tolled. She listened. 'There's the angelus bell in Barron.' Suddenly she became the bright, capable housewife. 'Jer will be back in an hour. Will you stay and have lunch with us, Tom?'

'No!' he said brusquely, and grabbed his overcoat and dived into it. 'But there's one thing I'll tell you, Rita!' He snatched up his hat and his gloves. 'If I met you not five years ago but ten I'd have given up God Himself for you!'

He went out the door and down the cobbled path. She followed slowly after him. At the wicket-gate he paused and looked up and down the long, empty road.

'I'll never pass this road again.' He flipped his gloves against the white celluloid letters on the gate. 'Why did you call it Pic du Jer?'

He watched her great eyelids drooping. He watched the sinking of her amber head. She spoke as softly as if she were whispering to the three foreign words.

'To remind me of you.'

She did not raise her head again until his car started and his wheels spurned the gravel of the road. Then she walked out to the middle of the road to watch him dwindling away from her into infinity, diminishing like a dot of light until he vanished out of sight.

She looked around the level bog. Miles away the blue smoke of a turfcutter's fire rose out of the flat emptiness straight up into the blue sky. She heard nothing. Then she heard a soft wind and raised her eyes to the blue above her. A host of swallows were flying south. She watched them until they, too, became lost to sight. Soon it would be winter. The rains and the fogs. She turned briskly indoors to prepare a meal for her man.

Only once did she pause in her task, the knife in one fist, the apple in the other, to look out of the window and murmur aloud to herself, 'I know what he'll do. It's what I'd do. Drive past me every time he goes to Dublin.' She added, 'Until it wears off,' and went on with her work.

'Our Fearful Innocence'

My name is Jerry Doyle. J. T. Doyle, B.E. I am the County Engineer for W—. I have made this town my home since I first came here as Assistant C.E. twenty-one years ago. I am a bachelor. Aged forty-six. I live in this half-comfortable converted flat on the first storey of Jack Jennings's old wreck of a house on Martin's Quay. He lives above me. Our housekeeper lives above him, although she is beginning to say that the stairs get longer every year. Below me is Jack's shop. He is a ship chandler. Or was.

It is such a warm evening that I am sitting in my shirtsleeves by the open window, with my pipe, and a glass of whiskey in my fist – and this old red-covered notebook of Jill Jennings's on my lap. I have been playing golf all day, our own course, above the town, the bay and the sea, my lungs so full of fresh air that I feel too lazy to do anything but look out at the seagulls wheeling like ... well, as Jill once said, wheeling like seagulls. The smoke from Ed Slator's house half a mile away on Rock Point is as steady as if it was part of the chimney. Children playing below on the quay. The canon strolling back as usual to his presbytery, which means that in about fifteen minutes the bell of Saint Killian's will begin to ring for Benediction. Not that I shall attend. I do turn up to mass every Sunday, but purely *pro forma.* As the C.E. I have to keep up appearances. Since what happened to Jill I believe neither in God nor the Devil. And neither does Jack, whom I have just heard shuffling about upstairs. The poor old bastard ...

When I first met Jack Jennings he was about forty-two or forty-three; the grandson of the *Jennings and Son* spelled out in marbled chinaware lettering on the facia board over his shop window. He never altered the form of name on the board. This was stupid of him, and typically insensitive, because he and Jill had no children. But it was just like him not to change it – an obstinate, cantankerous old cuss if there ever was one. After all, when he married Jill Slator he knew he was marrying into a dynasty famous for long-tailed families. Some of them must often have given that sign a glance that was as good as a process.

I liked Jack from the start, in spite of the seventeen years between us. While he was able to do it we played golf together every weekend. We were never really close to one another, although sometimes we exchanged confidences, mostly about what we chose to call our philosophies. My nickname for him was Zeno because I maintained that he was a born cynic. In revenge he called me Pangloss, the eternal optimist, who 'felt best after meals'. We got on, give and take, kidding, jabbing now and again, never really quarrelling. We got on – the way people always do in small towns. In a big city we might never have bothered about one another. We were an odd pair. We still are. I only gradually realized that Jill was the real bond between us. As she still is.

She was ten years younger than him when she married him. She was about thirty-two when I first met her, and in spite of the fact that she was much older than me I thought her the most attractive woman I had ever met. I must have said so once too often to my secretary May Hennessy because she infuriated me one day by snorting, 'Of course you're in love with Jill Jennings.' I was so mad with her that I nearly ate her. Then, realizing that nobody would ever call her attractive – the poor thing is no oil painting – I had to explain that all I meant was that what I found 'attractive' about Jill was her personality. At which May snorted again. She is a good secretary but she does speak her mind. Which I like now. In this shut-mouthed town everybody else goes around hinting at things they have not the guts to say straight out the way she does. I used to think that it might be because she travelled abroad every summer, and was always full of talk about France or Portugal or Italy and how free life is there compared to Ireland.

Actually, what first attracted me to Jill Jennings was the

way she, too, used to burst out with whatever came into her head. She had wide-open eyes, earnest and challenging. Her profile went with that eagerness, face and figure advanced like a ship's figurehead by the slope of her neck, an effect accentuated by the way her beautifully curved upper lip protruded a shade over her lower lip. I loved the way she greeted me whenever we met in the street, the eyelids lifted delighted to see me but abusing the hell out of me for not visiting her more often.

At thirty-two she still had the face of a girl just let out of convent-school, looking everywhere for this wonderful thing called Life that she and her pals had been talking about, and whispering about and making big eyes about ever since they realized that within a matter of months they would be – heaven help the poor kids – free. How enchanting young girls are at that age, before vanity: unaware of their own looks, their school berets flat as plates on their heads, their pigtails tied with venom, as uninterested in the crowds on the shore as the morning sea. Within a year it is all gone, they have become demons, vulgarians, simpering at every male across the mirrors of their compacts.

Jill never knew vanity. She had glossy hair, the finest and lightest, always untidy, loosely pinned at the nape of her neck in tiny, wandering downy curls that delighted and disturbed me. If she had any fault her skin was too white. On hot days when her arms and shoulders were exposed I used to feel excited to think that all her body was just as white. She dressed in soft, fluffy blouses, light as shadows, or smoke, billowing carelessly. Being so good-looking, she had no need to bother about dress. Her eyes were as grey-green as that sea out there. There was something of the mermaid about her, so free, so fresh, so restless, landlocked, always hearing sounds or voices beyond the town, outside the harbour, this shallow bay.

I loved this old fabric of a house where she and Jim lived. It is now as rundown as Jim's shop but it must have been a fine house and a good business a hundred years ago before the bay became silted up. Now only a couple of coal-tubs and small cargo vessels occasionally moor at the quays, and even they have to wait on the tide to come in. I see one waiting outside the harbour now. High tide will be around ten o'clock. Then it will have to wind carefully through the buoys marking the channels to the quayside.

I loved to visit them on nights when the east wind rattled their windows or blew white spindrift across the water, nights when the three of us would sit before the fire and drink a jorum, and have long wandering arguments about the craziest things, always started off by her. 'What is true happiness?' 'Free Will versus Determinism.' One night after she had been reading some advanced book about religion she suddenly asked, 'Should Faith be based on Life or should Life be based on Faith?' Another night she burst out with 'What is Reality, anyway?' We kept at that one until three o'clock in the morning. Last winter I took down one of her books, *Madame Bovary*, by Flaubert, and when I came on Emma and her lover talking for hours about Great Art I thought to myself, 'That fellow had us cold!' There was no other house in town where I could have arguments like that. All they talk about is golf, and bridge, and business. But I liked best of all to visit her when she was alone. Otherwise, she tended to take possession of me, ignoring Jack – I do not believe he had read a dozen books in his whole life – lounging on the other side of the fire, puffing his pipe, staring glumly into the fire.

Like that wild March night, in my third year in W—. A force-ten gale howling outside, the rain turning to sleet that threatened any minute to become snow. Jill and I were gabbling away about a performance of *The Three Sisters* that I had driven her up to Dublin to see two months before. Jack, who had obstinately refused to come with us, was saying nothing. Just staring into the fire. From that she went on to talk about the Russian ballet – she had been reading Karsavina's memoirs and she had once been to see a ballet in London. I was not saying much. I was lying back in the old armchair before the fire, between the two of them, enjoying her chat, the fire roaring up the chimney at my feet and the occasional spat of sleet against the windows, pleasantly aware that every street in the town was empty, when, all of a sudden, Jack jumps up, says, 'I think I'll drop down to the Club,' and walks out on us. We listened to him clumping down the stairs and the front door banging. Then I heard the old Jennings and Son signboard below the window twanging and banging like a drum and I realized that on a night like this there would not be a sinner in the Club – unless it was old Campbell the caretaker sitting by the fire gushing smoke every three minutes into the musty billiard room.

'I'm afraid we've been boring Jack,' I said.

For a few moments it was her turn to stare glumly into the fire. Then as if the wind had hit her into a shiver, she shook herself all over, looked wildly all around the room and cried, 'Then why does he go on living here? This bloody place is choking the life out of the pair of us. It will choke me like a wood if I don't clear out of it. And clear out of it quick!'

'Aha!' I laughed. 'To Moscow? To Moscow?'

She glared, tossed her head, then leaned forward over the arm of my chair and gripped my hand.

'Did it ever cross your mind, Jerry, that if the three sisters in that play had gone to Moscow they might have been just as unhappy there?'

I barely stopped myself from saying that their brother was not all that unhappy – he at least had the comfort of his child. Instead I said hurriedly that, after all, Jim's business was rooted here, and she could not expect him at the drop of a hat to open up another chandler's store in some place where nobody knew him, and she had all her relations here, and after all, this was not such a bad town, it was lovely in the summer, with the bay, and the sea . . .

She threw away my hand and said crossly:

'Jerry! There is no such place as Moscow. If I went to Moscow I would hear nothing there but the same stupid, empty chitter-chatter that I hear day after day in this bloody town – and nothing at all going on inside me. That play about the three sisters is marvellous because it is all chatter outside, and all silence inside. The summer! Don't talk to me about the summer! On summer evenings I sit by that window for hour after hour looking at the seagulls wheeling like seagulls, or a yacht manoeuvring in or out, or some little cargo boat with Cardiff or Bristol painted on the stern coming alongside Harry Slator's coalyard, or edging out past the lighthouse, and I watch it until it rounds Rock Point past the chemical factory, out to sea. And what do I think of? Nothing! Unless it is about somebody like you whom I know and like. Like you, or May Hennessy who came here a couple of years before you. Another stranger. People who come and who go before this rotten town knocks the truth and the honesty and the guts out of them.'

'Well, it is a fact that May Hennessy is always coming and going. The most travelled woman in W—!'

She snorted at me.

'Is that all you know? May is a friend of mine. I know a lot about May. And May knows a lot about me. May Hennessy hasn't been out of this town for five years.'

'But she is always telling me about her travels! She knows the Continent like the palm of her hand.'

'All out of books. Five years ago May went to Brittany. I said, "Did you enjoy it?" She said, "All I used to do was to walk along the quay and look at the names at the backs of the ships, and think wouldn't it be nice to be going home." Home! All May Hennessy found in Brittany was this town.'

'Then why are you talking about leaving here? I hope you're not serious about that?'

'I am! I am going somewhere where there are no ships coming and no ships going, where there is nothing except me. No! Not even me! Someplace where I will be born all over again.'

I sat straight up.

'You don't mean by any chance that you are thinking of leaving Jack?'

She nodded, took my hand again and stroked it. Completely misunderstanding her, I felt as if the wind had burst roaring in through every window, door and cranny of the house and that it was sinking like a ship under us both.

'Jerry,' she said. 'You are an ambitious man. Aren't you? You want to be the County Engineer. Don't you? To be king of the castle? If you don't go away from here soon, and very soon, you will get exactly that – and this place will knock the truth and the honesty and the guts out of you too.'

On the instant I knew she was right. Because while one side of me was thinking what an honest, outspoken woman she was, the other part of me was thinking all the mean, petty things they would all be thinking, but not saying openly if she did leave Jack – the behind-the-hand whispering, the consternation of the Slators, and finally that total silence when the town would deliberately forget what it did not dare acknowledge.

She rose. I leaped up, and clipped her in my arms. The little curls on her neck seemed so tender and helpless that I wanted to bury my face in them. The smell of her skin overpowered me. I looked into her eyes and noticed what I had never seen before, the way hard, green little flecks pricked their softness. Before I could say what I wanted to say, her fingers stopped my mouth. Then she kissed me, chastely, not the way a woman kisses a man but the way a mother kisses her child. She held me away from her and shook her head.

'No, Jerry! Don't say it! You arc not in love with me. You are only in love with an imaginary me. Somebody you've made up inside your head. I saw it the first day we met.'

'But,' I cried, 'I have only just discovered the real you!'

'And before that? What real me were you in love with then? I am not real, Jerry. I have no world to be real in. Not yet! Now you had better go, before he comes back.'

I was in such a turmoil I could not have stayed near her. I ran out of the room. I felt that if I stayed there for another minute I would start tearing the blouse off her.

When the hall door banged behind me I could hear it echoing up through the hollow house with that muffled sound that always means snow. The quay was already white with it. The whole town was being smothered in it. It clung to the gas-lamps. When I came to the door of the Club I could barely see the light through the snow on its fanlight. Just as I passed it I became aware of a stream of light behind me and, turning, I saw him come out and start to beat his way home, head bowed, the snow flecking his hat and shoulders. He walked against the wind and snow with the gait of an old man. In a moment he vanished into the darkness, as silently as the snow.

Before April ended she had vanished. I did not need to ask anybody what the Slators thought. One day as I was passing Tom Slator's coalyard he hailed me cheerfully and delivered the agreed formula.

'Hello, Jerry! Did you hear the great news? Jill is after buying a country mansion in County B—.' His laughter pealed. Falsely. 'Ach, it's only an old lockhouse on the canal. A little hideaway for themselves. To get away from the roar and the rumble of W—! Hahaha! Of course between you and me I don't believe she'll ever persuade Jack to go down there. It's just another one of her artistic notions.'

It would work, and she would pay for it. To the 'men's club' side of the town she would henceforth be 'odd', 'queer', 'difficult', 'hard to get on with'. The man who remained would always be defended. What a town!

I did not dare visit her until that July. It was not an easy place to find, a small two-storey canal house, of no special distinction apart from its age, in a valley between pinewoods filled with shadows and sunbeams, silence and sloth. The noisy humming of flies or bees. A coot clucking. A heron flapping away. The only real sound was from the water gushing between the timbers of the lock gates. For a mile right and left of her cottage the sky dreaming in the smooth water of the canal. For the dozen or twenty days we get of hot summer it would be as lovely a retreat as it was on that warm day. But in the winter?

She was more beautiful than ever. I knew that she was thirty-five – a middle-aged woman – but she looked about twenty-five. She seemed what I can only call triumphantly lighthearted. Yet our talk was not the old, easy freewheeling talk of three months ago. I felt a distance of reserve in her. There were long silences when we walked, with her little Yorkshire terrier trotting before us along the towpath, or when I was driving her to the nearest village to do some shopping, or when, once, a Guinness barge passed slowly through the lock and we watched the men lean against the gates to slew them slowly open, and then watched it go slowly dud-dudding away from us along the perspective of the canal until it looked no bigger in the distance than a toy boat. That was the only time I probed her.

'Are you never lonely here?' I asked her.

'Not at all!' she said, in astonishment. 'I have so much to do! Reading about the antiquities around here. I have an old bicycle to visit them. Studying the river flowers. Watching the birds. And it is extraordinary how much time I can spend on the house. It will take me years to get it the way I want it. Dreaming and thinking.'

The only word that held me was *thinking*. Thinking what?

As I was about to leave her she asked me if I would drive her as far as the next lock. (When I said she could drive with me to the end of the world, she laughed and said, 'That *is* the end of my world.') She wanted to buy freshly laid eggs from the wife of the lock-keeper with whom, now and again, if she wanted to hear a voice, she would pass the time of day and, perhaps, glance at the daily newspaper.

'Though it is always,' she smiled, 'yesterday's newspaper!'

This lockhouse was an exact replica of her own. Like the cells of certain monastic orders that are identical the world over, so I suppose is every lockhouse on these decaying canals that slowly creep across Ireland. We sat for a while in its poky kitchen chatting with the woman. Then she did something that I can never forget. She had brought a few sweets for the two small children there, and as she sat, the sweets in her lap, the two little girls standing on either side of her, she put an arm around each, saying, 'One for you' and 'Now one for you,' until the few sweets were evenly shared. The mother fondly watched the group. I went to the door to look out. I could not bear to watch it.

During the three years that she stayed there I never let two months pass without visiting her. I never again spoke to her of my feelings for her. There was no need to. We both knew. Nobody else from W— visited her. Two or three times I told Jack I had 'dropped in' on her. Each time he asked if she was well – no more. She told me he had written once inviting her to return, and that she had several angry letters from her family telling her it was her duty to return. In the spring of her third year I thought she looked ill and said so to Jack. The next I heard was from May Hennessy, who told me that she had suddenly been taken to the County Hospital of B—, in an advanced stage of leukemia.

From that on the family became full of solicitude and pity for her, telling us all that the one wish she and Jack had was that she should leave the hospital and come home. I guessed that she would be too weak to resist them. And that, in fact, was how, in the end, everything was done, all the whispering ended, the scandal smothered and forgotten, if not forgiven.

The last time I saw her was on a June afternoon, just like this one, lying in this front room, her bed near the window so that she could look out over the bay. She was thin and pale, her eyes made wider and brighter by the smallness and pallor of her face. There were half a dozen Slators there, keeping up a cheerful chatter about her. She was not talking, but once she smiled joyfully at the lace curtains blowing in through the open window, and said to me, 'They are like a ballet.' At which I remembered that snowy night three years back when she and I had been talking about *The Three Sisters*, and Jack had suddenly gone off in a sulk to the Club, and she said she was going to go away and be born again, and I began to wonder if she saw all life in the forms or shapes of a ballet that you cannot explain or reason about, but that, somehow, in their own way, say, 'This is right, this is the way it all is really when it is right.' But even as she said it, my eye fell on the black, gold-edged missal by her bed and I wondered if she had, in her weakness, surrendered to all the habits and ways against which she had once decided to rebel. A moment later her face contorted and she said, 'I must ask you all to leave now. I must ask nurse to do something for me.' I never laid eyes on her again. Two mornings later May Hennessy told me she was gone.

It was the right word. Gone she has but I have never felt that she has died. I don't believe it still. All my memories of her are of a vital living woman. I have no other image of her. As I looked out of my office window that morning at the sea, I felt what I still feel – she has gone back into it.

For everybody in the town except Jack and me that was the end of her story. Her death broke him. I never met him that he did not start talking about how lovely and spirited a creature she was, a greathearted woman. In my misery I began to haunt him, though I was never sure from one day to the next whether it was through friendship or hate. Still there must have been some compassion in it because when he said to me one day, 'Jerry, I can't go on living in that empty house,' I said, 'It's too big for you. Why don't you break it up into two flats and rent one to me? We'd be company for one another.' He jumped at it. He retired to live on the third floor, we put his old housekeeper up under the roof, and he rented me these rooms over the shop, furnished as they stood with all the bits and pieces of antiques she used to buy at auctions, and the shelves full of her books, even the ones she had taken with her to the lockhouse on the canal. He said he didn't want any of them near him. They only kept on reminding him of her.

That is fifteen years ago now, and I never stop thinking of her, coming back and back to all those questions that began to torment me from the morning she left us. Did she win? Or did she lose? What, in God's name, was she thinking during these three years of solitude when she was trying to be born again? What in God's name, did she think could, should or would happen to her? Did, in fact, anything at all happen to her? Not, of course, that I think of her all day long. I haven't the time – the year after she died I became (as she prophesied) the County Engineer. I am overworked. There are more things I want to do for this town than would keep any man busy for twenty hours a day. And not even a man as madly in love with a woman as I was and as I still am with her can think for every moment of his beloved. But often, on evenings like this and at odd moments, at noon, or late at night, she ambushes me. I see her again gabbling in this room, or walking in that lost valley, under the rain or the sun, and I wonder again what went on inside her, or whether the leaves, or the clouds or the mist ever told her what she wanted to know.

I sometimes now believe they said nothing, because, one night, I found among her books this red-covered notebook – a handwritten journal that she kept during those three years. I stayed awake half the night reading it over and over again hoping to find the answers to whatever it was she wanted to know. Not a clue! She had divided each year into the four seasons, and in each section she had merely written such pointless, passing things as 'I saw a kingfisher today', followed by the details of the place and the hour and the weather. Or she wrote, 'It is raining, the drops slide down my window, through it the trunks of the pine trees look wavy and puckered and corrugated. The water of the canal is pockmarked. The reeds are bowed down by the wind and rain.' Or she has scribbled down some quotations from whatever book she had been reading, like: *'A little kingdom I possess / Where thoughts and feelings dwell, / And very hard the task I find / Of governing it well.* By Louisa May Alcott, when aged 13.' Or this one: *'The longest journey / Is the journey inward.* By D. H.' whoever he is! Or there are small sums of housekeeping money added up. Or she wrote down some details about some old abbey she had visited on her bicycle. A schoolgirl could have written it all.

The next morning I brought the journal to my office and threw it on May Hennessy's desk.

'I found this last night among Jill Jennings's books. It's apparently her journal. She kept it when she was living by herself in Bunahown.'

I watched her open it at random, reluctantly, almost with distaste. She read a bit. She turned over another thumbful of pages and read another bit.

'I thought,' I said, 'there might be something in it about what she used to be thinking. But there isn't!'

She looked up at me sullenly.

'What would you,' she asked, 'be thinking, if you were her?'

'I might be thinking of God, or Life, or "What is Reality?" or I might be thinking why I could not get on with *him*. Wouldn't you?'

She lowered her head, turned another clutch of pages, and spoke without raising her head.

'She had only one thing against Jack Jennings.'

'What?'

She slapped the book shut and handed it to me with 'This is all about birds.'

'What was the one thing she had against Jack?'

'He is impotent.'

I shouted it at her:

'You have absolutely no right to say a thing like that! It's not true!'

'It is true. I have every right. She told me.'

For a moment we glared at one another.

'But if that was so she could have had an annulment of the marriage in five minutes! Annulments are granted every week of the year for that!'

'And would you,' she said, with contempt, 'expect her to expose him before the whole town? To shame him for the rest of his life?'

I walked from her to the window and looked down into the busy square. How many of them knew?

'So,' she said quietly to my back, 'she went away. It's as simple as that.'

I heard her typewriter clacking away behind me. I snatched up the book and left her. I didn't do a stroke of work that day.

But it is not as simple as that! She never really did go away! She remained. He remained. Both of them remained. She still remains. You cannot just toss aside two lives with 'A man and a woman who married badly,' or 'If she lived anywhere else she could have divorced him and married again.' If! You can do anything, if ... And if ... And if ... There is always that human and immortal If. God's curse on it! Am I one of those damfool Americans who think there is nothing on earth you cannot do? There are things nobody can do! The number of times I have wanted to do something as simple as widen a road, and knew I could only do it if I bulldozed some old woman's cottage that stood in the way, and that she would not give up, not if we gave her a new house a hundred times more comfortable. I once heard that in the middle of Chicago, where real estate is worth millions, there is an old fellow with a farm that he simply will not sell. How often have I wanted to dredge that bay out there, and I could do it in three months if the money was not wanted worse for something else. To build houses, to clear the slums. Why are there slums in America as bad as anything in Singapore? Why are there wars? How many men and women in the world wish to high heaven they had never married and yet they cannot leave one another because of their children, or their compassion, or pity, or their memories of their first happiness that is stronger than the cold years that, God knows why, froze their love to death.

Is that my answer? That she did not marry him for love. Only for pity. Did he tell her before they were married? But that is incredible. The poor bastard probably did not know until he married her. How long did it take her to understand?

Years? Of bewilderment, then terror, then misery and pity for them both. But I still do not know what she meant by being born again.

'I bought four eggs today from Mrs Delacey at the lock-house. Four lovely brown eggs with a feather clinging to one of them.' 'Poor Jerry visited me again today, I wonder what brings him so often.' She knew perfectly well what brought me. 'My wild cherry is a cloud of white blossoms.' What the hell have feathers and cherry blossoms to do with anything?

There's a plane passing over. To London? To Paris? To Rome? If anyone in it looked down at us what would he see? Nothing but an empty harbour, a huddle of roofs, a membrane of blue smoke. He would not see the Slators, or me, or Jack, or the tumbledown backyards, with their rusty sheds, and the valerian growing out of old walls, places I'm going to tear to bits some day if . . . If! And if!

That grey moon up there won't be bright for two more hours. Nor the lighthouse blink. Nor the tide in. The bay looks lovely when the tide is in. A skin of pure water. Moontracked. On a moony night like this, when the whole town is sound asleep, what would I not give to see her come floating in, look, and look, and wave one white arm to me before she turns for home again?

Brainsy

The night Tom Kennedy landed off the bus in the long street of Coonlahan to begin his career as a teacher in the Abbatian Brothers' College (popularly known as the A.B.C.) it was raining softly but implacably. He passed no remarks on the rain. He gave one look at Coonlahan and noted the hour: exactly seventy minutes before closing time. The next thing he did was to ask the driver if he could trouble him to show him where the hotel was. The driver laughed. No trouble at all. No hotel. But he might get some class of a room in that tall house down the street that old Mrs Gaston called a Guest House. 'Don't give her more than a quid. She never has any guests.' The old lady showed him by candlelight to a room high up under the roof, large, damp and cold as an aerial vault. That done, he went out at once, shot another despairing look around him and turned into the first pub he met to drown his shame. That telegram from the Brother Superior – 'COME AT ONCE BEGIN DUTIES TOMORROW' – could mean only one of two things. Either somebody else had come before him, looked at Coonlahan and spat on it; or nobody had wanted to come there at all. He drank steadily until the barman put out the oil lamps, clambered up to his room, emptied his pockets on the bed and counted his coins with a shaking finger to see if he had the price of his fare back to Dublin. He found that of the five pounds with which he had started from Dublin all he had left was eleven shillings and two pennies, and stared down through the mist around the street lamp opposite his window at his past and his future . . .

One look at him, a couple of questions and any stranger would have had it all. He looked about forty-five (he was thirty-six); his hair was grey as a badger; his lower eyelids were as pink as a bloodhound's; his trousers gave him legs like an elephant; he walked like a seal; and he had been on the booze for some fifteen years. As for his qualifications to be a teacher of English: he had, some eight years before, managed to scrape up a B.A. (pass level), by attending night courses at University College, Dublin, while concurrently (also previously and subsequently) failing at every odd job he had tried – clerk in a travel agency, copywriter for an advertising agency, door-to-door canvasser for the *British Encyclopaedia*, sub-editor for *The Irish Digest*, sub-sub-editor for a comic weekly called *Hullaballoo*, an auctioneer's clerk, a bookie's sidekick and a collector for a pious organization advocating total abstinence from all spirituous liquors. Only three days ago he had been sacked from that job for arriving on the doorstep of the Parish Priest of Killiney at eleven o'clock at night, speechless and footless. It was then that he decided that there was only one thing left for him to do – take up teaching. Searching the next morning through the small ads in the educational column of *The Irish Independent* he had come on one for the post of English Teacher in the A.B.C. of Coonlahan, in County Kerry. He had written off at once to the Brother Superior saying that he held a first class honours B.A. and had had three years' experience in England, adding, truthfully, that twenty years ago in Cork he had himself been a pupil of the Abbatians. He sent off the letter and prayed that something else except teaching would turn up in the meantime. To his dismay all that turned up was the telegram.

When old Mrs Gaston woke him up in the morning, groaning at her long stairs, he found that although the village consisted of a single Main Street it was a fine, wide street of multicoloured houses, and the sun shone so warmly on it that roofs exhaled a gentle steam. From his high window he saw a majestic range of mountains, a vast moorland broken here and there by tiny farms and he could just see a gleaming spit of ocean away off to the west. Better still, when he found the school – grey, square, two-storied, cross-crowned – down a side road, beyond the church that concluded the street at that end, the Superior, one Brother Angelo Harty turned out to be a kindly, hulking old man who welcomed him warmly, asked him no questions and, before introducing him to his own pupils, courteously led him around the other seven classrooms to meet his future colleagues – six Abbatian brothers in the old blue-black soutanes with the bony collars, and one lay teacher, Dicky Talbot, a cheerful, skinny little man, wearing pince-nez glasses on a promising prawn-red nose. They all greeted him in the most friendly manner.

'And this,' said Angelo, as he threw open the seventh door, 'is Brother Regis. Our history teacher.'

Tom stared through the ageing mask before him and slowly held out his hand to his oldest schoolboy pal, Brainsy Carty. As slowly, Brother Regis did the same, and then it was a cheerful 'Hello, Tom!' and an astonished 'So it really is you?' and he was back in the Abbatian Brothers' College in Cork, aged thirteen.

For four years – the purest, sweetest, loveliest years of his life – he and Brainsy had sat side by side on the same bench, for every class, every day. They used to meet every afternoon after school. They spent every holiday together. Days of Damon and Pythias. Exchanges of soul years: their diaries, their dreams, their heroes, their poems. Brainsy's 'All hail to Napoleon, dreamer and doer of might,' for Tom's 'O sweetest Virgin, free me of my fetters, / Send my prayer upward to the sky, / That I may suffer among the lonely lepers, / As Father Damien did in far-off Molokai.' Years when Brainsy's ambition was to climb the mountains of India or explore 'the untracked Amazon'; when Tom, if he could not be another Father Damien, wanted to be a Trappist monk, pray all night, work all day, never speak and dig a foot of his grave every week. Years when, because Tom had no father and Brainsy's mother was also dead, they agreed that it would be marvellous if Tom's mother married Brainsy's father and they would always live together like brothers. They had wept openly when at seventeen Brainsy's father sent him to Dublin to be trained as a teacher, and Tom's mother sent him off to a seminary in County Limerick to become a Capuchin priest. From that moment the pattern of their lives was set. Brainsy got what he wanted, a teacher's job in Dublin, and Tom was fired from the seminary, his Master of Novices dryly intimating to him that his mother (who had died, in the meantime) might have had a vocation for the priesthood, but he ... Well, he was turned twenty-one now. He had better go up to Dublin and look for a job.

Dublin? Tom's first thought was of Brainsy.

They were soon sharing a small flat, going halves in everything, eating and drinking together, chasing girls together, loyally deceiving them for one another, agreeing that if either of them wanted to bring a girl to the flat the other would walk the streets until he saw the window blind up and an umbrella standing against the light to show that the storm was over; though, in practice, it was always Tom who walked the streets. He liked the company of girls, but, as the saying goes, he never 'touched' them. As for their arguments – Brainsy being Brainsy – they were never in short order. For the time was now long gone since Brainsy's hero was Buonaparte at Lodi, or since he wanted to climb great mountains and explore great rivers. His obsessive interest now was in the marvels of modern science. His heroes were men like Bohr, Rutherford, Thomson, Einstein, Planck and Millikin. His villains were every priest, nun, monk, bishop and archbishop on up to the Vatican and the cardinals of the curia. It was a change that bewildered Tom until he remembered those odd questions at school that had won Brainsy his nickname. ('But, Brother, if it is a sin to kill, what about the glories of the religious wars?' Or 'But, Brother, if birds have wings why haven't we?' Or 'But, Brother, if we become dust when we die why can't Catholics be cremated?')

Their dissent only troubled Tom when their roles began to interchange, like a castling in chess; as when Brainsy might yield that if there ever was any truth in religion the last time it was seen was when it was hiding in the catacombs; and Tom would find himself conceding that, yes, it was there all right, but maybe it was really to be found only in our memories of a divine shadow passing along the shores of Galilee? Which would take them on to the analysis of the Gospels until, in agony, Tom began to find his shadow slowly turning to a wisp of smoke. One July night he came tramping home eagerly from his job to have it out, once and for all. He found a note on the table saying, 'Good-bye, we will meet in the great Hereafter.' Since then he had had neither sight nor sound of him until this minute.

Brainsy's smile went back into his mouth. His hair became grey, his back stooped. All that was left of his youth was the broken perpendicular furrow that used to come and go between his eyebrows like wind on water. It seemed now to be dug in there as permanently as the broken line of life in a man's palm. Or, Tom thought, as Angelo led him out of the classroom, like a sentence that starts one way and ends another – Was that an anacoluthon? – like say, 'If I don't mend my boozy ways what, in God's name, is going to be the end of *me*?' Though, God knows, he thought, following Angelo's broad back down the corridor, anacoluthing like blazes as he went, the truth is isn't it an extraordinary fact, like Brainsy and me, why must everybody in Ireland live like an express train that starts off for heaven full of beautiful dreams, and marvellous ambitions and, halfway, bejasus, you switch off the bloody track down some sideline that brings you back to exactly where you began, with all your machinery falling out of you in bits, and every wagon branded 'What's-the-use-of-doing-anything-at-all?'

Angelo paused with his hand on the doorhandle of Tom's classroom. He turned to say curiously, 'So you know Brother Regis?' A soft babel went on inside. Tom said, cautiously, not knowing what Brainsy might have told him about his own past, that, yes, they had both been at school together in the A.B.C. in Cork.

'But of course, that was years and years ago. He was a very clever boy at school. Oh, very talented! One of the stars of the A.B.C. And friends in Dublin tell me that he became a marvellous teacher.' He smiled ingratiatingly. 'At school the boys used to call him Brainsy. A nickname, like that, from boys, don't you think, Brother Angelo, is a great compliment?'

Looking steadily at his new teacher, the old man took out his snuffbox, opened it, dabbed in one fat thumb and slowly approached the nicotine to each hairy nostril. Still looking steadily at his man, he slowly replaced the box in his trousers pocket through a slit in his soutane.

'Brainsy? That's not bad, you know. It's extraordinary how penetrating boys can sometimes be. And how cruel!'

'He has been a monk now for how long?'

'Twelve years.'

'Always here?'

'He spent nine years in his old school in Cork.'

Nine years in a big city? And now shunted down to this back-of-beyond? Puzzled as well as worried, Tom ventured a probe.

'I never expected to find him down here.'

There was a sudden silence behind the classroom door. Had the boys heard them talking? In the silence, through the open window of the corridor, he heard the juniors downstairs repeating in unison the voice of a teacher guiding them through a reading lesson, first his deep voice, phrase by phrase, then their piping voices repeating the words after him:

'THE RHINE-O-SAYROS,' the deep voice boomed. 'The rhine-o-sayros,' the children piped. 'IS A WILD BASHTE.' 'Is a wild bashte.' 'HE WOULD ATE YOU.' 'He would ate you.' 'AND DESHTROY YOU.' 'And deshtroy you.'

When Angelo's answer came it was a shade too delicate.

'Well, you see, our Superior General thought he might find it a bit more easy away down here in the quiet of the country.'

It was the word *away* that gave him away. Whenever somebody has what we politely call a nervous breakdown we always say, 'He has been away.'

For several weeks all that Tom saw of his friend was when they passed one another in the corridor between classes, and without halting, Briansy would lift a hand, smile faintly and say something like 'All going well, I hope?' or 'Bad weather, isn't it?' Tom, deeply hurt, decided finally that if this was the sort of relationship the fellow wanted now he could play that game too – 'Morning, Brother! Nice day, isn't it?' – until, bit by bit, he began to get a hint here and a hint there of the kind of tensions that tauten life in small communities like the A.B.C.

He got his first small shock the day he overheard two boys refer to Regis as Brainsy. It could only mean that Angelo had, unguardedly, mentioned the nickname to one of the brothers who had, at once and maliciously, passed the arrow on to his boys. For a boy to give a nickname like that to another boy was a chummy thing to do. To give it to a teacher was like sticking a firecracker into his tail. He got a more painful hint the day he was trying to persuade his class that when Oliver

Goldsmith was writing *The Deserted Village* in his miserable London garret he was all the time sadly remembering the village where he was born, in Ireland.

'Take, for example, the lines . . .'

At once an ink-fingered hand shot up. It was Micky Brennan, the son of a local publican, a boy he had already come to recognize as one of the smartest boys in the class.

'I know the lines, sir,' Micky said eagerly, and started to quote them fluently and feelingly, from

> In all my wanderings round this world of care,
> In all my griefs – and God has given my share –
> I still had hopes my latest hours to crown,
> Amidst these humble bowers to lay me down . . .

on down to:

> And, as an hare whom hounds and horns pursue,
> Pants to the place from whence at first she flew,
> I still had hopes, my long vexations past,
> Here to return – and die at home at last.

Immediately Brennan had begun to recite the lines the whole class began to titter. (At what?)

'That's very good, Brennan. But how do you happen to know the lines so well?'

Another boy spoke up, a rough fellow named Harty, the duffer of the class and, Tom suspected, the bully of the school – he had already had to stop him, one day in the yard, from punching a boy half his size and weight.

'He knows them lines, sir,' Harty growled, with an envious look at Brennan, 'only because Brainsy . . .' There was a general titter at this slip of the tongue; if it was a slip. 'I mean Brother Regis, sir, is always quoting them to us at History. He says he's very fond of 'em.'

The whole class laughed openly; Tom understood; and in his fright passed quickly on to something else. If these giggling brats had been smart enough to read Brainsy for Goldsmith he had no need to persuade them to read Lissoy for Auburn. As he looked around at their innocent-wicked-probing eyes he knew that it would not be long before they saw through him too.

What nickname had they, maybe already, given him? And did this sort of thing run through the whole school, through the monastery, all through Coonlahan?

Where he now lodged was with a young carpenter and his wife in a tiny pink house rising directly from the pavement that ended with the school and the monks' dwelling place. Beyond that the road became grass-edged and the countryside began; though within a month, merely by facing the window of the small front room of his lodgings as he ate his dinner – at half past three every afternoon – watching the rare cart or the rare pedestrian that passed slowly by, it came to him that Coonlahan was a place where the life of the country had neither beginning nor end. Like any one of the little white-washed farmhouses on the level bogland that he could see through his window it was just another dot in space and time. That donkey cart trundling by with its roped pyramid of turf to be sold from door to door brought the bogland into the Main Street. The pasturers plodded in every evening with a small herd of black cows, their udders dripping, eager to be milked in somebody's backyard. Coonlahan's one water pump stood on top of three rectangular steps at a fork in the road just beyond the school, its timber casing always wrapped in posters advertising hay or land for sale, so that he occasionally saw the waterman's two barrels, covered with wet sacking, pass his window to the lazy cry of 'Pennyabucketthewa-a-ather!' The carpenter's wife, like many other women in Coonlahan, kept chickens in her backyard – he once saw a hawk swoop down on the hen run to carry off a chicken between its claws; and one hard, wintry morning he found her in floods of tears – a fox had stolen in at night and killed them all. 'I'm beginning to think,' he said to her, 'that the whole village ought to be stockaded!' Yet, one lovely afternoon in the following April he was to see a host of swallows pour in at one end of the Main Street and out at the other as if there were no village there at all. No wonder that old bus driver had laughed at him the night he asked for 'the hotel'! In a place where there was no railway, no cinema, no library, no bookshop, no dancehall, nothing but a handful of shops and pubs? Where, all through the long autumn nights, he soon found that there was nothing whatever to do – after he had corrected his pupils' homework or prepared his own – but to read, or sit with the carpenter and his wife in the back kitchen playing cards, or listening to voices from Dublin fading and returning on the dying batteries of the radio.

At such dead hours he would occasionally wonder what Brainsy was doing at that moment down the road. What did they all do once school was over? One afternoon he had seen two of them playing handball against the gable of the school. Another day he had watched a few of them aimlessly pucking a hurling ball in an empty field, shouting like boys, their soutanes doffed, their bony collars scattered on the grass like crescent moons. On fine afternoons he regularly saw some of them passing his window in pairs to walk, as he sometimes did himself, out some country road until the sun set. Coming on Dicky Talbot one October night in Brennan's pub, he asked him, 'How do ye pass the winter nights here in Coonlahan?' Dicky, married, with eight kids, said he had never needed to consider the problem.

'I mean, the brothers,' Tom said testily. 'Do they play cards? Do they ever read? And if so what?'

'I suppose they read the newspaper. Though it must be a bit of rag by the time it has passed through all their hands I imagine they read *Our Boys*, or look at the clerical weeklies. They have some sort of a ragtime library of their own but I have no idea what's in it. Textbooks? Lives of the saints? As you know, there's no library here. All the County Librarian can do is dump a couple of cases of books in the back porch of the chapel once a month. A couple of years back he offered them the run of everything he has in his H.Q. in Killarney, but only one of them ever availed of the offer.'

'I bet that was Regis!'

'The very man. But they soon put a stop to his gallop.' Dicky laughed at the happy memory. 'They caught him one night reading a book called *Is There an Afterlife?* by some Calvinist divine named Vaughan. They raised blue hell and bloody murder over it. They complained about the poor old County Librarian to the Parish Priest and to the County Committee. A bright boyo, he said he thought the author was Cardinal Vaughan.'

'You're surely not suggesting that Regis was having religious doubts? I mean, did the book deny the existence of immortality?'

'Amn't I after telling you the book was by a Calvinist? And the world knows that no Calvanist could exist for one minute without heaven for himself and hellfire for everyone else. Doubts? Not at all. It was simply the question mark after the title. They weren't going to stand for that! Doubts? Regis have doubts? You obviously don't know our Regis. His trouble is that he's full to the butt of the lugs with certainties. He's the Savonarola of Coonlahan. He's the scourge of the monastery. He thinks they're all a soft, flabby, half-pagan lot, and he's always telling them so. You should hear him saying, "He that is neither hot nor cold I spe-e-ew him out of my mouth." Or you should have been here last year when he made them all agree to give up cigarettes for Lent, and then caught one of them sucking a butt in the jakes. He reported the poor bastard to the Superior, the P.P. and the Bishop. What do they do at night? Sit around and eat one another, I would imagine. Have another pint.'

Tom brooded over that conversation. 'Simply the question mark after the title . . .' That would be right up Brainsy's alley. He decided that he must have a talk with him alone.

It was a frosty afternoon in mid-November before he got his chance. He had finished his dinner and was reading the Dublin paper (it never came in before three o'clock) when his eye was lifted by the lone pencilled shadow of one of the brothers passing swiftly outside the lace curtains. He recognized Nessan, the man who taught the kids Irish, and was just deciding that he was hurrying on some errand down the street when he saw Brainsy slowly passing by, also alone. He seized his umbrella, hat and overcoat and hastened after him. Ahead of him he saw Nessan turning right for the open country, with Brainsy about a hundred yards behind him. He caught up with him.

'Hello, Regis.'

'Hello, Tom.'

'You seem to have lost your companion.'

'He's my non-companion,' Brainsy said gruffly. 'I prefer my own company.'

'Oh? Am I intruding on some great thoughts?'

Brainsy relaxed into a smile as frosty as the grey field beside the road.

'Divil a thought, great or small. Walk along with me and leave us be talking. All that fellow,' nodding his chin towards Nessan's back, 'ever talks about is crossword puzzles. "What is a four-legged domestic animal in three letters beginning with C?" If you say cat he says cow. If you say cow he says cat. Lovely afternoon, isn't it? How's everything with you? Getting along all right?'

Tom let him talk school talk for a bit. Then he drew closer.

'You know that boy Micky Brennan?'

Brainsy's smile became a trifle softer and sadder.

'A bright boy, an inquiring boy, he reminds me sometimes of myself when I was his age.'

'He stood up in class one day and recited a whole chunk of *The Deserted Village* for me. *In all my wanderings round this world of care* ... You know the lines. He tells me you taught them to him. I never knew you were a Goldsmith fan.'

'As a matter of fact, I am very fond of that poem. Every historian ought to be. It touches on quite a number of modern problems. *Ill fares the land, to hastening ills a prey*. And so on. Poor Oliver knew it all. An exile himself.'

'Who always wanted to go home in the heel of his days? I often wondered whether he had a home to go to. As well I might. Since my mother died I have no home to go to. Is your dad still alive?'

Brainsy said, 'No,' and halted and looked off to where the far mountains rose clear and sharp against the frosty twilight.

'Home?' he said softly. 'The word has various meanings, of course. *Lead, kindly light ... The night is dark and I am far from home*.'

'Newman. The lighthouse in the Strait of Bonifacio. A great stylist.'

'A great teacher. When I read him I feel the next world revolving about me.'

'But you believe in the next world.'

'Meaning?'

'Meaning that I gave up all that sort of thing years ago.

Thanks to you, Brainsy.' Brainsy lifted shocked eyes to him. 'You haven't forgotten all our talks in Dublin? Day after day. Night after night. Year in and year out. After you left Dublin I stopped going to church, chapel or meeting. I hope you won't report that to your superior? I don't want to lose my job – just yet.'

They walked on in the frosty silence. After a bit Brainsy spoke.

'I accept no responsibility for your state of mind. You are a grown man. But if that is your state of mind what are you doing here?'

'It's a living.'

Their feet rang on the hard road.

'Well! You are a layman. So I suppose a living is a good enough reason for you to be here. I might do better to ask what am I doing here?' He pointed forward with his umbrella to his lone chaperon. 'Or what is that fellow doing here? Or what are they all doing here?'

'Teaching?'

Brainsy halted again. The line between his eyebrows went red as a scar. His voice became hoarse with fury.

'Teaching what? Isn't that the beginning and end of it? Isn't that what I'm always saying to these fellows? If every single thing we say and do and teach doesn't give the youngsters the feeling that this ball of the world is carrying us inch by inch towards another world where is the sense in any one of us giving up everything to become brothers? But do we do it? Angelo teaches them Latin. Perhaps you can tell me, because he can't, since when did Cicero or Ovid become pillars of Christianity? Oh, laugh away! That's what they do! That man there teaches the Irish language. He thinks he's doing great work for Ireland. He might just as well be teaching them pagan Greek. This year your lads will be reading *Macbeth* or *Julius Caesar*. What's so very Christian about either of them? It may all be a great joke to you. You've just said you have no beliefs. But I have my beliefs. And it's no laughing matter for me.'

He shivered and they resumed their walk.

'Tom! Do you know why I left you that time in Dublin? I'll tell you why. It's not nice. But I'll tell you. It was a Saturday. If you remember? You were working that day, I wasn't. It was a lovely sunny day. I took a girl down to Brittas Bay. She was eighteen. A sweet, lovely, innocent girl. I sometimes still pray for her. It was a real Irish July day, little showers of rain, great steamy clouds rising up all around us, everything bruised black and blue, the hills, the white fields, the blue sky. We swam and we lay down on the cool sand. Not a soul along the beach for miles and miles. The usual opening gambit. Slipping the strap of her bathing dress off her shoulder. When I did it she looked up at me and I never saw such terror, such contempt, such disgust, such disappointment in any human being's eyes. She looked at me as if I was filth. I put back the strap and said, "Forget it." I couldn't think what else to say or do. After a while she got up and said, "We'd better go home now, Jerry, you've spoiled everything." The whole way back to Dublin we didn't say one word. When she left me I went back to the flat and I looked at it. Everything ready. The half-bottle of whiskey. The two glasses. The couch in the corner. The sun pouring into the room. It looked exactly what it was. Sordid. That was my moment on the road to Damascus. It came to me like lightning that I was a bad influence on everybody, including you, Tom, and that if I didn't leave the world entirely I was done for. Inside a year I became an Abbatian brother.'

Ahead of them Nessan halted on the brow of a little hill looking at the sky. Hesperus. He could have been one of the Magi. They paused to let him walk on.

'And you have been happy ever since?'

'Within three years I realized that all I'd done was to jump out of the frying pan into the fire. I had thought I had a vocation...'

'Like me in the Capuchins!'

'... Instead, all I was doing, year after year, was shoving a few score of boys through some examination or other to get some lousy job. Would you give up the whole world just for that? After that it became more and more clear to me every year that if that was all my vocation was good for I was a fool, we were all a lot of fools, and the whole blooming thing was a cod.'

Whom hounds and horns pursue. Until the hare is torn to pieces. They thought he might find it more easy down here in the quiet of the country. Or was it because he was the kind of brainy teacher they couldn't afford, or the expensive makings of one? One small head that, as Goldsmith did not say about the village teacher, could never carry all he thought he knew?

That month ended it. A leak in the roof of the school made Tom's class uninhabitable, and for three weeks, while they were replacing the slates, he had to keep moving his class from room to room. For those three weeks he had a chance to watch them all teaching. None of them interested him except Brainsy, and he was a magician. With him the boys were not in a class at all; they were in a circus, on an ice-hockey rink. His trick, though it was his nature rather than a trick, was to keep them doubling after him all the time, never letting them rest for a minute. He was so good that Tom used to set his class to some written exercise so that he could pretend to be looking out the window while listening, entranced, to the chase going on at the other end of the room.

One such day he was standing like that, looking down into the kitchen-garden of the monastery, with Brainsy behind him luring them on to discuss the suppression of the monasteries. For forty minutes he started argument after argument. 'Sullivan, how would you like it if you saw your father's grazing land being taken away from him?' 'Yes, but supposing it didn't belong to him? Supposing that it originally belonged to the Church?' 'Brennan, what about all those executions of multitudes of poor people wandering all over the country, driven to terrible crimes by hunger? How far was it just, or unjust, to hang them?' Then, at a great leap, he was on to the humanity of John Howard and his plans for Prison Reform. 'Cassidy, what do you make of that idea?' 'Whelan, have you any idea where that humane spirit began in England?' 'Walsh, what about the Church, for example? Was it a humane idea when the Church began to teach that hell is not just fire eating the body but torment eating the soul?' 'Foley, what do you think? Was that a humane idea? Or was it even more inhumane?' 'What do you all think? Which was the more humane in that terrible century, the Pope or the King?' It was then that Tom heard the doorhandle click and, turning, saw old Angelo slide out as softly as he had, apparently, come in.

The very next day Angelo called Tom out of his class and informed him, in the corridor, that after the Christmas holidays he must, in addition to English, teach History.

'But,' Tom cried, 'I never studied History. And Brother Regis is a dab at History. He's marvellous at it. You heard him yourself.'

'I have heard him many times, Mr. Kennedy.'

'Then you can see for yourself that I couldn't come within a thousand miles of the way he does it. Compared to him I'm a complete ignoramus! And the boys are mad about his ideas on History!'

Angelo let out an exasperated sigh. He took out his snuffbox, but he was too upset to use it.

'I am very sorry, Mr Kennedy, but you will just have to do what I say. All you need do is to read the set texts and keep a couple of pages ahead of the class. And,' suddenly and uncharacteristically getting excited, 'I want you to know that I don't care two pins whether the boys are interested in Brother Regis's ideas, or your ideas, or anybody else's ideas, or not. My position is quite simple. I want my boys to get through their examinations, and that is all I want. And the plain fact of the matter is that since Brother Regis came here three years ago we have had more failures in History than in any other subject on the entire curriculum. And I'm not one bit surprised. Unless you can explain to me what on earth History has to do with such matters as whether there is real fire in hell or not. Look!' He was trembling in every limb, and his round, soft face had become as purple as a swede turnip. 'This little community of ours was as cosy and happy a little community as you could find in the length and breadth of Ireland until Brother Regis was sent down here on top of us to enjoy the peace and quiet of the country. Peace and quiet? God help us! Since that man joined us there has been neither peace nor quiet in this place. Do you know that last night, in our quiet little library, he and Brother Nessan, two brothers in religion, literally, literally I say, came to blows – I never thought I'd live to see it – before all the brothers. And about what, Mr Kennedy? About the nature of hellfire!' He gripped his soutane across his chest as if he were getting a grip of himself. On the spot he became quiet. 'You will take History in the New Year. Have no fears – you can't be worse than your predecessor. And for the rest of the year I will raise your salary by twenty-five per cent.'

That night Tom decided, over his fourth pint of porter, that Angelo could sack him if he wanted to; but he could not and would not do this to his best friend. In the morning he found he had no option. An ambulance stood outside the monastery door. The sergeant of the Guards and a plainclothesman were talking with Angelo and Nessan inside the gate. Every window in the school was full of white faces. Dicky Talbot whispered to him that Regis had been missing since midnight and that the Guards and the brothers had been out searching for him with lamps until three hours ago, when he was found, unconscious, in a ditch beside the road, presumably knocked down by some yob in a passing motorcar. He was now lying in his bed in the monastery, still unconscious, about to be taken to the County Hospital in Tralee.

He was still unconscious when Tom went to Dublin that Christmas; he was unconscious on his return; he remained unconscious for, in all, sixty-six days. A month later he was discharged from hospital, as well as ever, meaning, as he himself said over a cup of tea in Tom's lodgings, 'Hale and hearty! Except for a bruised liver, a broken leg, two smashed fingers, three ribs that creak whenever I try to touch my toes and a silver plate in my skull.'

'Well,' Tom joked, in the merry tone we all reserve for such doleful occasions, 'you gave us a nice fright! I expected to hear any day that you were dead.'

From his armchair Brainsy gave him a queer look.

'So I was,' he said quietly.

'Was what?'

'Dead.'

'You look very much alive now, anyway.' Tom laughed uncomfortably.

Brainsy's mouth went tight. The frown between his eyes caved in. This apparently, was no laughing matter either.

'There is no least doubt about my death, Tom. I have had

plenty of time since I came back from the grave to think the whole matter out completely. I have been asking myself a great many interesting questions. And I have arrived at a very simple conclusion. When I was knocked down that night on the highway I was given a blow on the head that plunged me into a state of total oblivion for sixty-six days. I lost all my faculties. I fail to see what more could have happened to me if my heart had stopped beating. I was, in a word, humanly speaking, dead.'

With anybody else Tom would have scoffed or made polite, meaningless noises. He opened his mouth to make one, leaned forward, leaned back; did the same again, did it a third time; and sank back into his armchair. He felt like a lunatic rowing an imaginary boat. You always had to come to the point with Brainsy.

'But your soul was alive!' he said at last.

Brainsy smiled and to enforce the smile adopted, at one and the same moment, a Kerry brogue and what used to be called an Oxford accent – the common Irish way of being superior without seeming to be lofty.

'Oho! Aren't we a darlint boy! So, now, oo doo believe in the sowl, eh?'

'Well, no! Or, only as a metaphor. Such as, "Brevity is the soul of wit." Shakespeare. Or, "O God, if there is such a thing as a God, please save my soul, if I have such a thing as a soul." Renan. But, I don't believe in the soul in your sense of the word.'

Brainsy smiled.

'After my experience on the road to Tralee I don't believe in anything any longer. How could I? A material man, with no material faculties whatever, but endowed with a soul? That's not a man, that's a vegetable. Are we horseradishes or potatoes? Of course,' he mused, 'there were philosophers who believed, and some may even still believe, that vegetables and animals have souls.'

'God knows,' Tom conceded, 'there are times when I think the one half of me isn't much better than a potato.'

Brainsy waved a languid hand.

'Now you are postulating two souls. One rational, the other

irrational. The heresy of Photius. Condemned by the Council of Constantinople in 869.'

'But, surely,' Tom pleaded, 'my soul isn't working all the time? I mean when a pint of porter is flowing down my gullet. Or when my eye looks at you now drinking that cup of tea...'

'You are now denying the principle of unity. Condemned by the Council of Vienne in the thirteenth century. Recondemned by Pius the Ninth in 1857. It is the whole man who sees and drinks, not your boozy, bloodshot eyes or your big, thirsty mouth. Soul and body drink together. "I drink," said Aristotle, "therefore I am." '

Tom stared goitrously at his friend.

'Brainsy! I'm lost. Would you mind telling me what exactly we are talking about?'

'About a fantasy. Believed in by millions. Real to millions. I sometimes wonder,' he considered, pulling his left ear, 'whether the idea had any existence at all in Western Europe before Aristotle?'

Tom's voice rose to a squeak of desperation.

'Are you saying now that Aristotle invented my soul – if I have such a thing as a soul?'

'The origin of your soul? If you have a soul? That is very difficult. Saint Augustine suggested that it may have come out of your father's cock. *Incorporeum semen* was his elegant phrase. That was called Generationism. Others thought that God creates the soul and pops it into the embryo in, I can't remember, was it the third or the fourth month? That is Creationism. But that raises an extremely awkward problem. It means that God would have had to stain it deliberately with Original Sin beforehand. No. Tom! It's all a lot of scholastic nonsense. Man was born with a brain. Without a brain he is a beast. Or he is dead as a man. When that fellow left me that night on the road I was no more than a rabbit that somebody took by the hind legs to bash its head against a rock. I died.'

'But your doctor,' Tom cried, 'will tell you that your organs remained alive, your heart, your guts, you were fed intravenously, you breathed, you aged, your tissues went on growing.'

'As your whiskers will keep on growing in the grave. As

snakes galvanize after you cut them in two. What is it to be dead? Tom if anybody knows I should know. I went into black darkness. And there was nothing there.'

The image of Brainsy lying in black nothingness flooded such horror into Tom that he leaped up and, as if he was at a retreat, or a mission, or a revival meeting, or listening to Billy Graham, he shouted out, 'I believe! I believe in the soul! I cannot believe in a man without one!' and he banged the polished round table that the carpenter had made for his wife, with its lace doily under a little silver vase bearing its one artificial rose.

'Anyway!' he cried triumphantly. 'The simple proof of the matter is that you are here now, alive and kicking. If you died, tell me who or what is this sitting there now in front of me talking all this balderdash?'

Brainsy rose on his walking stick and took his black hat.

'I do not know, Tom. I do not know who I am. Or where I came from. Or what I am. That is something I shall have to find out. I'd better go. Whatever I do and wherever I go I seem to have a bad influence on everybody, and upset everybody.'

'Everybody?' Tom asked fearfully, following him to the door. 'Have you been talking like this to anybody else?'

'Why not? I explained it all to Angelo. I explained it all to the Bishop. Oh, yes,' he beamed, seeing Tom's eyes widen, 'they brought the Bishop to me.'

'And what did his Lordship say to you?'

'What could he say? He just kept looking at me. He mentioned Lazarus. "But, my Lord," I said, "Lazarus was not dead. If he was dead when Christ came, you must believe that he was already judged by God and either resting in what your Lordship calls heaven, or suffering in hell. Or can your eternal God upset his own eternal judgements?" That floored him. He left me without another word and I have not seen or heard from him since. Oh, by the way, Tom, I'm forgetting my manners. I never thanked you for that nice cup of tea.'

It was this cheerful mention of the cup of tea that most frightened Tom. The man had no idea at all of what lay ahead of him.

'What are they going to do to you now?' he asked, at the front door.

'Angelo tells me I'm to teach Geography. A safe subject? "What are the chief rivers of France? What's the highest mountain in the world?" Or that's what he thinks. Geography has changed completely since his day. It is everything now – anthropology, sociology, the sudy of environments, economics, human values, history, religion, science. I'm going to have a lovely time with Geography.'

He waved a hand and limped away back to the monastery.

'I'll pray for you,' Tom called after him, and slowly closed the door.

He did not see him for three weeks. One reason was that since Lent began he had gone completely off the drink, but all this so upset him that every time he neared a pub in the Main Street he had to rush past it and start counting the days to Easter Sunday. The man *was* a bad influence! Nevertheless he could not help wondering how far the story had travelled. On the Sunday before Good Friday he met Dicky Talbot as he came out from mass, and asked him for news of Regis. Dicky stared at him, laughed long and loud, and then fell silent for a full half-minute, staring at him.

'You know,' he said at last, 'Coonlahan must be one of the most extraordinary little places in the whole world. It has one street, one large church, one small convent, one monastery of microscopic proportions, four pubs, it contains about fifteen hundred people, and I'm sure every person here thinks he knows everything about everybody. And he mostly does. But as for what goes on in the convent or the presbytery, or the A.B.C., the three of them might as well all be in Siberia. I swear that at this moment there could be three nums nailed up by the ears to the back wall of the convent and nobody would know anything about them for six months. Look at you! You are teaching here, and you actually have to ask me where Regis is! For the last week he's been out in the kitchen-garden working as a lay brother.'

'You mean they wouldn't even let him teach Geography?'

'Angelo watched him doing it for a week and whipped him out of it like a shot to go downstairs teaching spelling to the kids. You know the way the kids chant their spelling after the teacher. "C.A.T. Cat. C.A.T. Cat. C.A.T. Cat." Sometimes it's about the only sound you'd hear from one end of Coonlahan to the other. Angelo went into Regis's spelling class one day and he nearly had a fit. Regis had them chanting, "D.O.G. God. D.O.G. God. D.O.G. God." '

Tom wiped his forehead. Dicky looked up and about the sky.

'Grand day, thank God!' he said. 'The first week of April. Nice time for planting spuds. If you go out into the walled garden any afternoon you'll probably find him hard at it.'

It took Tom until Thursday to overcome his dread of the encounter; then, miserably, when he knew the brothers would be out walking, he made his way to the kitchen-garden. It was a warm, sunny day. The remnant white plaster and exposed sandstone of the backs of the houses in the Main Street were islands of red sausage-meat in seas of snow. The gate twanged behind him. The lovely evocative small of manure. The tops of the new potato ridges already beginning to whiten in the sun. In one corner an old, whitehaired brother digging stolidly. Brainsy sitting on an upturned bucket apparently lost in the passing clouds. His dusty soutane was rucked up by a cincture of twine, his sleeves and his trousers' ends were turned back, heavy boots on his stockingless feet. When he heard the gate he lowered his head to see who his visitor was, waved, got up with the help of his stick and, as graciously as if he were welcoming Tom into his drawing room, indicated a grassy patch where they could lie in the sun and out of the turn of the spring wind.

Tom looked at him apprehensively. He seemed entirely at his ease. Even the furrow between his eyebrows was pale and shallow. They laid down, facing one another, each on his elbow. Tom produced cigarettes, lit for them both and it was all suddenly as cosy as if they were back in Dublin years ago, talking from bed to bed about the doings of the day, or about girls, or the gossip of the pubs, or the days when they were boys together in Cork.

'How's the old leg?' he asked.

'It works. It will never be up to much. I'll always have to use the stick.'

'And how's the old head?'

'Oh! That never stops. Around and around like a mill horse. Clop. Clop.'

'And how's all the old rest of you?'

'Fine! I get pains now and again. But when they're bad I take pills.'

'At this rate you can't be much use as a gardener, can you?'

'Paul,' nodding to the far corner, 'does all the hard work. I plant, or weed, or anything I can do on my knees. I've got very interested in cooking, too. They used to have a lay brother doing that – he was a ship's cook before he joined the Order – but they've promoted him to teaching the infants. Within a month or two I bet you they will all be eating better than they ever did in their lives. Oho! There's plenty of work in the old horse still.'

It seemed to Tom that he was being much too chipper about it all.

'And how are they treating you?'

'I rarely see them. Lay brothers can, if they want to, sit in the library, but in practice they rarely do. Paul and I live, eat and amuse ourselves in the kitchen. In there at night we are like an old farmer and his son. Reading, or listening to the radio, or playing draughts or chess – he's very good at them both. I read a lot. The County Librarian has promised to keep me well supplied in that quarter.'

'And they don't mind?'

'They don't mind anything I do any longer. I am a man who has lost his faculties. I am off my chump. They are all right. They're a dull bunch. But never forget it, Tom, there is such a thing as Christian charity. I have never in my life experienced such kindness as I have since they shunted me out here.'

Away in his corner Paul's spade rang on a stone. A swallow did a jet dive down and out of the garden. Brainsy was talking of how Paul and himself spent their day. Ten mouths for breakfast, washing up after it, making the beds, sweeping and dusting the whole place and then off down the Main Street with two big woven shopping bags.

'We're not the most popular customers.' He grinned. 'Probably because they are afraid to cheat us.'

Their shopping done, they might leave the bags behind some counter and go out the road for a stroll, but not before Paul had satisfied his one secret vice.

'He loves his bottle of stout. So, in with us by the back door to Brennan's pub, upstairs to his parlour and he has his little tipple there like a lord.'

'And you?'

'As you know, I never drink stout. And we can't afford anything else.'

'That's where the ferry boat left you, Brainsy! Guinness and godliness, it's a great combination. You can't whack it.'

'Meaning that you are back on the booze?'

'I wish I was. I'm dying for Easter Sunday to come. Four more days! My stomach thinks my throat is cut. It's very decent of them to give you money for the stout.'

'They give us no money. Poverty, Chastity and Obedience. That's the rule. But we cheat them a bit on the shopping.'

They gossiped about the town. Little gossip. About the tiniest things. Paul knew every hole and corner of the place, every man, woman and child in it. Towards the end Tom said, 'I hope you're not corrupting poor old Paul with all your wild talk. Aren't they afraid you might?'

'I can say anything I like to him. In fact, I say the most outrageous things to him. And they don't mind. He is stone deaf. He's far more likely to corrupt me. He cheats like the divil at chess. There last night when I was waiting for him to make his move I saw a mouse coming out of its hole along the floor under the wainscoting. It had an eye like a robin. I winked at it. It winked at me. I said *Quutch*! The next thing there was old Paul saying, "Checkmate!" I swear to high heavens he pocketed a pawn while I wasn't looking. We fought all night over it.'

He laughed so heartily that Tom's heart sank. What a way to pass a life! There was a long silence between them. Another swallow swooped in and out of the garden.

'They're coming back,' Brainsy said and Tom, thinking he meant the brothers, got up to go. Brainsy showed him where they were having the peas, and the cauliflowers, and the scarlet runners. Tom looked at them and did not see any of them.

When they came, at last, to the gate Brainsy held his hand in a long, hard grip and the furrow between his eyes became intense.

'Look, Brainsy!' Tom cried, holding the holding hand just as tightly. 'If you don't believe in any of this stuff why don't you for God's sake chuck it all up and clear out?'

'And where,' Brainsy asked sadly, 'would I go?'

'Come back with me to Dublin. I'll be quitting here in June. We'll start together all over again.'

'And what would I do? All I'm any good for is teaching. And they've taken that away from me. After all this hullaballoo you know well that I'd never get another job again.'

Their hands parted. He opened the rasping gate. Tom passed through it. They looked at one another through it.

'Don't worry about me, Tom. You know where I live. Come and see me anytime. I'll be all right. All I'll ever miss will be the old chat.'

He raised his hand as if in blessing, and went back to his garden. Tom watched him limping away, turned, went out to the road and shuffled down to the Main Street, where he saw a great host of swallows blowing in through one end of it and out through the other. He went into the first pub he met, and he drank there until he was drunk. It was a habit that would stick to him all his life, always sober as a judge through Lent, always as drunk as an owl on the eve of the Crucifixion. In the dark pool of his pint he saw what the swallows would see: the wide bogland, brown-yellowy, seaweedy green, and the small road driving through it, and the far mountains with their clouds, and a few clustered roofs far below with one or two specks of humans moving between them, and one upturned garden with thickly ivied walls, good for nesting, and a man lying there on his back gazing up at them.

But, O swallow, swallow, swallow! That is the only man I have ever loved. And he is dead.

Thieves

From the beginning it was Fanny Wrenne's idea. The whole gang must go up in a bunch to the cathedral for their Easter Communion. This time a real pilgrimage! It would be like walking to Jerusalem. What was more, they must go up there for first mass. Clamorously the gang danced around her.

'Six o'clock mass! We'll have to get up at four. It'll be pitch-dark. There won't be a soul abroad. We'll be all alone. We'll have all Cork to ourselves. Everybody but us snoring.' Fanny added her masterstoke. 'And after mass, do ye know what we'll do? Buy a bag of broken biscuits and be munching them all the way home.'

It was one stroke too many, as they found when they scattered, racing in all directions to beg pennies from their fathers and mothers, their uncles and their aunts, for the bag of broken biscuits.

Were they gone clean out of their little heads? Were they mad? Kids of nine and ten walking halfway across Cork in the dark of an April morning? To a cathedral that was miles away? Supposing it was raining! And what about if they lost their way? Whose idea was this anyway? Fanny Wrenne's. That kid was ever and always creating trouble.

In the end only two of them met at the bridge that morning. Fanny, because she always got her way, because her mother was dead, and her father away at sea, and she an only child, and her old Aunt Kate was a softie. And Dolly Myles, because her father neither knew nor cared what any one of his eleven children did, and because her mother knew that Fanny Wrenne could be relied on to look after anybody anywhere – a dark, sturdy, bosomy, bottomy boss of a robin who would spend her life bullying every other little bird in the garden away from the crumbs that God meant for all. As for poor Dolly, she was born to be bossed. Eyes as blue and as blank as a doll's, her hair as fair, her cheeks as pink, and her adenoidal lips hanging from her nose in such a sweet little triangle that old gentlemen were always stopping her in the street to pat her curly poll.

They approached one another across the bridge like two dwarf ghosts. Upriver all they could see was the bright window of the waterworks shining down on the smooth curve of its lasher. All they could hear was the faint hum of turbines, and even that came and went on the morning wind. Downriver they saw nothing at all but the daffodil of the first gaslamp, and, far away, one vast cloud reflecting the night glow of the city. Overhead the sky was as black and blue as a mackerel.

Fanny had brought her Aunt Kate's best umbrella. It was red, it bore a red tassel, its handle was a scarlet bird's beak with a glassy eye embedded on each side of its head. She brought it because Dolly had told her the night before that her mother had a good friend named Mrs Levey who lived near the cathedral in a place called Flatfoot Lane. Fanny immediately said they would call on Mrs Levey on the way to mass, and give her the umbrella as an Easter present. In return she would be certain to give them a penny each as an Easter present, and with the two pennies they would buy the broken biscuits on the way home.

The gaslamps were no better than candles. Between their wavering scraps of light they could not so much see the footpath as feel for it with their feet. They walked hand in hand. They did not speak at all. They met nobody. They heard nothing but their own footsteps. Every house was as dark as a prison wall. Then, suddenly in one house they saw a lighted upstairs window. It made them speak. Who could be awake at this hour? Somebody sick? Somebody dying? Staring up at it, Dolly put her arm around Fanny's waist and Fanny clutched the umbrella to her like a baby. Could it be a robber? They hurried on fearfully. Soon they began to dawdle. Once, they looked back towards the west and were glad to see a star floating behind a black cloud. Ahead of them the sky was paling and opening but there was no star to be seen there at all. They sat on a low wall to rest and began to argue about how many broken biscuits you could get for tuppence. They started off again, still arguing, took two wrong turnings and were only halfway up the long sloping street to the cathedral when Shandon Tower exploded into three-quarters chime so close to them that Dolly let out a squeak of fright. *Do. So. La. Re . . . Re. La . . .*

'It's all right,' Fanny soothed. 'We've lots of time. So long as you know where Ma Levey's house is. And,' threateningly, 'I hope to God you do!'

Dolly looked down a dark laneway to their right. 'I know it's up here somewhere.' She looked across the street at the maw of another alley. 'Or could it be that way?' Blankly she looked back down the hill. 'Or did we come too far?' With a wild rush of assurance she chose the first laneway, and in a second, they were swallowed into its black gullet, running around and around in a whale's belly, through dusky gullies and dark guts, thin defiles and narrow, whirling shafts, dead-end lanes and turn-back cross trenches, all nameless and all smelly, only to find themselves ejected exactly where they began just as a soft sprinkle of April rain began to fall. Seeing that Fanny was about to shout, Dolly got her shout in first. 'It must be the other way!' Again they were blown about like two bits of white paper through more revolving lanes, dykes, alleyways and passages, lined with more dwarfs' houses and whitewashed cabins, some thatched, some slated, each with its holland blind drawn down tightly, all of them so close together that a woman could, without moving her body, have stretched her hand from her own door to her neighbour's for the loan of a sup of milk or to return yesterday's newspaper. In every one of those cobbled lanes there was a runnel, already trickling with rainwater. There was barely room for it between the lines of cabins. There was no room at all for a footpath. They circled and descended, climbed and came down again, twisted and turned until a vast giant suddenly soared up above them with a great black clock face that silently said five minutes to six. At the sight of Shandon Tower where she least expected to meet it, Dolly burst into tears and Fanny, in a rage, pointed the bayonet of her umbrella at her belly.

'The house!' she screamed. 'Or I'll spit you up against that wall.'

'But,' Dolly wailed, 'I was only up here once. And I was with me mudder. And it was two years ago. And I was only seven.'

'Find that house!'

'If we could only find Flatfoot Lane, I know I'd know the house.'

'How would you know it? This place is maggoty with houses.'

'It have a white card in the window with Mrs Levey's name on it.'

'March!'

Dolly snuffled and pleaded.

'Why can't we keep the umbrella. It's not your umbrella. You stole it. And if it goes on raining we'll be drownded.'

At this sign of grace the sky ceased to weep, but the devil smiled. By magic there appeared, just above their heads, a bright red board that said FLATFOOT LANE. Here there were real houses, small but two-storied, in red brick, with two windows above and one window and a door below. More cobbles, no pavement, another gurgling refuse-runnel and at the end of it a blank wall. They raced up one side of it and down the other, and, at last, there, between looped lace curtains, was the white card. It said in black print MIRIAM LEVEY. Beneath the name it said LOANS. On its green door there was a brassy knocker shaped like an amputated hand. Fanny seized it, sent a rattle of gunfire echoing up and down the lane, and looked at the upstairs window expectantly. Nobody stirred. She looked across the lane and could just see the tiptop of the clock tower, a tiny green dome carrying a big golden salmon, its weather-vane gleaming in the risen sun and stirring faintly in the morning wind. Still, no sound, not a breath, not a thing stirring except when a white cat flowed along the base of the enclosing wall and leaped over it like a wave.

'Maybe,' Dolly said hopefully, 'she's dead?'

Fanny sent another dozen rounds of riflefire up and down the lane. They heard the upper window squeak open, saw ten bony fingers slide over the windowsill and Mrs Levey's tiny witch's face, yawning up at the sky from underneath a cellophane bag full of white hair in blue curlers. She yawned for so long that they thought she would never close her gummy mouth again. When she had finished her yawning she peered sleepily around the lane, said, 'Pusspuss! Pusspuss!' and finally looked down at the two white children. Fanny cheerfully waved the red umbrella at her.

'Good morning, Mrs Levey. Me Aunt Kate sent us up to you with this gorgeous umbrella for a present for Easter.'

'Your Aunt who?' she asked, and the word 'who' turned into another prolonged yawn. She peered down at the pair of them, shook her head, said, 'I'm afraid, child, I don't know no aunts at all. But, anyway, whoever she is...' Another yawn. 'Or whatever it is, leave it there on the windowsill and I'll get it when I wake up,' and withdrew, and the window banged.

Fanny gazed reproachfully at Dolly, who, knowing what was coming, lifted her blonde eyebrows, put her hand on her hip and, self-dissociatingly, began to examine the architecture of every house along the opposite side of the lane.

'So that,' Fanny said scornfully, 'is your ma's lovely friend?'

'That,' Dolly piped, without as much as a backward glance, 'is your aunt's lovely umbrella.'

'A mangy ould maggoty ould moneylender.'

'Our credit was always good,' Dolly said loftily.

Fanny looked imploringly at the sky. The great gong saved her, booming the full hour, and all over the valley lesser bells softly announcing the angelus.

'We'll be late,' she shouted, threw the scarlet object on the windowsill and they scurried off back to the open street of the hill.

In the valley spires and chimneys were now tipped by the sun. Between these hill-houses the only sign that the night was going was a man who raced before them, lamplighter by night, lampquencher in the morning, plucking the head off every daffodil as he ran.

They hastened into the cathedral, panting. It blazed with lights, candles and white chrysanthemums. Not more than a couple of dozen worshippers. The priest, robed in the violet of Lent, was standing with his back to the altar, reading from a book the gospel story of the woman caught in adultery. ('What does that mean?' Dolly whispered, and Fanny whispered, 'Watering the milk.') Afterwards, Dolly said the bit she liked was where Jesus said to her, 'Run along with you, now, but don't do that any more,' but Fanny said the bit she liked was where Jesus kept stooping to the ground, writing some strange words whose meaning, the priest said, nobody will understand to the end of time. After that the sermon began and it went on so long that their heads began to nod, and they had to nudge and kick at one another to wake up, then making shocked faces and giggling, or, for fun, pretending to yawn like Ma Levey in the window. At last the priest ended his sermon, throwing his white wings open to say, 'Three weeks after He forgave that unfortunate woman they murdered Him, calling Him a criminal, but three weeks from now He will rise again as, in a few minutes, He will appear amongst us in the shape of a white circle, shining and immortal. Leave ye all kneel down now and prepare to welcome Him as He descends from heaven.'

The time for communion came. Side by side, their hands joined like the angels in holy pictures, their eyes modestly cast down, they walked slowly to and from the altar rails, as Sister Angelina at school had taught them to do. Slowly, the mass ended. There were more public prayers after it, and then they were standing in the porch, the city below them, the morning about them, the gaslamps all quenched, the pavements dancing with rain. A postman's black cape shone. A milkman, hooped against the wind and rain, raced from his cart to pour milk into a saucer-covered jug on a doorstep, leaped back into his chariot and drove off with his whip sailing behind him like a flag.

'What about the umbrella?' Dolly said accusingly, and, because of the rain, longingly.

'Why don't we take it back?' Fanny cried, and hand in hand they galloped down the hill and back into Flatfoot Lane. The trickle of rainwater still ran whispering down the central runnel. In an upstairs window an old man, slowly and dexterously shaving one side of his face before a small square mirror balanced on top of the window sash, suspended his razor to watch them gallop through the rain, halt before the white card and stare at the empty windowsill. Fanny rattled the hand on the green door and peered upward, the rain pouring down her face. The upper window squeaked open and Mrs Levey looked down.

'Oh, Law!' she said mildly. 'Is it ye again?'

'We made an awful mistake, Mrs Levey, we brought you the wrong umbrella, would yeh ever throw it down to us and we'll bring yeh the right one tomorrow morning at exactly the same time.'

The old face withdrew. After a moment the red object came sailing out through the window over their heads, plonked on the wet cobbles and the window banged shut.

The umbrella was as old as sin. It bulged like a carrot. It was tied by a bit of string. It had a black bamboo handle. The old man in the opposite window, one half of his face red, the other half white, hailed them.

'Use it, girls,' he shouted. 'That's rain! Oho!' he assured them, waving his frothy razor, 'I see it all. Ye gave her yeer lovely new umbrella and she throws ye back her leavings. Just like her!' he roared at the top of his voice across the lane. 'The bloody ould Jew' and returned to his tender shaving.

Fanny picked up the carroty umbrella, untied the bit of string, shot the gamp open above her head and from it there showered scores and scores of pieces of paper that the wind at once sent blowing wildly all over the cobbles. The old man, watching, let out a roar of delight that drowned the last strokes of the seventh hour. Others who must also have been watching from behind their curtains, slammed up their windows, leaned out, cheered and bawled and pointed joyfully to one another.

In astonishment the two children stared around them at what they had done. Up and down the lane, more and more doors opened and more people pointed, laughing and shouting in chorus, 'Levey the thievey, the dirty ould sheeny, rob ye and leave ye!' Overhead the old woman's window opened. She leaned out, screamed like a peacock, vanished and the next minute shot past them, a man's overcoat over her head and her nightdress like a shawl, racing hither and thither barefooted over the wet cobbles after her dockets. As she raced and stooped and picked, the whole lane kept bawling their horrid chorus at her. Only once did she pause and that was to shake her skinny fist at them. Then, suddenly, there was total silence. She had collapsed on her hunkers in the middle of the lane, her withered arms raised to the pouring sky, her mouth wide open, pleading to it in some strange language. As suddenly she fell silent, her head and her hands sunk into her lap. Slowly, a handsome young man came forward in his bare feet to lift her. After him an old woman came, and then another, and another, began to pick up the bits of paper, until one by one all the watchers were silently gathering up her dockets and pressing them into her crumpled hands. The two children ran.

Not until they halted at the river did Fanny notice that the rotten scarlet thing had accompanied them. She threw it over the quay wall, where, by stretching up on their toes to look, they could see it floating slowly away on the outgoing tide.

'Down the river!' Fanny hooted.

'Under every bridge,' Dolly giggled.

'Out to sea!' Fanny shouted.

Laughing they turned for home, stamping into the puddles of the rain, screaming with delight as they kicked arcs of water at one another. They lifted their wide-open mouths to the trees along the Mall trying to catch the falling drops. When they came to the iron railings opposite their own parish church of Saint Vincent they swung on them like two white wheels to see the rain falling up, and the church spires pointing down, the whole world standing on its head. By the time they came to their own bridge the rain had petered out, the sky was white and blue, the river water was smooth, the fields beyond it were empty and wet.

'Anyway,' Fanny said, 'even if we got the pennies we couldn't have bought broken biscuits. Not a shop open.'

They saw a light in a cottage, and a light in a villa on the side of the hill, and one window in a house beside the river was reflected longingly in the pure water. Dolly cocked her head.

'Listen!' she said.

They listened. Far away, around the bend of the road, from maybe half a mile away they could barely hear it. It would be lighted, and empty. The first tram.

Of Sanctity and Whiskey

As Luke Regan drove down to Saint Killian's for the first sitting he kept shifting around the fading cards of his schoolboy's memories of the place and wishing the press had never got on to this thing. It was a pleasant idea, of course, and he could understand the columnists playing it up – but the stupid things they wrote about it! 'Former pupil returns to his old school to paint his old teacher.... This portrait of a distinguished Headmaster by a distinguished Academician is certain to reflect two sensibilities in perfect rapport with one another.... This new portrait by Mr Luke Regan, R.H.A., of Brother Hilary Harty, the retired Head of Saint Killian's College, should record not one journey but two journeys from youth to maturity....' He had already confided to his boozing friends that he found the whole bloody thing extremely embarrassing; not least because he could see that they thought he was just boasting about it. He had only been in that school for three years, between the ages of twelve and fifteen. It was forty years ago. He had not the slightest recollection of this Brother Hilary Harty, and he felt sure that the old man could not possibly remember him.

Hilary Harty? He hoped he was not that old snob they used to call Dikey, a fellow with a face like a coffin and eyes like a dead hen. Could he be Flossy, who used to collect jokes in a notebook as fat as a Bible: a head and a face like a turnip; purple, orange and green – that would be a nice palette to have to work with! Without affection he remembered Popeyes, always blinking at you like the flicker of a motorcar that the driver had forgotten to turn off. But his name was Hurley. Now, little Regis would be a marvellous subject – a pink-and-white angel face with a fierce furrow between the eyebrows. That would be a challenging puss – if you were lucky enough, and had time enough to get him talking about himself. But Hilary? The name rang no chime, sweet, cracked or otherwise. 'Two sensibilities in perfect rapport with one another . . .' Had none of these fellows ever been to school themselves? Didn't they know well that no boy ever knows anything human at all about his teachers? Men dressed in black soutanes and bony collars, with names like ships, or stars, or horses – Hyperion, Aquarius, Berengarius, Arkel – floating into your classroom every morning, saying, 'Irregular verbs today!' or 'Did we polish off Queen Anne yet?' and if you didn't know your stuff, giving you three on each hand with the leather strap stuck in their black belts like a policeman's truncheon. All any boy ever wants from any teacher is that he might give you a bit of a chance now and again; understand, or know, or guess that the real reason you did not know your history, or your maths, was not because you lost the book, or had a headache, or broke your pen but because you saw Molly Ryan yesterday with high leather boots halfway up her fat legs and you simply had to dodge out that night to be gassing with her under the gaslamp by the back gate, watching her swinging her pigtails and admiring her toes just to provoke you. Little Regis would have understood; he was the only one of them who understood anything. He would give you a good clout on the ear, look at you hard and say, 'I'll give you this one chance, Master Regan, but if you ever do it again I'll have the hide off you.' And you loved him for it. But the rest of them? Human? The shock he got the day he saw Popeyes laughing with a woman in the Main Street! (Jesus! I must have been a right little prig in those days!) Not to mention the evening he saw Monsieur Joffre, the French teacher, coming out of a pub wiping the froth off his Clemenceau moustache. And by the same token not a drop must pass his lips while he was doing this portrait. Not with two hundred quid from the Past Pupils' Union depending on it. Anyway, he had been off the booze for four months now. 'Drop it, Luke!' – his doctor's last words. 'Or it will drop you into a nice, deep, oblong hole up in Glasnevin. Ninety per cent of your bloodstream is pure alcohol, and you know where that finally lodges?' – and he had tapped his forehead. 'D.T.'s. Epilepsy, Neuritis, Insanity, God knows what!' The memory of it frightened him so much that when he was passing through Kilcrea he halted for one last, one absolutely last quick one before he arrived. And, just for precaution's sake, he packed a bottle of Paddy Flaherty in his hold-all in case he got a cold, or needed a little nightcap to send him to sleep after a day's revving-up at the easel.

The only change he could see, guess, presume or infer in Coonlahan was the rows of cars parked on each side of the Main Street. Surely, in his time, there were only a few horse-drawn carts or donkey-butts? Chromium everywhere now and neon strips. The street's surface, asphalted, recalled mud and cowdung on market days. With relief he saw a neat-looking hotel called The Shamrock, and booked himself in there.

'How long, Mr Regan?' the freshfaced young woman said with a welcoming smile.

'How did you know my name?'

'Ah, sure the whole town knows about the painting.'

He winced.

'Four nights, please.'

'Only four?'

He winced again. In the Academy his colleagues called him Luca Fa Presto, after a certain Neapolitan painter who could finish any picture in twenty-four hours.

'It's a small portrait. Head and shoulders.'

Did she think he was going to live in the monastery? All the same he felt a bit ashamed that he was not. There were painters who would have done it, toiling to reveal the habits of a lifetime in a face. Degas must have done it before he began his *Uncle and Niece*. Manet must have known every damned thing about those three people he imprisoned behind the green railing of *The Balcony*. Courbet had put a whole countryside into those three men in *Bonjour, Monsieur Courbet*. Still, when he had driven out of the town and come to the big iron gateway, with SAINT KILLIAN'S COLLEGE half-mooned across it in gilded lettering, and saw the half-mile of avenue leading straight as a ruler up to the barrack-bare front of the college, grim as a tombstone against the sinking sun, he wondered whether Degas, or Monet, or Courbet, or Rembrandt, or Holbein or any of them would have wanted to soak himself in so dreary a joint as this either in the name of literal truth or ideal beauty. Wishing that he had had another drink in The Shamrock before facing this Brother Hilary Harty, he rang the bell.

A cheerful little lay brother, spry and bright as a monkey, showed him into the front parlour where, with painful clarity, he remembered the evening his mother had handed him over there to a matron named Miss Wall and with a face like one. The literal truth of the room leaped to the eye: linoleum on the floor, horsehair chairs, a round table glistering with a mock walnut veneer, a gas-fire unlit. As for ideal beauty: pictures in monochrome, *The Agony in the Garden*, the ghostly face of Christ on the pious fraud called *The Veil of Veronica*, somebody's *Annunciation*, and was that Breughel's *Tower of Babel* lifting the clouds? The Past Pupils' Union was going to make him earn every penny of this two hundred quid. The door was hurled open, a powerful-bodied old brother strode in, jolly-faced and beaming, and on the spot the setting sun hit his face and everything became joyous and splendid and okay.

'Luke Regan!' he all but shouted. 'After all these years!'

And the two of them were laughing and shaking one another's hands as energetically and boisterously as only two men can do who do not know one another from Adam. But what a head! Ripe for marble! For marble and porphyry! Nose rubicund, eyes blue as gentians and an astonishingly protruding lower lip, the sure sign of a born talker. Hair white, thin on top but curling like the last of the harpers around his neck. Manet be blowed! Poor old Rembrandt! It was going to be the portrait of his life. Green curtain behind, ochre streaks of sunlight, buckets of carmine, lumps of it laid on with bold hard brushstrokes – half-inch brushes at that. Energy, strength, tenderness, humour! No more of that blasted pink toothpaste enamel that he had been floating all over the gobs of endless company directors for the last ten years. Not, to be fair, to flatter them but to flatter their stupid wives. 'Oh, Mister Regan, I think Eddie is much younger than you are making him out to be!' Or 'D'ye think, Mister Regan, you could make the tie a bit smoother like? The way you have it makes him look old and careless like.' Meaning, 'My God, man, do you want people to think *I'm* that old?'

'Brother Hilary, when do you think we can begin?'

He was so excited that when he got back to The Shamrock he had to go into the bar for a large one to calm his nerves. In its gold pool he saw the title on the catalogue of the Academy, where the portrait would be shown publicly for the first time. *The Old Dominie*. By Luke Regan, R.H.A. Not for Sale. Or what about *The Good Shepherd*? Or maybe, *Ex Cathedra*. Or *Post Multos Annos*? With a neat gold tab at the bottom of the frame saying, *Gladly wolde he lerne and gladly teche*. Tactile values? His fingers involuntarily began to mould the face. The man sitting beside him said, 'Hello, Mister Regan.' He sighed and did not deny it.

'My name is Halligan. Harry Halligan. We all knew you were coming. All Ireland knows about the painting. You have a great character there in old Leatherlip.'

'Leatherlip?'

Far away a bell chimed harshly, curtains parted on a small red light at the end of a mile-long corridor.

'Don't you remember? Or didn't ye call him that in your day?'

'How extraordinary! We did call one fellow that. But, surely, not *this* man?'

'*Tempus fugit*. It's twenty-five years since I was at Saint Killian's. He was slim then, bushy black hair, eyes like a razor blade. You knew him in his thirties. And you really can't remember him?'

'He will come back to me. I'll quarry him out. That's how a painter works, working in and in, burrowing, excavating. It's like archaeology, you don't know what you are looking for until you find it. Sooner or later the face speaks.'

Halligan half-turned to the woman on his left: a bosomy, high-coloured little blonde. Horsey type.

'Let me introduce you to my wife. Valerie, this is Luke Regan the famous painter.'

She gave a cool hand and a cooler 'Howdyedo?' in a loud Anglo-Irish voice. No smile. Regan could feel the antagonism in her, and wondered at it. They had two more quick ones together before Mrs Halligan abruptly hauled her husband off with her. Regan took a last one by himself for the road to sleep.

Because of the light he decided to use the front parlour for a studio. It had three tall windows facing north. He could come and go without bother. By two o'clock, when his man would be free and the light good for two hours or so, he had managed to get a throne fixed up, a green curtain hung for background, his easel and work table ready and the inflatable lay figure that he always travelled with (one of his neatest Fa Presto tricks) draped with a black soutane that he would be working on every morning.

'I can't believe, Brother Hilary,' he laughed, as his charcoal lightly and rapidly sketched in the outline, 'that you are really seventy-five. You look about fifty.'

He always talked while he worked to keep his subject from stiffening or sagging.

'Aha!' the old boy laughed triumphantly. 'Mixing with youth all my life, that's what does it. That,' finger magisterially aloft, 'and the regular life. A dull life I suppose, not like you, out in the world, travelling, meeting interesting people, doing interesting things. But I have had my compensations. No worries, no regrets, no tensions. The rut, Luke. The beaten path. The ascetic discipline. Simple food. Good country air. Constant exercise. No excesses of any kind. You wouldn't grow fat on my kind of life, my boy. But that's what turns every monk into a man.'

When he came to the mouth he stared long and hard at the protruding lower lip. Again that far-off bell. Leatherlip? The eyes were curiously small but they gave out sparks when he talked. He would have given anything for an early photograph of the softer eyes of the boy buried behind those sharp orbs. He saw that the nose was red because it was veined all over. If this were a company director he would have said at once, 'Chronic alcoholic.' He knew rosacea when he saw it. Chiefly in elderly women. The wages of virtue. Chronic tea-drinkers. Gastritis. Monastery food. Probably an ulcer. Teeth browning from age and pipe-smoking. There would be black centres on the tip of every one of them. He frowned again at the big lip. A hard mouth in a jolly face. Now, what in hell did that portend? Silence. A good subject – he held the pose patiently.

'The rut?' he murmured, looking up, looking down. 'The

beaten path? "The path of the just is as the shining light that shineth more and more unto the perfect day." '

'I'm glad to see that you read your Bible, Luke.'

'Now and again, Brother. A little to the left, Brother. Thank you, Brother.'

The light on the lip threw an interesting shadow. The nose became gory.

'Ah, yes!' concentrating on the jutting lip. 'Now and again ... "Return, return O Shulamite. Thy belly is like a heap of wheat set about with lilies ... Thy neck is as a tower of ivory ... Many waters cannot quench love, neither can the floods drown it." '

He glanced up. The eyes were blazing, the whole expression of the face had changed, the brows gathered down fiercely, the cheeks as scarlet as the nose. His charcoal flew, dragging down the eyebrows. That revealing wet light on the lip, thrust out a whole inch – that, above all, *that* he must keep.

'I think, Mister Regan, I think, Luke, it might have been better if you had concentrated on the New Testament.'

By a forty-year-old reflex he glanced at the black belt around the belly to see if he still carried the strap. No time for that now. Now? Memory was now!

'Now, Brother, I begin painting.'

As he mixed his colours he cooled, a sign that he was in tip-top form. He knew they called him Luca Fa Presto. Bloody fools! You boil at the inspiration. You go cold as ice in the execution.

'You're dead right, Brother,' he said soapily. 'The new Covenant. There is the true wisdom. I learned that here in Saint Killy's.' (Funny how the old slang name came back to him. It was all creeping back to him.) 'I often think, Brother, of those wonderful words of Saint Matthew. "Behold the birds of the air ... They sow not, neither do they reap ... Consider the lilies of the fields ... Even Solomon in all his glory was not arrayed like one of these." '

To his relief the mollified voice quoted back to him.

' "Behold, a greater than Solomon is here." '

He looked up at the veined nose. The tuning fork for a study in *rouge et noir*. He touched the canvas with carmine.

'Oh, a beautiful saying, Brother! A darlint saying, Brother. And so wise, Brother. So very wise.'

Not too red now, for Christ's sake. No wife, but the Past Pupils' Union would have to be pleased. And, after all, two hundred johnnyogoblins in this job! A long silence.

'And there's another fine phrase. Muscular Christianity. A Jew invented that. Disraeli. A great man in lots of ways.'

'A Jew?' said the voice coldly.

'By the way, Brother,' he said hurriedly. 'Talking of muscle. When I was here in twenty-six, Brother, the Gaelic Football team was going great guns. How is it doing these happy days?'

The old man beamed and told him. The rest of the sitting went as smooth as milk. The only other little lurch came when he looked out at the sky, threw down his brushes and said that the light was going.

'Can I see what you have done so far, Luke?'

He handled it with expert joviality.

'We never do, Brother, not until we've polished off the victim.'

They parted in laughter and with warm handshakes. He took the key of the parlour with him; he would be working on the lay figure in the morning.

Halligan was waiting for him in the bar; alone this time. Seeing that his glass was at low tide, Regan invited him to freshen it up.

'I won't say no. How's the masterpiece doing?'

A stocky man. Heavy hands, but they could be a craftsman's. A fawn waistcoat with brass buttons. Ruddy cheeks. A gentleman farmer? A fisherman? Not a doctor – no doctor would dare drink at a public bar in a small town like this. The wife had had the smell of money.

'He's coming back to me slowly. Another sitting and I'll have him smoked out.'

'What,' eagerly, 'are you finding?'

Regan eye-cornered him. This fellow might be a member of the Past Pupils' Union.

'A splendid character. I was just wondering did he ever teach me history?'

'Were you a senior?'

'I was only what we used to call a gyb. A Good Young Boy. I came here when I was twelve. Straight from the nuns. Our Ladies of the Holy Bower. You wouldn't think it now to look at me, but I used to be their little angel. Curly hair. They used to make me sing solo at Benediction. In a lacy surplice, purple soutane, red tie. They spoiled me. It was only by the blessing of God I didn't turn into a queer. I may tell you the change from there to here was pretty tough. I only stayed three years.'

'No, you wouldn't have had him. And,' surveying him humorously, 'you may have been a little angel, Mister Regan, but you've put on a bit of weight since then. Thirteen and a half stone? He only taught the seniors, and after he became Headmaster he had no fixed classes at all. Anyway, his particular obsession was English Grammar. He was dotty about it. He was a bit of a megalomaniac, really. Couldn't give it up. Even after he became Head he used to rove around the school from class to class leathering it into us. Of course he's retired now, but I'm told he still does it. Did he never come into your classroom to wallop *I seen* out of you and *I saw* into you?'

Halligan laughed as if in happy memory of the walloping, and, on the spot, Regan had his man whole and entire. The terror of his very first day at Saint Killy's often repeated, seeing the lean black ghost come floating in. Like a starved wolf. One hand waving the leather strap behind his back like a black tail. The rasping voice. 'What is a relative clause? What is an adverbial clause? Decline the verb *see* in the past tense. No, it is not! Hold out your hand. Take that. And that. And that.' And, always, the one thing all boys loathe in teachers, as sarcastic as acid. Oh, a proper bastard!

'Do I take it, Mister Halligan, that you didn't particularly like it at Saint Killy's?'

'I got on there all right. I was good at games. And Leatherlip was mad on games. "The Irish," he was always telling us, "are famous all over the world as sportsmen. Strong men." It was he started boxing at Saint Killy's. He used to knock the hell out of me in the ring. I got so mad at him one day that I deliberately gave him one right under the belt. And I could hit hard at that time. When he got his wind back he nearly murdered me. He was the only fly in the ointment.' He leaned over and whispered: 'I often thought afterwards that he was the only wasp in the ointment.' He glanced quickly around the bar and said in a loud voice, 'Mind you, Brother Hilary is a great organizer. He built up a great school here. We are all very proud of Saint Killian's in this town.'

('Fuck *you*!' Regan thought.)

'And most justifiably so, Mister Halligan. By the way are you a member of the Past Pupils' Union?'

Halligan smiled crookedly. His voice fell.

'I didn't tell you I'm the local vet. I look after the Jersey herd up there.' He beckoned to the barmaid. 'The same again, Miss Noble.'

'Family?' Regan asked.

'Three boys.'

'They at school here?'

Halligan shuffled his glass a bit.

'Not exactly. You see . . . Well, the fact is Valerie is a Protestant. We met at the hunt. Actually, she's a niece of Lord Boyne's.' (A good connection for a vet, Regan thought.) 'Before I married her I knew I'd have to do something to smooth the way for her. For myself, of course, I didn't give a damn. To hell with them. But for poor little Valerie . . . You live up in Dublin, you can do what you like there, you don't understand what it's like in small places like this. But,' he winked, 'there's always ways and means. Two months before I got married, do you know what I did?' He nudged and again winked. 'I joined the local Knights of Columbanus. And, by God, it worked. Though I'll never forget the first time I went to the Club after the wedding. The Grand Knight got up and he says, "Since our last meeting I suppose you all know that one of our brothers got married." Christ Almighty, I thought, here it comes! He's going to give me hell for marrying a Protestant. I'm going to be ruined for life in this place. Far from it! He complimented me most warmly. I drove home that night singing like a bird. I knew I'd done one of the smartest things in my life. After a year I dropped them. But when it came to where we'd send the boys to school, Valerie and myself had one hell of a fight. I said we simply had to send them to Saint Killy's. We started with the oldest boy. The very first day he came home from school with his two hands red as pulp from Leatherlip's strap. After that Valerie put her foot down. We came to a sensible compromise. We sent them all to school in England. One of the finest Catholic schools in the world. Nobody could object to that.'

'Very shrewd. Very wise move. And after that, no opposition? Miss Noble, fill 'em up again."

'Not half! The day I whipped Tommy out of school Leatherlip wrote me a stinker. He went all around town saying I was a snob, and a lah-di-dah, and an Anglicized Irishman, and a toady, and God knows what else. Just to show you – it wasn't until he retired that I got the job of looking after the college herd.'

Regan laughed.

'Elephants never forget.'

'It's no joke,' Halligan whispered solemnly. 'Don't delude yourself. That man never forgets anything. Or anybody.'

'I wonder,' Regan said uncomfortably.

Just then Valerie Halligan came in. He noted that after one quick one she hauled her husband away. From her manner it was plain that she did not approve of his latest drinking companion. This time Regan did not wonder why.

Not that he had ever been much leathered by anybody at Saint Killy's, and never once by Leatherlip. On the contrary, he had often wished he would leather him after the day he called him out of the class and sat him on his knee, and said to the rest of them after he had leathered them all, 'Look at this clever little boy. He knows what a dependent clause is. And he's only twelve, and straight from the nuns, as small and fresh and rosy as a cherry. Why don't you slobs know it as well as he does?' His nickname became Cherry. They called him Leatherlip's Lapdog, or Leatherlip's Pet. They used to corner him and say things like, 'Cherry, if *he* comes in today for more frigging grammar your job is to suck up to him. Get him into a good humour or he'll leather us and we'll puck the hell outa you.' He used to try, but it was always the same, 'See this bright little boy!' And, after school, they would shove him, and taunt him and puck him. Once he deliberately tried to get leathered by failing to write out six sentences the night before on *shall* and *will*. The strap was swished, the brows came down, a grey spittle appeared at each corner of the big lip. Terror shook his bones.

' "I *will* go there tomorrow." Is that correct?'

'No, Brother. Plain future statements in the first person must always have *shall*.'

' "We would not win a single match with a team like that." Is that correct?'

'No, Brother. Plain conditional statements in the first person must have *should*.'

'Come here to me, boy. Now, listen to that bright little boy, straight from the nuns . . .'

For three years he had suffered hell from the benign approbation of that accursed old fathead.

'Miss Noble, the same again. No, make it a double this time.'

He went to bed plastered.

'Well, Brother Hilary, I hear nothing all over the town but people singing your praises. You've made a great job of this college. The doyen of Saint Killian's.' The old monk beamed softly.

'Ah, well, Luke, I've done my humble best. But, mind you,' rather less softly, 'I had to fight all the way.' Far from softly: 'Opposition. I had to keep my hand on my dagger every moment of the day.'

'Aha, but you fought well, Brother. You fought the good fight, Brother. "To give and not to count the cost, to fight and not to heed the wounds." '

'Who said that?' – suspiciously.

The lip out again with the lovely wet light on it. Porcine. Sensual. Lickerish. Loose. Deboshed by pride and righteousness. Daringly he slapped on a fleck of viridian. And, by God, it was just right. He kept him waiting for the answer.

'Saint Ignatius Loyola said that. A great body of men, the Jesuits.'

The two eyes cold. Turquoise? No! Pine-needle blue? Hell's bells, snow and ice are the one thing no Irish painter can ever get right. Nor the British. Nor the Italians. You have to live with the stuff like the Dutch and the Scans. The gore of the cheeks would have to bring it out. Cherry? Damn you, I'll give you cherry. No ablution here. Warts and all. Maxillae of an anthropomorph. Ears of a bat. That time he had to sit on his lap in class! The hair stuck out of his ears.

'Have you ever had any Protestants in Saint Killy's, Brother?'

The little finger dug into a hairy ear and wagged there twenty times.

'I don't approve of mixed marriages and I don't approve of mixed schooling. Protestants haven't our morality, Luke. The morality of every Protestant I ever met was written into his chequebook. They are completely devoid of our mystical sense of the otherworld. Not like you and me. I don't like Protestants. You mentioned some Jew yesterday. I'll be frank with you, Luke. I don't like Jews either.'

'Oh, you're on to something there, Brother. A cunning bloody race. Very able, though. I was talking about Disraeli.' He seized his palette knife for the coarse, oily skin of the cheeks. 'Do you remember what he said the time Dan O'Connell taunted him with being a Jew. "Yes, I *am* a Jew, and when ancestors of the right honourable gentleman were brutal savages in an unknown land, mine were priests in the temple of Solomon." '

The old warhorse out on grass. Teeth bared. Sepia? Burnt siena?

'For Heaven's sake, Luke! I do wish you'd stop talking about Solomon!'

'All the same, Jesus was a Jew.'

'One of the mysteries of the world!'

'And he chose the Jews.' Laughing delightedly at the furious face on his canvas he quoted. 'How odd / That God / Should choose / The Jews." '

In laughter the ritual answer pealed from the throne.

' "Oh no, not odd. / They hoped to God / some day / He'd pay." '

They both cackled.

'Ah, Brother, you understand it all!'

'We understand one another, Luke. Two comrades in Christ!'

He worked on. From the distant playing fields young voices cheered. A long silence. When he looked up he saw a profile.

The old man was gazing at the moony face of Christ looming through the Veil of Veronica.

'Do you know Greek, Luke? A pity! There is a wonderful Greek word. *Archiropito*. It is the perfect word for that image of Christ. Painted by no human hand. Painted by the angels. The day I became Headmaster I bought three dozen copies of that angelic image. I put one in every classroom. I gave one to every brother to hang over his bed.'

He sighed. Regan looked at the fraud. Then he looked at his portrait. Never had he felt such a sense of power, energy, truth to life. The light was fading. 'Tomorrow is Sunday. I might do a little work on the background. Then on Monday we'll have the last sitting.'

'And then,' as eagerly as a boy, 'I can see it?'

A laggard nod. As they parted the old man put his arm around his shoulder.

'My dear friend!' He sighed affectionately. 'Take care of yourself, Luke,' who gave one backward glance at his easel; the face was virtually finished, the body half finished, the soul naked. Areas of bare canvas at the edges surrounded it all like a ragged veil.

That evening the Halligans came together, had one quick one and left, promising to call on Sunday afternoon and go out to the college for a secret look at the unfinished masterpiece. He stayed on alone. The Saturday night crowd was dense. He felt he was drinking with half the town. He was the last to leave the bar, pushed out, blind drunk, by the barman and old Noble. He took a bottle of whiskey to bed with him. He woke late. The angelus was slowly tolling and under his window hollow feet were echoing along the pavement to last mass. He drank some more and slept some more. He was wakened by the maid knocking at his door to ask him did he want to eat something. He ordered her to bring him up a bottle of whiskey. When she returned she stamped the bottle distastefully on his chest of drawers and banged the door after her. Halligan came up at four, refused to drink with him, said that Valerie was waiting outside in the station wagon, helped him to dress and all but carried him downstairs. He was tolerantly amused by his stumblings and fumblings as he tried to get into the car, but

Mrs Halligan was not. 'Oh, for Christ's sake!' she growled at her husband. 'He needs to be pumped!'

When they had pushed open the hall door of the college and crept cautiously across the empty hall to the parlour, she had to take the key from his helpless hand to open the door. They entered twilight. Regan dragged back the window curtains, bade Halligan switch on the light and with one forensic arm presented them to the easel. For one minute's silence he watched Halligan's mouth fall open and his eyelids soar. Her eyelashes peered.

'God almighty!' Halligan whispered. 'You have him to a T.'

'T for Truth,' he cried triumphantly.

Halligan turned to his wife.

'What d'ye think, Valerie?'

She looked at him, she looked at Regan, she looked at the portrait. Then she edged Halligan aside, stood before the portrait and, one hand on her hip, extended her silence to two minutes.

'Isn't it stu – PEN – dous, Valerie?'

She walked away to the window, did a tiny drum roll with her nails on the glass, turned to them and spoke, quietly, coldly and brassily.

'Don't be a damn fool, Halligan. Mister Regan! I know nothing about painting, but I know one thing, for certain, about that painting. Nobody will buy it. Not here, anyway. Are you, Halligan, going to get up in the committee of the Past Pupils' Union and say that portrait is stupendous? Vote for it? Pay for it? And hang it? And where? There's only one place in this town where you could hang that picture – in the bar of the Shamrock Hotel, where everybody would laugh their heads off at it and then go out and say it is a public disgrace. And do you think even old Noble would dare hang it? You can vote for that picture, Halligan, over my dead body – we've had trouble enough in this town and I don't want any more of it. And I'll tell you one other little thing about that picture, Mister Regan. If you show it anywhere in this country you might just as well go out and hang yourself because it would be the last portrait you'd be asked to paint as long as you live.'

Regan laughed at her.

'To hell with their money. I'll show it at the Academy. I'll sell it there for twice the price. It'll be reproduced in every paper in Dublin! In every art magazine in the world!'

Halligan looked at him with funky eyes.

'Luke!' (And if Regan had been sober he would have known at once by that use of his first name how grave the issue was.) 'Valerie is right. Listen! Would you do one thing for me, and for yourself and for God's sake. There must be a second key to this room. Anyone might come in here at any moment.' He cocked a frightened ear. 'Any second that door might open. Would you take it back to the hotel for the night, and tomorrow morning look at it calmly and coldly and make up your own mind what you're going to do about it. You know,' he wheedled, 'they might even start pawing it!'

'Pawing? Wise man! Shrewd man! Monkey, monkey,' he approved. 'See all, hear all, say nothing. Let's get it out of here.'

They restored the twilight, the hallway was as empty as before; they drove fast, back to the empty, Sunday afternoon Main Street. Outside The Shamrock she put her head out through the window of the wagon to say, 'I'll give you one minute, Halligan, no more.' They were lucky. They met nobody on the way to the bedroom. They stood the portrait on the mantelpiece. They sat side by side on the bed and looked at the scarlet, scowling, wet-lipped face of their old master staring down at them. Halligan accepted one slug from the neck of the bottle, slapped his companion on the back and ran for it. Regan lay back on his pillow, emptying the bottle gulp by gulp, rejoicing strabismally at the face on the mantelpiece that, like a wavering fire, slowly faded into the veils of the gathering dusk.

'*Archiropito!*' he wheezed joyfully as he drained the bottle on its head, let it fall with a crash to the ground and sank into a stupor.

It was dark when he woke. He had no sense of time, of date, of day or night. He thought he heard noises downstairs. He groped for the bell, found it and kept pressing it until the door opened and, against the light, he saw the burly figure of old Noble.

'Mishter Noble, shend me up a bottle of whishkey if you please.'

Silence. Then:

'I will do no such thing, Mister Regan. If I was to do anything I'd send for a doctor. Sleep it off.'

The door closed and he was in darkness again.

'The bitch!' he growled, knowing that she had tipped off the old man. *Must* have a drink! If only ... Suddenly he remembered. That bottle he had bought on the way down from Dublin. Had he drunk that too? He rolled out of bed, crawled on all fours to the light switch, at last found his hold-all and there was his golden salvation. The colours of the little map of Ireland on the label swam – purple, and red, and yellow and green. With his teeth he tore off the thin metal covering on the neck, wrested out the cork, twisting its serrated edge, lifted the bottleneck to his mouth, engorged the sweet liquor as if it were water and sank on the floor in a coma. The maid found him there in the morning, and ran from him down the stairs, screeching.

He recovered his senses only for the few minutes during which he was being put to bed in the monastery. Hilary had him brought there immediately he was informed of his sorry condition by old Noble, then by the community's doctor who had driven him at once to the college door, wrapped in blankets, still in a stupor, his breath coming in gasps, his forehead glistening with cold dots of sweat. It took three brothers to lift him from the car and carry him upstairs to Hilary's bedroom. Harry Halligan and Valerie Halligan, also alerted by Noble, came after them, carrying his few belongings stuffed into his suitcase and his hold-all. As they packed them, her eye roving about the room saw the portrait on the mantelpiece.

'Halligan,' she ordered. 'Take that thing down and burn it.'

He looked at her, looked at the closed door, told her to lock it, took out his clasp knife and cut the canvas from its frame. But when he approached the empty grate his nerve failed him.

'I can't do it, Valerie. It's like murder.'

She snatched it from him, tore some paper linings from the chest of drawers, crumpled the canvas on top of them in the grate, put her cigarette lighter to the paper and they watched everything burn to ashes. They drove to the college, laid his two cases inside the door, and drove rapidly down the drive for home and a couple of stiff ones. In the middle of her drink, and her abuse of him, she looked at him and laughed, remembering from her schooldays.

'"To be thus is nothing, but to be safely thus,"' jumped up to ring old Noble and warn him never to mention their names to anybody in the college about this affair.

'Rely on me,' the old voice replied. 'We're all in it together,' from which she knew that he, too, had seen the portrait.

Hilary sat by his bed during his few, limp moments of consciousness.

'My poor Luke,' fondling his icy palm. 'What on earth happened to you at all, at all?'

'Brother,' he said faintly. 'Can I have one, last little drink?'

The old man shook his head, sadly but not negatively.

'Of course you can, Luke. I'll leave you a glass of the best here beside your bed for the night. Tomorrow we'll cut it down to half a glass. Then, bit by bit, between us, with God's help,' glancing up piously at the veiled face over the bed, 'we'll wean you back to your old self.'

In the morning a young lay brother stole into the room with a nice hot cup of tea for the patient. He found the glass dry and the body an empty cell. Touched, he was like stuffed leather.

The obituaries were invariably kind. They all stressed the burned portrait, the symbol of every artist's indefatigable pursuit of unattainable perfection. They slyly recalled his convivial nature, his great thirst for friendship, the speed with which he could limn a character in a few lines, the unfailing polish of his work. But as always, it was some wag in a pub who spoke his epitaph.

'Well, poor old Lukey Fa Presto is gone from us. He wasn't much of a painter. And he had no luck. But what a beautiful way to die! In the odour.' His glass raised. All their glasses lifted. 'Of sanctity and whiskey.'

With solemn smiles they drank.

The Kitchen

I was there again last night; not, I need hardly say, deliberately. If I had my own way I would never even think of that house or that city, let alone revisit them. It was the usual pattern. I was in Cork on some family business, and my business required that I should walk past the house and, as usual, although it was the deep middle of the night the kitchen window upstairs was dimly lit, as if by a lamp turned low, the way my mother used always to fix it to welcome my father home from night duty. She usually left a covered saucepan of milk beside the lamp. He would put it on the stove to heat while he shook the rain from his cape on the red tiles of the kitchen, hung his uniform on the back of the door and put on a pair of slippers. He welcomed the hot milk. It rains a lot in Cork and the night rain can be very cold. Then, as happens in dreams, where you can walk through walls like a pure spirit and time gets telescoped, it was suddenly broad daylight, I was standing in the empty kitchen and that young man was once again saying to me with a kindly chuckle, 'So this is what all that was about?' It was five past three in the morning when I sat up and groped wildly for the bedside light to dispel the misery of those eight dismissive words that I am apparently never going to be allowed to forget, even in my sleep.

It is a graceless lump of a house, three storeys high, rhomboidal, cement-faced, built at the meeting point of a quiet side street curving out of an open square and a narrow, noisy, muddy, sunless street leading to one of the busiest parts of the city. Every day for over twenty years I used to look down into this narrow street from the kitchen window – down because of the shop beneath us on the ground floor, occupied in my childhood by a firm of electrical contractors named Cyril and Eaton. Theirs was a quiet profession. Later on, when the shop was occupied by a bootmaker we could hear his machines slapping below us all day long.

My guess is that the house was built around 1870; anyway, it had the solid, ugly, utilitarian look of the period. Not that my father and mother ever thought it ugly. They would not have known what the word meant. To them, born peasants, straight from the fields, all the word 'beautiful' meant was useful or prolific; all 'ugly' meant was useless or barren – a field that grew bad crops, a roof that leaked, a cow that gave poor milk. So, when they told us children, as they often did, that we were now living in a beautiful house all they meant was that it suited our purposes perfectly. They may also have meant something else: because they had been told that the house had originally been put up by a builder for his own use they considered it prime property, as if they had come into possession of land owned by a gentleman farmer for generations. Few things are more dear to the heart of a peasant than a clean pedigree. It keeps history at bay. Not, of course, that they owned the house, although they sometimes talked dreamily about how they would buy it someday. What a dream! Landless people, in other words people of no substance, they had already gone to the limit of daring by renting it for twenty-six pounds a year, a respectable sum in those days for a man like my father – an ordinary policeman, rank of constable, earning about thirty bob a week.

Their purpose in renting so big a place was to eke out his modest income by taking in the steady succession of lodgers who were ultimately to fill the whole house with the sole exception of the red-tiled kitchen where the six of us lived, cooked, idled or worked. I do not count as rooms the warren of attics high up under the roof where we all, including the slavery (half a crown a week and her keep), slept with nothing between us and the moon but the bare slates. Still, we were not really poor. Knowing no better life, we were content with what we had.

During some forty years this was my parents' home; for even after my brothers and I grew up and scattered to the corners of the compass, and my mother grew too old to go on keeping lodgers, and my father retired, they still held on to it.

So well they might! I was looking at my father's discharge papers this morning. I find that when he retired at the age of fifty his pension was £48 10*s.* 8*d.* a year. Fortunately he did get a part-time job as caretaker of a garage at night which brought him in another £25. 5*s.* 5*d.* a year. Any roof at ten bob a week was nicely within his means. It must also have been a heart-break to his landlord, who could not legally increase the rent.

One day, however, about a year before I left home – I was the last of us to go – my father got a letter which threatened to end this agreeable state of affairs. When he and my mother had painstakingly digested its legal formalities they found to their horror that the bootmaker downstairs had, as the saying goes, quietly bought the house 'over their heads', and was therefore their new landlord. Now, forty-odd years in a city, even in so small a city as Cork, can go a long way towards turning a peasant into a citizen. My father, as a lifelong member of the Royal Irish Constabulary, then admiringly called the Force, had over the years imbibed from his training and from the example of his officers, who were mostly Protestants and Gentlemen, not only a strong sense of military, I might even say of imperial, discipline but a considerable degree of urban refinement. My mother had likewise learned her own proper kind of urban ways, house-pride, such skills as cooking and dress-making and a great liking for pretty clothes. At times she even affected a citified accent. When they read this letter and stared at one another in fright, all this finery fell from their backs as suddenly as Cinderella's at the stroke of midnight.

They might at that moment have been two peasants from Limerick or Kerry peering timidly through the rain from the door of a thatched hovel at a landlord, or his agent, or some villainous land-grabber driving up their brambled boreen to throw them out on the side of the road to die of cold and starvation. The kitchen suddenly became noisy with words, phrases and names that, I well knew, they could not have heard since their childhood – evictions, bum bailiffs, forcible entry, rights-of-way, actions for trespass, easements, appeals, breaches of covenant, the Land Leaguers, the Whiteboys, Parnell and Captain Boycott, as if the bootmaker downstairs slept with a shotgun by his bed every night and a brace of bloodhounds outside his shop door every day.

Nothing I said to comfort them could persuade them that their bootmaker could not possibly want to evict them; or that, from being a land-grabber, or even a house-grabber, he was just an ordinary, normal, decent hardworking, city-bred businessman, with a large family of his own toiling beside him at his machines, who, if he wanted anything at all, could not conceivably want more than, say, one extra room where he could put another sewing machine or store his leather. And, in fact, as he patiently explained to my father, that was all he did want; or perhaps a little more – two rooms, and access for his girls to our private W.C. on the turn of the stairs. He must have been much surprised to find himself thrown headlong into the heart of a raging rural land war.

I left home that year, so I cannot tell if there was or was not litigation at this first stage of the battle. All I knew for certain is that after about a year and a half of argufying, both parties settled for one room and access to the W.C. The rest I was to gather and surmise from their letters to me. These conveyed that some sort of growling peace descended on everybody for about three years, towards the end of which my father died, my mother became the sole occupant and the bootmaker, seeing that he now had only one tenant over his head, and that with expanding business he was even more cramped for space than before, renewed his request for a second room.

At once, the war broke out again, intensified now by the fact that, as my mother saw it, a bloody villain of a land-grabber, and a black Protestant to boot, was trying to throw a lonely, helpless, ailing, defenceless, solitary poor widow woman out on the side of the road to die. The bootmaker nevertheless persisted. It took him about two more years of bitter struggle to get his second room. When he got it he was in possession of the whole of the second floor of his house with the exception of the red-tiled kitchen.

Peace returned, grumbling and growling. Patiently he let another year pass. Then, in the gentlest possible words, he begged that my mother might be so kind, and so understanding, as to allow one of his girls, and only one, to enter the kitchen once a day, and only once, for the sole purpose of filling a kettle of water from the tap of her kitchen sink. There was, to be sure, he agreed, another tap downstairs in his backyard – a dank five-foot-square patch of cement – but it stood outside the male workers' outdoor W.C., and she would not, he hoped and trusted, wish any girl to be going out there to get water for her poor little cup of tea? I am sure it was the thought of the girl's poor little cup of tea that softened my mother's heart. She royally granted the humane permission, and at once began to regret it.

She realized that she had given the black villain a toehold into her kitchen and foresaw that the next thing he would want would be to take it over completely. She was right. I can only infer that as the bootmaking business went on expanding, so did the bootmaker's sense of the value of time. At any rate he was soon pointing out to my mother that it was a dreadful expense to him, and a hardship to his staff, to have to close his shop for an hour and a half every day while his workers, including his family, trudged home, in all weathers, some of them quite a long distance, for their midday meal. If he had the kitchen they could eat their lunch, dryshod and in comfort, inside half an hour. He entered a formal request for the kitchen.

Looking back at it now, after the passage of well over a quarter of a century, I can see clearly enough that he thought he was making a wholly reasonable request. After all, in addition to her kitchen my mother still possessed the third floor of the house, containing three fine rooms and a spacious bathroom. One of those rooms could become her kitchen, another remain her bedroom and the third and largest, which she never used, would make a splendid living room, overlooking the square's pleasant enclosure of grass and shrubs, and commanding an open view up to the main thoroughfare of the city – all in all as desirable an apartment, by any standards, as thousands of home-hungry Corkonians would have given their ears to possess.

Unfortunately, if I did decide to think his request reasonable, what I would have to forget, and what he completely failed to reckon with, was that there is not a peasant widow woman from the mountains of west Cork to the wilds of Calabria who does not feel her kitchen as the pulse and centre of her being as a wife and a mother. That red-tiled kitchen had been my mother's nest and nursery, her fireside where she prayed every morning, her chimney corner where she rested every night, the sanctum sanctorum of all her belongings, a place whose every stain and smell, spiderweb and mousehole, crooked nail and cracked cup made it the ark of the covenant that she had kept through forty years of sweat and struggle for her lost husband and her scattered children.

Besides, if she lost her kitchen what would she do when the Bottle Woman came, to buy empty bottles at a halfpenny apiece? This was where she always brought her to sit and share a pot of tea and argue over the bottles and talk about the secret doings of Cork. Where could she talk with the Dead Man, collecting her funeral insurance at sixpence a week, if she did not have her warm, red-eyed range where he could take off his damp boots and warm his feet in the oven while she picked him dry of all the gossip of the narrow street beneath her window? She had never in her life locked the front door downstairs except at night. Like the door of any country cottage it was always on the latch for any one of her three or four cronies to shove open and call out to her, 'Are ye there, can I come up?' – at which she would hear their footsteps banging on the brass edgings of the stairs while she hastily began to poke the fire in the range, and fill the kettle for the tea, or stir the pot of soup on the range in preparation for a cosy chat. All her life her neighbours had dropped like that into her kitchen. They would be insulted if she did not invite them into her kitchen. She would not have a crony in the world without her kitchen. Knowing nothing of all this, the bootmaker could argue himself hoarse with her, plead and wheedle with her to accept the shiniest, best-equipped, most modern American-style kitchenette, run by electricity, all white and gleaming chromium. Even if it was three storeys up from the hall door it seemed to him a marvellous exchange for this battered old cave downstairs where she crouched over a range called the Prince Albert, where the tiles were becoming loose, where he could see nothing to look at but a chipped sink, one chair, a table, one cupboard, a couple of old wooden shelves and a sofa with the horsehair coming out of it like a moustache. He might just as well have said to a queen, 'Give me your throne and I'll leave you the palace.' While as for proposing as an alternative that she could keep her old kip of a kitchen if she would only let him make a proper kitchen upstairs for himself, his family and his workers . . .

'Aha, nah!' she would cry at me whenever I visited her; and the older and angrier she became the more did her speech revert to the flat accent of her flat west Limerick, with its long vanishing versts of greasy limestone roads, its fields of rusty reeds, its wind-rattling alders and its low rain clouds endlessly trailing their Atlantic hair across the sodden plain. 'Is it to take me in the rear he wants to now? To lock me up in the loft? To grind me like corn meal between the upstairs and the downstairs? A room? And then another room? And after that another? And then what? When he'd have me surrounded with noise, and shmoke, and shmells, and darkness and a tick-tack-turrorum all day long? Aha. My mother, and my grandmother before her didn't fight the landlords, and the agents, and the helmeted peelers with their grey guns and their black battering rams for me to pull down the flag now! It's a true word, God knows it, them Proteshtants wouldn't give you as much as a dry twig in a rotten wood to light your pipe with it. Well and well do I remember the time ould foxy-whiskers, Mister Woodley the parson, died of the grippe away back in Crawmore, and my uncle Phil stole out the night after his funeral to cut a log in his wood! While he was sawing it didn't the moon come out from behind a cloud, and who do you think was sitting on the end of the log looking at him out of his foxy eyes? Out of my kitchen I will not stir until ye carry me out on a board to lie in the clay beside my poor Dinny. And not one single minit before.'

Which was exactly what happened, six years later.

All in all, from start to finish, my mother's land war must have lasted nearly fourteen years. But what is fourteen years to an old woman whose line and stock clung by their fingernails to their last sour bits of earth for four centuries? I am quite sure the poor bootmaker never understood to the day of his death the nerve of time he had so unwittingly touched.

After the funeral it was my last task to empty the house, to shovel away – there is no other word for it – her life's last lares and penates to a junk dealer for thirty shillings. When it was all done I was standing alone in the empty kitchen, where I used to do my homework every evening as a boy, watching her cooking or baking, making or mending, or my father cobbling a pair of shoes for one of us, or sitting at his ease, smoking his pipe, in his favourite straw-bottomed chair, in his grey constabulary shirt, reading the racing news in the pink *Cork Evening Echo*.

As I stood there I suddenly became aware that a young man was standing in the doorway. He was the bootmaker's son. Oddly enough, I had never spoken to his father, although years ago I had seen him passing busily in and out of his shop, always looking worn and worried, but I had once met this son of his in the mountains of west Cork – fishing? shooting? – and I had found him a most friendly and attractive young fellow. He came forward now, shook hands with me in a warm, manly way and told me how sorry he was for me in my bereavement.

'Your mother was a grand old warrior,' he said, in genuine admiration. 'My father always had the greatest respect for her.'

We chatted about this and that for a while. Then, for a moment, we both fell silent while he looked curiously around the bare walls. He chuckled tolerantly, shook his head several times and said, 'So this is what all that was about?'

At those eight words, so kindly meant, so good-humoured, so tolerant, so uncomprehending, a shock of weakness flowed up through me like defeat until my head began to reel and my eyes were swimming.

It was quite true that there was nothing for either of us to see but a red-tiled floor, a smoke-browned ceiling and four tawny distempered walls bearing some brighter patches where a few pictures had hung and the cupboard and the sofa used to stand. The wall to our right had deposited at its base a scruff of distemper like dandruff. The wall to our left gaped at us with parched mouths. He smiled up at the flyspotted bulb in the ceiling. He touched a loose tile with his toe and sighed deeply. All that! About this? And yet, only a few hours before, when I had looked down at her for the last time, withdrawn like a snail into her shrivelled house, I had suddenly found myself straining, bending, listening as if, I afterwards thought, I had been staring into the perspective of a tunnel of time, much as I stared now at him, at one with him in his bewilderment.

I thought I had completely understood what it was all about that morning years ago when they read that letter and so pathetically, so embarrassingly, even so comically revealed their peasants' terror at the power of time. I had thought the old bootmaker's mistake had been his failure to understand the long fuse he had so unwittingly lighted. But now – staring at this good-humoured young man who, if I had said all this to him, would at once have understood and have at once retorted, 'But even so!' – I realized that they, and that, and this, and he and I were all caught in something beyond reason and time. In a daze I shook hands with him again, thanked him again for his sympathy and handed him the keys of victory. I was still dazed as I sat in the afternoon train for Dublin, facing the mile-long runnel that burrows underneath the city out to the light and air of the upper world. As it slowly began to slide into the tunnel I swore that I would never return.

Since then I must have gone back there forty times, sometimes kidnapped by her, sometimes by my father, sometimes by an anonymous rout of shadowy creatures out of a masked ball and sometimes it is not at all the city I once knew but a fantastically beautiful place of great squares and pinnacled, porphyry buildings with snowy ships drawing up beside marble quays. But, always, whatever the order of my guides, captors or companions, I find myself at the end alone in a narrow street, dark except for its single window and then, suddenly, it is broad daylight and I am in our old kitchen hearing that young man say in his easy way, 'So this is what all that was about?' and I start awake in my own dark, babbling, clawing for the switch. As I sit up in bed I can never remember what it was that I had been babbling, but I do understand all over again what it was all about. It was all about the scratching mole. In her time, when she heard it she refused to listen, just as I do when, in my turn, I hear her velvet burrowing, softer than sand crumbling or snow tapping, and I know well whose whispering I had heard and what she had been saying to me.

She was a grand old warrior. She fought her fight to a finish. She was entirely right in everything she did. I am all for her. Still, when I switch on the bulb over my head I do it only to banish her, to evict her, to push her out of *my* kitchen, and I often lie back to sleep under its bright light lest I should again hear her whispering to me in the dark.

Also in Penguins

Stories of Sean O'Faolain

In these short stories, ranging from Dublin through the hills, lakes, and valleys of Donegal, and counties Mayo, Limerick and Cork – everywhere where life has been (and is being) lived in its tragedy and comedy – Sean O'Faolain, one of the greatest living Irish writers, captures the variety and richness of Irish – not to say human – experience.

Also available in Pelican

The Irish

Not for sale in the U.S.A.